Anothr

Print ISBN 978-1-912604-13-5

Dedication

For my husband and wonderful family who have helped me
through a dark few months.
Thanks to you, there is light at the end of the tunnel and it's
getting brighter every day.

Prologue

L ying on her side in the road, Hannah looks at a sandal a few feet away. It's similar to hers, but she can't see it clearly because her left eye keeps rolling inwards. No, the sandal isn't hers, there's a spatter of red on the heel.

Something feels very wrong inside her head, and her right eye watches a pool of dark liquid spread out from underneath her across the tarmac. There is a taste of metal in her throat. Hannah thinks she hears a scream and a babble of voices. A woman's face comes close to her own. Her mouth moves, but Hannah can't make out what she is saying. It is as if they are separated by thick glass. The woman smiles, though tears run down her cheeks. Does she know her?

Hannah watches images flick in quick succession across the woman's face.

The road … traffic racing along as if each vehicle is afraid of coming last … it's raining … Hannah needs to cross … a tissue on foggy spectacles … waiting … linking arms with someone … laughing?

Green

Amber

RED

A gap between cars … preparing to cross … a sharp elbow … sandal strap snapping … panic … running …

A man's voice comes as if from a long way off. 'Don't move her. You could do more damage!'

'Damage? Is someone hurt?' Hannah thinks she says these words but can't be sure as her lips are numb. She looks at the woman again; tears still wet her cheeks, but there is a dark hole growing at one side of her face. It looks like a full moon aligning with the sun.

A searing pain explodes behind Hannah's eyes and she wants to scream, but her mouth is full of vomit and her limbs thrash themselves against the surface of the road.

In the dark, she prays the pain will stop, and seconds later it does. She hears a man's voice loud in her ears counting up to five, over and over, and in perfect time with the counting, she feels a rhythmic thump against her ribs.

At last, the man's voice is fading, and she is thankful. The darkness is a circle and a bright pinprick of white light expands from its centre, until it is all that she can see.

Chapter One

My fingers tremble as I hold them poised above the keyboard on my work desk, so I tuck them under my armpits. I look at the computer screen and then switched my gaze to the rain on the window, focus my mind, fight to keep a hold on the present, but the past fights harder. Memories stored deep, perhaps almost forgotten, like daffodil or crocus bulbs can often emerge from the thickest frost. I tell myself that thirty will be knocking at my door in a few months and school is a long time gone. I close my eyes but it's no use. A wrecking ball of nineteen-year-old images smash into my consciousness …

SMACK!

Automatically my shoulders jerk up round my ears, but lower again as I realise someone has popped bubblegum behind me. Synthetic strawberry sweetens the air. Perhaps a bit of gum has landed on my new school cardigan. My hand travels up my sleeve but stops when laughter trickles through the group of children blocking my way. Their ringleader, Megan, steps forward.

I notice a loose thread on my sock. Yes, I remember snagging it on the rabbit hutch before school this morning. I close my eyes and conjure an image of Boris, wiggling his nose and twitching his ears.

I swallow.

I wish I was home with him now.

I open my eyes, but don't look up, just dig the toe of my shoe into the tarmac on the playground. The baking sun has softened the surface, and from the little hole I make, sticky black molasses releases the acrid smell of bitumen.

Perhaps if I keep looking at the thread on my sock and picture Boris in my mind, they'll all get bored and that bitch Megan will leave me alone, but my heart's racing, sweat beads my top lip, and a tide of anxiety sweeps Boris away.

A phone ringing somewhere in the office brings me back to the present. I open my eyes, take a moment to calm my breathing. Of all the unwelcome memories trapped within the folds of the past, this one escapes most frequently and is the most vivid. Though it is a grim day outside, I can feel the sun's heat on my skin, the bitter taste of humiliation; the feeling of helplessness and self-loathing in my eleven-year-old heart.

Occasionally there would be a trigger, but not today. Today I'd been sitting at the keyboard, fingers flying, constructing an invoice for Clear View Glass & Co. Just another day, another typical task, but then my hands started to shake, and I'd stared through the window at the rain and thump: there I was back in the playground.

The rain gathers strength, lashing the pane as slate-grey clouds crowd in, weighting the day, anchoring my thoughts to the past. Just another day, but perhaps that is the problem. Everything since my school days is different, yet nothing has really changed. I can tell the rest of the memory is there just waiting, but I'll be damned if I'll give in this time.

I rest my fingers on the keys but can't resume typing, just look at the deluge outside and wonder what the hell I'm doing with my life. A rasp of stubble against dry fingers accompanies a deep sigh close to my ear. My gaze leaves the clouds and telescopes back into the office. I don't need the reflection on the window to tell me that the boss, Kevin Morley, stands inches away from my right shoulder.

'Lu, did you hear me?'

'I heard you sigh,' I answer, but keep 'and your infuriating habit of stroking your chin every waking moment' in my head.

'That's because you took no notice when I spoke to you. Away with the fairies this afternoon, eh?' Kevin draws his fingers over his chin again and I wish I could block my ears.

'Just looking at the rain, the clouds, you know?'

Kevin makes a noise in his throat that sounds as if he is trying to laugh but his vocal cords are too serious to permit it. 'Well, some of us have work, no time for cloud gazing. I asked you if you'd ring Mrs Percy about rearranging her patio door fitting.' He jabs a finger at a telephone number on the pad in front of me. 'Sarah double-booked her yesterday. I swear that girl has a brain the size of a peanut.'

'It would fit with the wages you pay us then, wouldn't it?'

Kevin's jaw drops. His fingers hover above his stubble but don't make contact; his lips part but apparently have trouble forming words, so his tongue just clicks the roof of his mouth instead. If he is surprised at my comment, then I'm stunned. I had wanted to give him smart answers many times before but had never dared. Only five years older, he talks to me as if I am an infant.

'I beg your pardon?' Kevin manages to wrestle his expression from startled into neutral, though I assume that his one raised eyebrow is supposed to intimidate me.

I clear my throat and consider the choices. Do I continue to speak my mind, or pull my horns in and, snail-like, retreat into my shell? Megan had forced retreat. Even aged eleven she had been far more intimidating than Kevin. Since that day I had been a snail. In fact, long before that day.

Never being what my mother called 'much of a mixer,' I'd always gone off on my own, or with Boris, preferring to read in the shade of the cedar tree during the summer holidays, rather than having a laugh with friends … not that I had many. I became a dab hand at pulling my horns in and never saying boo to a goose. That phrase always struck me as odd. Just why on earth would a person want to—

'Hey! What's the matter with you today? I asked you a question and I'm still waiting for an answer,' Kevin says.

I watch him add another raised eyebrow and folded arms to his repertoire and note that he's echoed almost exactly what Megan had said on that long-ago day.

'I think you heard me, Kevin.' My words taste sweet on my tongue. Without realising it, I have opted to keep my horns out.

'I did hear you, Lucy, but I am perplexed as to how you think you can talk to me in that rude and offhand manner!'

'It's Lucinda. And perplexed? What a very old-fashioned word. I do like it though, don't you?'

'What? I *really* cannot believe—' he begins, but the door opens and Sandra, his PA, comes into the room.

'Sorry, there's a problem. An irate customers on the phone.'

Kevin clicks his tongue against the roof of his mouth again and frowns down at me. 'This isn't finished,' he says, and taps his knuckles on my desk. 'Not by a long chalk.' He rasps his stubble and leaves.

The time flies for the next hour. I don't look at the weather, nor allow my thoughts to wander. I don't want to think of the consequences of my unprecedented behaviour – and consequences there will surely be. Kevin Morley would never let me off the hook. He's cut from the same cloth as Megan, though her cloth was hessian to his silk. Her cloth still had the pins in it and was trimmed with barbed wire. Once her cloth was drawn over the skin, it wounded – left scars.

Just before four thirty, Kevin strides from his office, his serious eyes on mine. From the pegs along the door he selects a raincoat, snaps out the creases and drapes it over his arm with a flourish. I hide a smile. He looks ridiculous, though I presume he imagines himself to be terrifying – a matador entering the ring.

'I have to sort out an urgent matter so will be leaving early,' he says to the space just above my head. His voice comes from deep in his throat and his mouth is pursed so tight I wondered how he gets the words out. Eyes that normally hold little interest or expression sweep mine with clear contempt. 'We will discuss your disrespectful attitude in the morning. And let me be quite clear'—he nods three times and cracks his knuckles— 'you had better be damned well sorry, madam.'

The door closes behind him and I think about the next morning and if I am sorry or not. It will probably still be raining, and I'll be sitting behind the desk typing. I'd look up at the rain and the grey clouds would merge into one colossal mass and be sucked down to street level. They would muscle in, press against the window of the office and I would feel the air leave my lungs, and I'd struggle to remember who I was inside my oxygen-starved brain. But then it wouldn't matter who I was because my life was empty, and I'd see nothing in my future but rain, keyboards, egotistical raspy-faced bosses and memories of the past.

At the end of the day I stand, walk to the window, take a few deep breaths and look out at the shoppers on the high street avoiding puddles. I suddenly realise I'd not avoided puddles today. Today I had drawn something up from deep in my belly, something that resembled pride, guts and fight. Something that I didn't know was in me. So, no, I'm not sorry.

I press a few keys and the computer shuts down. My reflection frowns at me from the blank screen, the memory of that day in the playground crawls at the edges of my mind and Kevin crawls there too, rasping and sneering. Before I can change my mind, I start up the computer again and compose a letter of resignation. A police car is parked near my house. I look across at Mrs Heggarty's, she's forever complaining about the kids who lived on the estate. Dad says that she must have the local police station's number on speed dial.

I open the door, put my coat on the banister and try to calm my voice enough to be able to shout my normal greeting – difficult when my heart is beating so fast. I tell myself that Mum and Dad's reaction to me chucking the job won't be as bad as I imagine. Dad might even say I'd done the right thing. He's always the softer of the two.

'Hello, it's me!' I say and walk into an empty kitchen. Odd. Mum would normally be making dinner by now.

'In here, Lu.' The voice from the living room is Dad's but there is something not right. It sounds broken.

Dad matches his voice. He sits in his chair by the window, eyes staring from a slack white face. Opposite, on the sofa, two police officers nurse their caps. The female officer stands. 'Lucinda, please take a seat.'

I look into her sympathetic eyes and feel the room shift. I don't want to sit. 'What's happened?' I say, leaning my weight against Mum's chair.

'Please sit down, Lucinda.'

'No. Just tell me what you're doing here.'

The officer takes a deep breath. 'I'm afraid to tell you that your mum died in a road accident this afternoon.'

I sit down.

Chapter Two

It's ironic that it's sunny today. We have had rain, fog, and even sleet over the last week or so; why on the day of Mum's funeral is the sky a fairy-tale blue, why are the birds singing, and why is the world carrying on as if nothing has happened? My world is different from everyone else's. My world is small, dark and cold. There is no sun. Perhaps there will never be sun again.

I lean my head against the cool glass of my bedroom window and watch the funeral cars pull up outside the house. Dad, freshly shaved, scrubbed clean of despair and awkward in his new suit, goes down the path to talk to the funeral director. The fact that he's walking and talking, functioning like a real person twists my heart because I know it's all an act. Dad has been on autopilot for days, mostly allowing his brother Graham and sister-in-law Christine to organise everything, and wading through the dizzying mountain of bureaucracy surrounding a person's death. Our neighbour Adelaide pitched in too. I have been worse than useless. Last night Dad stood in front of me just staring. His red-rimmed eyes and milk-white skin under a greying beard told me the extent of his pain, but his words pretended otherwise.

'Tomorrow we have to be brave for your mum, love. We have to be strong and get through the day. I'll be here for you, don't worry.' Then his face had crumbled, and he'd turned away, walked out into the garden.

The reflection in my cheval mirror shows me a tall, pale woman in a red dress. The woman has very dark circles under her eyes, the colour of slate, and her black hair is scraped back into a ponytail. This can't be me, can it? My eyes used to be green, my skin peaches and cream. I remind myself that this was before my world became dark and cold. Before Mum stepped off the pavement, ran across the road … and into the path of a car.

'Lu … time to go, love.' Dad's soft voice from my doorway blocks the too-graphic images of what my mind imagines it must have been like for Mum that day.

I turn and look at him, well, past him really, because the pain in his eyes opens wounds that I'm trying desperately to keep closed. 'I'm ready,' I say, and follow him downstairs. I'm not, of course. If it were left to me I'd stay at home. Mum's gone. What's the point of gathering at a church to sing, pray and then watch them put her body in the ground? Aunty Christine said that funerals are for those who are left behind. If that's the case, then I want to be left behind here at home. Dad needs me, though, even if he says it's the other way around.

Everyone in the church is crying except me. I'm pretending that I'm somebody else, somewhere else. That's working by and large, but then I catch sight of Dad's shaking shoulders and I have to refocus. There's no shame in crying, is there? Though every time I feel like I'm about to, nothing happens. The last thing I want is to screw my face up and then no tears appear. People will think I'm nuts. I sigh and look round. The church is full of our friends and neighbours and even some people I don't know. Must be Mum's friends from work, I guess.

Outside the sun is still shining brightly, making a mockery of our solemn mood as we gather round the oblong hole in the earth. The vicar is saying lots of lovely stuff about Mum as if he knew her. She never attended church – well, apart from funerals and christenings – so it's doubtful that they were best buddies. Why am I being so horrid? The man is doing his best, everyone else seems to appreciate it, so why can't I? I look around the faces hidden behind a variety of tissues and handkerchiefs. There's a woman a little way off under a tree dressed in black and wearing a hat and sunglasses. I shield my eyes from the sun but can't make her out. No idea who she is. She obviously doesn't know about the request to wear bright clothes today. When she sees me staring, the woman pulls her coat collar up around her ears and walks away. Odd. I must remember to ask Dad who she was.

The earth is damp and cold in my hand. As I scatter it, I wonder what it's like for Mum to be inside the coffin in the ground right there in front of me. Then I scrap the idea, because Mum's not alive, is she? In the coffin is just the shell of the woman who brought me up. Her essence, spirit, has gone, leaving us with just memories. Dad throws his earth and a rose, his lip trembles and I slip my arm around him, feeling my body shake as the tremors of grief flow through his body. Uncle Graham takes his other arm and we lead him back to the car. It's as if we're all in some awful nightmare in which I'm playing a starring role but can't remember my lines. No amount of direction from the wings can prompt me, nor encourage a worthy performance. I'm just numb. Paralysed. Perhaps I'm dead too.

Chapter Three

If I had been told six weeks ago that I'd be grateful to see Adelaide Heggarty's pinched face framed by two arcs of pencilled eyebrow on my doorstep each day, I would have found it very hard to believe. When I was a kid, I'd asked my mum why Mrs Heggarty's eyebrows looked strange. Mum had explained that ladies of a certain age sometimes lost their eyebrows and chose to fill them in with an eyebrow pencil. It was clear to me our neighbour hadn't learned that skill very well and, as a result, looked permanently surprised no matter how she was feeling. Only a few months ago I had remarked to Mum that Mrs Heggarty must draw her eyebrows on with crayon, without a mirror, possibly in the dark.

Dad had picked up the baton. 'Yes. Just look at them. She'd do better to cut out bits of black felt and make Groucho Marx ones instead.'

This had brought near hysterics from Mum who'd been waving to the owner of the eyebrows from the window. When Mrs Heggarty had gone indoors, she'd thumped his arm. 'Steve! You're awful to that poor woman.'

'Poor woman?' Dad had said, holding an invisible cigar to the corner of his mouth, bending his knees and doing the Groucho walk around the living room. 'Oh, come on, Hannah. She strikes terror into even the hardest kids on the estate. All she has to do is wiggle those brows and they wet their pants.'

The memory brings a smile as I watch Mrs Heggarty cross the street and walk up our path. I want to share Dad's joke with her, but of course I can't. She would be upset and certainly wouldn't find it funny. Mrs Heggarty doesn't find things funny. If she smiles – a rare occurrence – it's a brief affair. Her small mouth, normally set in a thin line, twitches at the corners and then returns. It's as if her lips have never learned how to bend, or just don't have the willpower. Nevertheless, since Mum died she's been a godsend.

'Hello, Mrs Heggarty, how are you today?' I say, standing to one side as she breezes into the hallway.

'Oh, you know me, Lu. Always ready to do what's necessary.'

I think Mrs Heggarty's lips are gearing up for a twitch but at the last minute they stay put. 'Yes, I do. You have been really marvellous since …' I'm still not ready to say what had happened to Mum out loud. I can think the words to myself in my head, but if I try to speak them, my throat closes over.

'Nonsense, it's a pleasure. And how many times have I told you to call me Adelaide? Mrs Heggarty is very formal.' She checks her reflection in the hall mirror and runs her finger over one eyebrow. 'I do prefer it for people with whom I'm not too familiar, of course. It's just what I was used to growing up. Did I tell you that my mother always used the surname of her friends and they hers, even after thirty-odd years?'

'Yes, Mrs … Adelaide, you did.'

'And how is your dad today?' Adelaide looks in the mirror again, smooths the other eyebrow and pats her short grey hair.

I lead the way to the kitchen and switch the kettle on. 'The same, I'm afraid.'

Adelaide sets two mugs on a tray and opens the fridge. 'Well, that's to be expected. It will take some time – it hasn't been that long since the funeral.'

I sit at the table and watch Adelaide make the tea. She always takes over even the simplest of tasks and at one time it would have annoyed me. Now, however, I expect it, am grateful for it. I know I wouldn't have been able to cope with things day to day without her, and certainly wouldn't have coped alone with Dad.

After that dreadful evening when I'd walked in and found the police in the house, Dad changed into somebody else – a stranger to me. Apart from pulling out all the stops the day of the funeral, he'd locked himself down, shuttered his mind, become monosyllabic. I'd asked him if he knew who the mysterious woman was with the hat and sunglasses at the funeral, but he couldn't even remember seeing her. Each day I witnessed a little more of the life drain out of him along with his colour. Now he was completely grey.

Grey face, grey hair, grey man.

Last night I'd found him in the dark staring at the TV, the bright flash of scene changes lending animation to his face. I was reminded of the phrase 'he had become a husk of a man.' That described Dad exactly. A husk sitting in Dad's chair, all the goodness, vitality – juice of life – sucked away by Mum's decision to dash across a busy road. Evidently, she'd just left the hairdressers and must have opted for a shortcut to get to her car and out of the rain.

For at least four days after the funeral, unable to function beyond getting up and sitting in chairs, we had relied on Adelaide and occasionally Uncle Graham and Aunty Christine. Graham couldn't do much because he had to keep the carpentry business he ran with Dad going, and Christine had elderly parents to care for. So, given that I was in deep shock, Adelaide had volunteered to do everything for us, and all the time tears weighed heavy against the back of my eyes while my cheeks were dry deserts praying for thunderclouds. That wasn't normal, surely? Adelaide had reassured me it was okay that I couldn't cry, and that grief had no set pattern, nor master.

While my uncle and aunt had done the nitty-gritty after Mum died, Adelaide had arranged the funeral, contacted relatives, sorted the wake. She liked to be useful and she knew about death, having 'seen two husbands off' as she'd put it. I thought that sounded as if she'd set the dogs on them or something, rather than outlived them. Adelaide believed the most important things in life were serving church and community. She knew everyone's business and the names of all the neighbours. I liked to think that Adelaide might have escaped from a 1960s black-and-white film, in which women wore floral aprons, folded their arms, and talked in hushed tones over garden fences. Not that Adelaide would be seen dead in an apron of course. She was always neatly turned out in a skirt, smart jumper and pearls.

'No luck with that last job interview, then?' Adelaide says and places a mug of tea in front of me.

I pick up the tea and blow along the surface. I don't want to talk about the interview. Adelaide comes around every day to sit with Dad while I go out job hunting. Then she does the shopping, cleans the house or whatever needs doing until I return. Adelaide has a very strong feeling that Steve shouldn't be left alone. He has 'that look about him'. Thinking about Dad's vacant stare, I presume Adelaide can detect something about it that I can't. There isn't an argument there though. I feel much better when I'm away from the house and grateful that Adelaide is happy to stay with him.

Adelaide looks at me across the table, her eyebrows ratcheted up a notch, and I realise she is still waiting for an answer. 'Oh, sorry. No, not heard anything yet. The thing is, I'm not really as qualified as I need to be for the jobs I'm applying for now.'

'The manager of a clothing store, wasn't it?'

'Yep.' I drink the tea and look out of the window at a couple of sparrows fighting over nuts in the bird feeder. Under Adelaide's scrutiny I know how the nuts feel.

'Is that what you really want to do?' Adelaide opens a packet of chocolate digestives and pushes them across the table.

'Managing a store? It would be better than the last job.' Heat seeps up my neck. I take a biscuit.

'I think you do what really makes you happy. Don't just settle for something because it's better than the last job. You only get one life, so they tell me,' Adelaide says, and her lips actually twitch and curl fleetingly at the corners.

'That's what Uncle Graham said to me recently.'

'Did he?' Adelaide takes a sip of tea. 'I hope you listen to us, Lu. The world is your oyster and it's time to cast away stones.'

'Sorry?

'A time to cast away stones. It's from the Bible – Ecclesiastes if memory serves.'

'But what does it mean?'

'There are different interpretations, but most say it's about clearing land for planting. So, it's about new beginnings – starting again.'

I shift my weight and look out of the window at the bird feeder. My eyes have filled, and I don't want Adelaide to see. She will fuss and flap and ask if it was something she'd said to upset me. It is something she's said, but I'm not upset. Not in a sad way at least. Those words have reached into my mind and begun to unravel the knot of thoughts that have been getting more confused and difficult to untie since Mum died. I know I have to get out of the house right now in order to be able to make sense of the loose ends.

'Right. I'll be off. Thanks again for all you're doing and see you in a while,' I say, swivel in my chair, and stand up facing the cooker so I won't have to look at Adelaide.

'Okay. I'll go and have a little chat to your dad and then make a nice stew for later.'

I silently wish her luck with the little chat, as Dad hardly speaks nowadays, and the antidepressants don't seem to help. The doctor's decision to prescribe these drugs so quickly after such a trauma might have been a good one, but I suspect it will just make living even harder after he's stopped taking them. I frown at that as I close the front door behind me. I'm a fine one to talk.

Park benches, cinemas and coffee shops were the reality of my fantasies about job hunting and interviews these past few weeks. I walk up a grassy hill overlooking the urban sprawl of Sheffield and wish I was looking at the sea. Oceans and sandy beaches often visited me in dreams but living so far away from the coast means a trip to the seaside is rare. When I had managed to go there, it made me instantly calm. Calm is elusive in the city. It tends to get buried under traffic noise, tall buildings and litter.

I sit on a bench and look at a line of ants busying themselves along the length of a discarded cola bottle. Such purposeful little things directed by a collective conscience. My conscience has been troubled lately, which hasn't made thinking about the future very easy. I watch the ants move on to a sweet wrapper, the morning turns to afternoon and the sunshine chase cloud shadows down the hill.

The breeze plays with my hair and whispers in my ears, and the words of the wonderful Adelaide finally allow me to tie those loose ends. After today, I promise myself that there will be no more sitting on benches while ostensibly looking for jobs. No more lies. I will cast away stones, start again – literally.

In the weeks since Mum died, I'd filled my time with thinking. Tentative introspection swam in the submerged caves of my mind, graduating to soul searching and then, latterly, a brutally honest appraisal of Lucinda Lacey, the first thirty years. Those years have come and gone so quickly with little to show. I don't want the next thirty to play copycat. A nucleus of an idea has divided and grown, but my conscience, armed with sensible arguments, has restricted it time after time. The sensible arguments say:

It wouldn't be fair on Dad …
It could all go wrong and then you'd feel worse …
Flights of fancy are normal during the grieving process, you're not thinking straight at the moment.

The nucleus has been given its freedom today though and I feel giddy under the acceleration of its development and strength. I realise that I need to find out who exactly Lucinda Lacey is, and though it might be painful, scary, and hurtful to some, particularly Dad, I will return to the start and look for my birth mother.

Chapter Four

The pub smells of beer, sweat, competing perfumes and aftershave. I want to stand up and walk out of the door into the cool night air. I think about getting up and just leaving, because an hour is enough time to spend on anyone's birthday, thirtieth or not. I also think about telling my two friends from the old job that I am going to cast away stones, and then watch their reaction. Ellie and Sally would probably look more like meerkats than the abandoned puppies they had channelled when I said I really didn't want to celebrate at all. They would sit upright and raise their eyebrows in an Adelaidesque manner and—

'Your miles away, Lu,' Ellie says, tapping my hand.

'Am I?' I say, wishing I was.

'Yes, we just said we fancied getting a bite to eat here. How about you?'

'No, I ate earlier, thanks.'

'So, did we, but I fancy some chips,' Sally says with a giggle that sounds as if she'd borrowed it from a child. 'Shouldn't really, I've worked so hard to reach my target weight,' she adds, smoothing her short skirt over toned thighs.

'Well, you go ahead. I'll get off now, I have lots to do.' I stand and picture myself out in the street.

'No! You can't go yet, it's your birthday!' Ellie says, grabbing my hand and tugging me back into my seat. I don't want to be tugged back into my seat, especially as I had been so close to escaping.

'And what's so important that you have to do it at nine o'clock on a Thursday night, a thirtieth birthday night?' Sally asks, her amber eyes directly on me.

'I have to check my emails to see if there's been any progress on tracing my birth mother.'

Meerkats *and* goldfish. My smile forgets to be fixed and stretches wide across my face as I look at the raised eyebrows and open mouths of my friends. A fly lands on a sticky circle on the table that had once belonged to the contents of Ellie's cider glass and then buzzes past her nose. I will it to have a look inside her open mouth, but Ellie's hand flaps it away before it has a chance to consider it.

'Bloody hell, I had no idea you were adopted!' Sally says, her eyes round.

'It's not really something I talk about, or think much about, really,' I say, though the last bit is a lie. I have thought about it for many years, and about a year before Mum died I had made my mind up that I would try and trace my birth mother. It was just something I felt I had to do. The kind of 'in your gut' feeling that wouldn't be ignored. So around six months ago I hired a genealogist, Maureen Henson, to do some digging. One of the adoption websites I had been on had a forum and a member had put me in touch with Maureen. I had given her all the details from my birth certificate and my adoptive parents' information and asked her to act as an intermediary. She told me it should be fairly straightforward, and I should hear something in a few weeks.

Not long after, however, I had second thoughts, cold feet, whatever. I never answered Maureen's email I'd received about a month later. Not even opened it, just deleted it and emptied my recycle bin to be sure. I had sent one to Maureen though. Told her I didn't want to know what she'd discovered, if anything, settled the account and apologised for her trouble.

I worried that she'd found her. I worried that she hadn't. It was all too sudden, too stressful. I'd just not had the guts to find out, or to tell my parents of course. The time had never been right … until now. Yesterday I'd emailed Maureen, apologised again, and explained that I had decided to go ahead, asked if she'd found anything.

I smile at Sally's stupefied expression. 'But now I want to find my birth mother to try to make sense of my life,' I finish, though I hadn't known I was going to say it.

Ellie frowns, presses her lips together and leans forward. I can't decide if she looks worried or has a bout of stomach cramps. She sucks her teeth and shakes her head. 'I'm not sure that's a good idea, Lu.' Her dark eyes focus on mine and blink meaningfully a few times. I know that she is doing her sympathetic and 'I know better than you' look and wonder what she would say if I told her to mind her own bloody business.

'Luckily, I *do* think it's a good idea. I've thought about it very hard over these past weeks and I honestly think it's the best thing for me.'

Ellie clicks her tongue against the roof of her mouth and shakes her head. Then both she and Sally stop being interested in my news and watch a man from the next table get up and walk to the bar. They nudge each other and Sally whispers something to Ellie that I can't catch. Ellie catches it, evidently, snorts down her nose and fans her hand next to her cheek. 'I wouldn't't mind,' she sighs. She leans in close to me. 'Just saying what a gorgeous rear he has, and—'

'Evening, ladies,' the friend of the man from the next table says. He has appeared unnoticed and silently by my chair as if through a trap door. 'Dave over there is at the bar and we wondered if you'd all like a drink? My name's Harry.'

Ellie's colour deepens to a warm scarlet even though I doubt Harry had heard what she'd said about Dave. 'Oh, that would be lovely, wouldn't it, girls?' she says breathily and flutters her lashes.

I think she sounds as if she has asthma or has just run upstairs and looks as if perhaps she had something in her eye. I have never understood the commonly accepted change in behaviour of some women during interaction with a man they find attractive. I can't imagine how Harry would find it so.

'Oh, how kind. Mine's a white wine spritzer, thanks,' Sally says, twisting her curls into a ponytail and then letting them fall back around her shoulders, while all the time staring at Dave's behind.

Harry puts his hand on the back of my chair. I look up at him and he smiles. He has a nice friendly smile, dark blue eyes and light brown hair. He also has the same kind of stubble as my ex-boss, but as yet hasn't offered to rasp it. If Mum had been here she would have said Harry was a handsome and smartly turned-out chap. She would have encouraged me to get to know him and hoped we would hit it off, because it was about time I found a man. The thing is, I don't want to find a man. I decline the offer of a drink and, after Harry has gone, I say I'm leaving to check emails.

Ellie pulls her chin close to her chest and harrumphs. 'Do what you think is best. But, as I said, I think you should be careful about trying to find your mother.'

I am tempted to say that I think Ellie should be careful about drawing her chin in as it makes her look like a constipated Buddha, but that would be cruel.

Harry pops back to get his wallet just as I stand to leave. He sets his empty glass down on our table and says to me, 'Are you really thirty today? I couldn't help overhear your conversation earlier.'

'Yes, I am,' I say, aware of all eyes on my face as if searching for lines and wrinkles.

'Well, I would say you look more like twenty-five, and a model to boot.' Harry looks directly into my eyes. 'I think it's that blue-black hair, without a strand of grey – and those unusual moss-green eyes, of course.'

Ellie sniggers into her cider and I feel my colour rise. Then she blinks rapidly as if trying to dislodge the flash of jealousy I'd seen there and moves a hand of stealth towards a fly, which has graduated from the sticky circle to the rim of Harry's glass. I raise my hand and flap the fly away. 'That's kind of you to say, Harry. Not true, but kind,' I say, looking back at him just as directly. Though bold for me, it seems safer than looking at my friends. If I do I might lose my nerve and have to pull my horns in.

'Blue-black hair is very precise, isn't it?' Ellie says through a tight mouth as if she's afraid of allowing the fly access. 'What are you, a hairdresser?'

'Funny you should ask that, but yes.' Harry pulls a few business cards out of his wallet and hands them round to us. 'Just started my own business down in the precinct. Not doing too bad at all.'

'"A Cut Above, by hair artist Harry Clements",' Sally reads. 'We always go to Hair Today, don't we—' Sally's arm jerks under the impact of Ellie's elbow and she and I read the warning signal in our friend's eye. 'Oh, God. Sorry, Lu, I didn't think.' Sally speaks quietly to the floor.

I hadn't needed Sally's faux pas to remember what had happened to Mum as she left Hair Today. As soon as Harry had said 'hairdresser' I had been in the death day, by the side of the road in the rain, willing my mum not to cross.

'That's all right. It's easily done,' I say, and drain half my glass in one. The cool air from outside is calling and this time it won't be ignored. 'Thanks, girls, it was a lovely evening.' I gulp down the remainder of the wine and step away from the table.

Ellie stands and tries to grab my arm as I walk past. 'No, you can't go like this. You're upset.'

'No, I'm fine, honestly.' I muster a half-fixed smile that feels as if it wants to slide off my face.

'Yeah, well, you don't look fine,' Harry says, his kind eyes finding mine. 'Stay and have another drink. I don't know what the problem is but—' Ellie's nudging elbow sets to work again, and he shakes his head.

'Another time, perhaps? See you all,' I send over my shoulder as I hurry to the door and at last make my escape into the night. Adelaide is asleep in front of the ten o'clock news. Though relaxed, her face still hangs from the eyebrows of surprise and looks as if it can't quite make sense of a dream. I tiptoe past and pick up my laptop from the coffee table. I really ought to wake my neighbour, but an awake Adelaide will not allow the quiet time in my room

I very much need after the birthday disaster. Why hadn't I stayed for a drink with Harry? He clearly liked me, but it was the same old story. I have no confidence meeting new people, particularly where men are concerned. Something always feels awkward. Out of place.

The second escape of the evening is nearly complete until a floorboard announces my departure with a traitorous squeak.

'Lu, is that you?' Adelaide burbles. She sounds as if she's underwater.

Can I ignore her and dash upstairs to my room, stuff some pillows under the duvet and then hide in the wardrobe if Adelaide comes in to check? A second squeak says no. 'Yes, it's me,' I whisper, and give a little wave.

'Had a lovely time?' Adelaide rubs her eyes with the heels of her hands and gets up from her chair.

'It was great, thanks. Shall I walk you to your door?' I step into the hallway and flick the light switch.

'Fancy a cuppa first?'

Still with my back to her, I unhook a coat from the rack and hope my neighbour won't be offended when I decline. I fake a yawn and turn to look at her, but the yawn remains stuck, hippo-like, and I hear a choked laugh in my throat. I cover my giggles with another yawn and a cough because Adelaide's eyebrows are … gone. Well, not gone exactly, but the carefully crayoned arches have smudged along the bridge of her nose to the south and disappeared into her hairline to the north. Must have been when she rubbed her eyes.

I step behind Adelaide and help her into her coat. 'I'm so tired, I wouldn't be great company. We'll have tea tomorrow?'

'Tired, on your thirtieth birthday at only five past ten?' Adelaide raises the skin above her eyes. A bloodhound looks at me … a bloodhound with a smudged forehead.

Laughter bubbles in my stomach and though I try so hard to hold it back, it bursts from my mouth. I flap a hand in front of my heated face and say, 'I know! What a boring Betty I am, eh?'

Adelaide raises the folded skin above her eyes again. I've never seen a suspicious bloodhound until now. 'Hm. Never mind, I'll be off then. Your dad went to bed with a hot drink about an hour ago.'

Her tone sobers my mood, but I have to force myself to think of serious things when I look back at my neighbor's disappeared eyebrows. 'Oh, you are such a treasure. Thanks again for looking after him.' I touch Adelaide's arm lightly and reach for the door handle.

Adelaide turns a stiff back. 'No need to walk me, I'm perfectly fine,' she says, and leaves.

I pick up the laptop from the hall table and feel like an idiot. Poor Adelaide obviously realised I was laughing at her for some reason, but she wouldn't know why until she looked in the mirror at home.

Dad's gentle snoring snakes under his door and across the landing floorboards. I enter my room, change into my pyjamas and for a few moments I draw my legs under me on the bed and just listen to the computer booting up and the familiar house noises. The old building sounds like an elderly person relaxing stiff joints and settling down for the night. Clicks, creaks, soft taps from the boiler, and Dad's snores perform a comforting tune conducted by the rustle of tree branches outside my window.

If I really concentrate, hold my breath and half close my eyes I can almost see Mum wave from the dimly lit landing and say, 'Night, love. See you in the morning,' as she had on so many nights. Almost, but each time I try I can't hold her there. At the last moment her image is snatched away like smoke in the wind. She is gone and all I have left are memories.

At my desk, I scroll through emails full of adverts and offers, until I see the name I'd been hoping for. Maureen's. I look at the bold type on the email's subject line and poise my forefinger over the mouse; it trembles as if the left-click button is about to deliver an electric shock. I clench my jaw and place the pad of my fingertip on the mouse. Since that day on the bench I had decided to live life with my horns out, but once I open the email the future will stretch before me, unknown and untested.

Oddly, the future will also be my past. A circle of time joined end to end, spinning out of control on its axis – and the axis is me. My horns recede, but before I can retreat fully I close my eyes and force my finger down. I take a breath, open my eyes and read:

Hi Lu,

Good news! I have your birth mother's name and current address (see below). I found it back when you first contacted me, and, as intermediary, I tentatively touched base to see if she was indeed the one we were after. I gave her your basic info as we agreed. She was over the moon and even asked if I had your contact details. Of course, I very soon had to tell her that you had changed your mind, so didn't give them to her. But don't worry; you aren't the first to have had second thoughts!

So, I think it is best that you write a letter in the first instance and see what happens. As I said before, I am here to offer advice and support. As we discussed last time, these matters are rarely straightforward and often not like the programmes we see on TV. Email or give me a ring.

Best, Maureen.

Ms Mellyn Rowe, Seal Cottage, Tregrenas Hill, St Ives, Cornwall

I touch the screen with my fingertip and trace each letter of the name and address of my birth mother, static prickling every loop and curve. Then I fold my hands in my lap and the tears that have been so long overdue finally find release.

Chapter Five

July dawns are like notes of hope. They remind the days to be bright, fresh and summery.

Sometimes the days forget to read the notes or prefer to sit under rainclouds or hemmed in by thick walls of pollution. But sometimes they pay attention. Today is a note reading day. I watch from my window as the muted dawn light reveals the purple shadows and sages of the garden as a base coat, while gradually adding the bolder brushstrokes of sunlight to transform the canvas into a kaleidoscope of dazzling colour. In corner barrels, lupins boast pink and blue; in hanging baskets, yellow primroses glow under the blush of red geraniums, and, in the foreground, the huge white rose bush Mum had loved presents myriad of dew-covered buds, pregnant with fragrance.

In the four months since Mum has been gone, my life has become unrecognisable. Years of working in the office, going through the motions of repetitive nothingness, are over. Like the rose bush, my future has bloomed into an exciting prospect of something – something with promise and hope. I've always loved my adoptive parents, nobody could have wanted better, but I'm convinced that finding my birth mother will unlock the answers to questions I have kept hidden in my heart. Even the schoolyard memory has left me alone, so things must be looking up. I'm not looking forward to the immediate future though.

I find Dad in the kitchen, his back to me, reading the instructions on a packet of something. Over the last while he has thankfully started functioning again, but not enough to go back to work. Adelaide doesn't come over as much now, but she has brought him a load of jigsaws and he's completed at least one a day.

It's as if every time he successfully places a bit of shaped card into the appropriate space on the puzzle board he's helping to rebuild the pieces of his shattered life.

Dad turns to look at me and points at the packet. 'It says here that you have to fill this sachet full of milk and pour it on the porridge. What a daft idea.'

'Why daft?'

'Because it's a flimsy bit of paper and it will probably spill all over the shop. Why you bought this microwavable stuff I don't know.'

I can't tell him that it was Mum that bought it because he'd feel bad, and that's the last thing I want. 'Do you want me to make it? You sit down and have your cuppa.'

'Thanks, love.' He sits at the kitchen table and rustles a newspaper. 'No luck on the job front?'

'No, not as yet.'

He turns a few pages. 'Not to worry, you have to find the right one.'

'Yes. And thanks to you having me still live at home, I have enough in the bank to tide me over for ages yet.'

'Smashing.'

This is a ritual we go through every few days. It's as if we have a well-rehearsed script that has to be adhered to, and if we deviate from it the world as we know it would fall about our ears. I stir milk into the bowl, put it in the microwave and hope the scriptwriter isn't listening. 'Dad … I have something to tell you that you might not like.'

He looks up from the paper and frowns. 'What is it?'

The hum of the microwave sounds like a giant angry bee and it puts me off my stride. Since finding the email about Ms Mellyn Rowe I'd pictured the scenario a hundred times. Imagined what I'd say, what he'd say back, and how it would all pan out. Now, with Dad's anxious eyes on mine and the beep of the microwave coming in just when I'd plucked up the courage to open my mouth, the scenario turns into a blank screen.

Dad's face threatens to drain to grey again after so recently getting some of its colour back. 'How bad can it be? Just say it,' he says, folding the newspaper and setting it aside.

I pick up a tea towel and open the microwave door. 'Let me just get the porridge and—'

'Forget the bloody porridge. I can't eat it until I know what's made your face look like somebody has died …' He draws his hand across his chin. 'They haven't, have they?'

I take the porridge over to the table anyway and sit opposite. 'No, Dad. But it was because Mum did that I decided to do something.' I take a deep breath. 'I decided to find my birth mother and … well, I have.'

I look at him, but he shrugs his eyebrows and pulls the porridge towards him. He picks up the spoon but doesn't eat. Now the microwave has stopped humming there is nothing to break the silence apart from a few birds squabbling outside on the feeder. I wish he would say something. 'We got any honey for this stuff?' Is not what I expect, but at least it's a start. I get the honey.

'So how do you feel about it?'

Dad stirs honey into his porridge and shrugs his eyebrows again. 'I knew it would come one day. Even though you said you'd never want to find her when you turned eighteen.'

My scenario had involved shock, possible tears – his and mine – recriminations, and eventual acceptance. It had not involved calm porridge eating and shrugging eyebrows. I weigh my response carefully and then reply, 'I didn't at the time. Also, I thought it would be a slap in the face for you and Mum after everything you've done for me.'

'So how has your mum leaving us changed all that?'

Dad always makes it sound as if Mum hadn't died, just that the marriage had broken down. He can't bring himself to say the words. And how am I going to answer that question? 'It was a lot of things, coming up thirty, and I hadn't been happy for a while. You know, just drifting from one New Year's Eve to the next, wondering what the year would bring rather than making things happen? I'd made the decision to find her about a year or so ago, just never did anything about it.' He eats his porridge and looks at me. I look out of the window at the rose bush and wish Mum was here; she'd know what to say.

'When Mum …' I can't say it either, not out loud, not in front of him. 'I guess it was like a catalyst. I'd already set the ball rolling by quitting that awful job. The fact her life was cut short so suddenly made me realise how important it was to live mine, stop going through the motions, you know?'

'You've always been ashamed of being adopted, haven't you, Lu?' Dad wipes his mouth and sits back in his chair. I can't decide if he is angry, sad or both. His face is serious, yet his eyes are unreadable.

I want to say don't be daft, that's ridiculous, but instead find myself saying, 'Where's that come from?'

'From that day when you ran out of school when you were eleven. That vile Megan girl had bullied you about it.'

I really wish he hadn't said that because, wham! There I am in the playground again, surrounded …

Megan takes a step closer and pokes a long crimson-painted fingernail in my stomach. The pain is bearable, but the humiliation accompanying it sheathes the expectant silence. The air grows thin, harder to suck, while the atmosphere in the crowd becomes thick, palpable – heavy with anticipation. 'What the hell are you staring at your socks for, you nutter? I asked you a question and we're all waiting for an answer.'

The question had been asked only a moment or two ago but carries with it the weight of ages and stab of betrayal. I will never trust anyone again. Ever.

The sun sears a warning on the exposed skin at the back of my neck as my long black hair curtains forward, but I can't look up. A car drives past the school gates; the exhaust fumes mix with tar. There's a roll of nausea in my throat. 'I'll ask you one more time,' Megan hisses, poking me again, and someone sends a nervous giggle into the sepia sky. 'Then I'll do more than poke you. Is it true what Gill Morris says about you being adopted?'

The girl is so close now that I can smell the waft of cheese and onion crisps on her breath and the overpowering deodorant fails to mask the smell of sour sweat. The space between us is charged with electricity, a sure sign that Megan is high on adrenaline – itching to carry out her threat.

I have to give in.

Dad's voice snaps me back. 'You said you had kept it all a big secret until your friend betrayed you.' He leans his elbows on the table and stares into my eyes. I can see that he isn't angry now. Just sad. Really sad. 'Betrayed was the word you used. That's the kind of word you use when the secret you're hiding is big, bad and shameful.'

I close my eyes against the sadness in his, but all I can see is Megan.

I bite my lip as Megan grabs my hair and yanks it back, hard. 'Oi, I'm talking to you!'

I think about running, but Megan's hand is wound tight in my hair; I'm forced to look up into dark eyes framed by over-mascaraed lashes and cold with anger. Megan's nostrils flare, her mouth twists down at one side. She tugs my hair again and then the sting of a slap on my cheek competes with the ache in the back of my neck. To my shame, I feel my eyes fill. Megan's face and the gathered crowd merge together, become a dark smudge at the margins of my sight.

There is nothing for it. I open my mouth and into the silence I hear my voice, small and tremulous, say, 'Yes. I'm adopted.'

I force my eyes open and a surge of sadness engulfs me. I want to reach out and take Dad's hand. But I know that if I did, I would cry and be unable to stop. I take a swallow of lukewarm tea and say, 'I suppose I didn't want to believe that I was adopted. You know that day when you told me about it all when I was seven? It was as if I was in a bad dream, but the next day I woke up and found the dream was still real.'

'It wasn't easy for us either. Sorry we didn't do a better job,' Dad says with a wistful smile.

I can't bear to see the pain in his eyes – pain that I'm causing. 'No. Please don't think that. You didn't do a bad job.

You told me you could never love me more and that I was special because you had chosen me, wanted me so much. No. It was all me.' I rub my eyes and think about my seven-year-old self. Then I just let the words come.

'I felt bereft, as if someone had taken away my parents overnight, even though you were still there. And, as time went on, I wondered why I had been rejected by my birth mother. I blamed myself for her rejecting me, and then blamed myself again for feeling so resentful that you weren't my natural parents. I always felt different from everyone else somehow. Nobody at my school had been adopted as far as I knew, and the whole thing got so screwed up in my head until I didn't have much faith in who I was. I thought there must be something wrong with me. That bitch Megan really hurt me, and I don't mean just physically. She told me I was ugly and that there must be something really wrong with me for a mother not to have wanted her baby.'

Dad puts his hand on mine and mutters a curse under his breath. I blink away tears and hear ... *Shrill laughter blending with the bell sounding for the end of lunch break. I continue to look down until the crowd disperses, their footsteps echoing away across the black expanse of tarmac.*

Hatred for Megan, Gill, but mostly for myself swells and fills the empty centre of my chest. Megan is an evil bitch, Gill is my only real friend and she'd betrayed my confidence, but it was true what Megan said. I have thought the same things about myself every day since I'd been told I was adopted. There must be something really wrong for a mother not to have wanted her baby.

Perhaps it's true that I'm ugly. Perhaps it's something else. Whatever it is, it's in me, about me ... because of me.

I look up and around the empty playground. The breeze picks up dust and sweet wrappers, drops them at my feet and then whisks them away again. A tall figure steps out from the shade of a classroom door, but before the teacher can spot me, instinct sweeps me out of the school gate.

Aching lungs slow my pace and, minutes from home, I lean my head against a bus stop to catch my breath. Panic flutters as realisation dawns that I've truanted, would be found out and would be confronted with the disappointed faces and concerned questions of my parents. We would all be called into school – perhaps even by the head teacher – and I would be punished.

Dried bits of metallic paint have become indented in my forehead from the bus stop. I pick them off and walk on. School is not an option this afternoon. An image of Megan's hateful eyes won't leave and my cheek throbs. I swallow tears and force Boris back into my mind. Only a little while now before I can hold him against my face, inhale that woody smell of straw and carrots on his fur and tell him everything. He will understand, even if nobody else does …

There's no stopping my tears now and I curse myself for getting in a state. This won't help the situation. I draw deep breaths in … out … in, to try and calm myself.

'But why didn't you talk to us?' Dad's eyes are moist too and he reaches for my other hand. 'We always asked if we could help, said we would help you contact your birth mother when you turned eighteen if you wanted, told you the little information we had about her being a young girl and living in Cornwall. You just said you didn't want to know.'

'I know. I was just too confused and upset about it all to tell you how I felt. In fact, I didn't know how I felt. I do now, though. Took me long enough, eh?'

Dad nods and squeezes my hand. 'So how do you feel?'

'I feel more grateful to you than you could ever know for looking after me and I love you so much, Mum too.' I blow my nose on a bit of kitchen roll and look away. If I look at Dad I will crumble again. 'But I need to meet this woman who gave birth to me. See if I have anything in common with her, find out more about my birth father if I can. I suppose it's like you doing your jigsaws. You need all the bits before you can have the satisfaction of seeing the whole picture.'

'But of course. That's only natural, love.' Dad gets up and put his arms around me. 'As I said, I always knew it would happen. It was you who didn't.'

I stand and hug him tight, my face in his shoulder, breathing the comforting smell of the soap he'd used since forever. 'You're not mad with me?'

'Course not, Lu, you're my daughter. I love you and want whatever you want,' he says thickly.

We stay like this in silence until Adelaide walks in a few minutes later with another jigsaw under her arm. She looks at our tear-stained faces, raises her eyebrows and heaves a sigh. 'I can see that a nice cup of tea is called for here.'

Dad and I give each other a look and bite back laughter. Thank God for Adelaide.

Chapter Six

The old brown leather suitcase that we'd had since I was a child sits next to two holdalls, a pair of walking boots and an iron – still boxed – in the boot of my car. I always pack too much when I'm going anywhere, but this lot for just one week in Cornwall is a little over the top, even by my standards. The iron is especially excessive as I never use one, but I remembered Mum saying, 'Be prepared for every eventuality,' so I'd put it in at the last minute.

Sunday morning in our street looks the same as it does on every other day except that privet hedges look less green, the windows hide behind curtains, flowers in gardens seem a little more faded and the garden gnomes look hung-over. It's as though the week had been so hard to deal with that the collective energy of houses, humans, plants and gnomes alike have been reduced to emergency levels only. Today, the first of August and the third of a heatwave, adds an extra layer of apathy and inertia, unbroken even by the tolling of St Bartholomew's bell calling all parishioners, willing or reluctant, to morning service.

Adelaide closes our front door behind her and hurries down the path towards me. 'Right, I'm off to church and I've just popped the roast in, so it will be well on the way when I get back.' She cocks her head birdlike to one side and looks me up and down. 'Now, don't worry about anything while you're away. I'll look after your dad. This is your time, go for it, as you young ones say.' Her lips twitch at the corners and then lift for at least two seconds.

There's an unexpected lump of emotion growing in my throat, and before I can talk myself out of it I step forward and put my arms around her. She feels solid and dependable and I wonder what I'd do without her. Adelaide says something that sounds like *awumah* and pats my back a little too hard.

'I can't begin to thank you for everything you've done lately, Adelaide,' I say, looking away from her moist eyes in case mine try to copy them.

Adelaide flaps her hand and looks into the boot of my car. 'Nonsense, I did what any good neighbor worth her salt would have done.' She eyes the iron and frowns.

'We both know that's not true,' I say, closing the boot and leaning my hip against it. 'You made me realise it was time to cast away stones and that is the most important thing ever.'

Her mouth twitches again and she nods. 'Good. I'm glad. And now I'd better pop off or I'll be late. Safe journey.' She touches my cheek lightly and then I watch her small figure hurry away down the street. As she passes each house, it seems to me that the privet hedges and flowers regain their colour, the windows throw back their curtains and the garden gnomes stand to attention and salute her. Okay, perhaps the last bit is taking things too far.

Behind the wheel of my car I turn the key in the ignition and glance up at the bedroom windows to see if Dad has broken his promise. No. There's no sign of a face or even a shadow behind the curtains. We had said goodbye inside and I told him not to wave from the window. Now he hasn't I wish I had allowed it; the whole point in him keeping away was so that I wouldn't be sad. But I'm sad anyway.

I tell myself off – it's only for a week. Myself isn't having that though, and answers that it isn't about the timescale, but about the enormity of what I'm actually doing. My life will be changed no matter what the outcome. I put the postcode for Mellyn Rowe's house into the satnav and it confirms what I already know. Five hours and fifty minutes in present traffic. I wonder how long it would take in past or future traffic. If only I had a time machine. I tell myself off again for procrastinating with stupid thoughts. This time, myself doesn't answer back.

Two hours down the M1 the air-conditioning gives up and resorts to huffing lukewarm air at me as if in reproach; the heatwave must have been too much for the ancient system. I have to open the window and then spend the next five minutes wrestling one handed with the wind, which insists on whipping my hair across my eyes. I scrabble in my bag for a clip or hair band, then I remember they're in the suitcase. A sign at the side of the road says Services in three miles and I decide enough is very much enough.

Sucking an ice cube, I sit at a corner table and watch a tide of people flow in and out of the doors. Some bob towards the bookstore, others to the fast food outlets, and others rush past on a strong current, red faced and determined, towards the sign for the toilets. I love the transience of these places. People passing through, all going to different destinations, all with their own stories to tell. I guess there won't be many that are off to meet their birth mother today.

On the table I smooth out the letter I had received in response to my own. All the adoption agencies, and indeed the genealogist, Maureen, had advised a letter as first point of contact. I read it again now and a few butterflies shiver their wings in my stomach. In three hours or so I will be coming face to face with her.

Dear Lu,

I was overjoyed to get your letter! When your eighteenth birthday had passed, and after a few years I'd still not heard from you, I thought you had decided not to find me. Then Maureen wrote to me and said you were looking for me but then you changed your mind. I don't blame you of course; it can't have been easy for you. Thank you so much for your phone number, but I really think it would be great to meet face to face as you suggest. I'm sure I would become too emotional on the phone and not be able get my words out properly.

I quite understand that you want to stay at the hotel in town, as we don't really know each other, but the door to Seal Cottage is always open.

I can't wait to meet you. I have so much to ask you, and I'm sure you feel the same! Let me know when you are coming, and I will put the bunting out!

Here's my email, it might be quicker than snail mail – trowe@hotmail.co.uk

Love,

M x

In the two weeks since I'd received it, I'd read it so many times that the paper had grown soft from all the folding and unfolding. Now when I place it on the table it opens all by itself. I can hardly believe it's real. Everything has happened so quickly. I trace the lines with my fingertips and think about how cheerful she sounded.

Then I trace the word 'love' and wonder if she could mean it. I wasn't sure how I felt at all. I certainly didn't feel love, but perhaps she did. I had seen accounts on TV and read in books where the birth mother had kept a much treasured and dog-eared photo and had said that she had never stopped thinking about or stopped loving the child she'd put up for adoption.

I watch programmes about reuniting loved ones, such as *Long Lost Families*, like others watch favourite soap operas; I just can't get enough of them. Since my decision to find Mellyn, my appetite has become even more voracious. I'd re-watch some and play in my head the meeting that I'd have when I found my own birth mother. My imagination often changes things around, but the meeting would always be emotional and always have a happy ending. Of course, I have to prepare myself for the opposite. The last few months have taught me that life isn't a fairy tale.

They say that blood is thicker than water, don't they? But what if blood isn't enough? Even though she carried me for nine months and gave birth to me, it doesn't mean that I'm immediately going to like her, does it? She might be so different to me that I could never warm to her. She might be a racist, right-wing, card-carrying Nazi. Then what? People say it doesn't matter what your parents are like, they are still your parents, and deep down you love them.

But what if I don't? Okay, I know I'm not expected to feel love for her yet, but what if I never do? What if I can't stand the sight of her and want to leave after five minutes?

I finish my drink and notice my hands shaking as I set the glass back down. This what-if scenario isn't helping, and I need to clear my head before I meet her. Going in with a head full of what ifs and preconceptions will just fuck everything up. Sometimes if you expect the worst, then that's what happens. That wouldn't be fair on her or me, would it?

This is my cue to get up, go to the loo and get on with the journey. My resolve is just a bit battered, that's all. It's to be expected. My spirits rise as I walk into the Ladies' – I can do this. Then doubt wallops me over the head. Perhaps I should just turn the car round and go home. Maybe I was right the first time when I changed my mind about finding her. Why not just leave the past alone? What's the good of poking it, putting it under a microscope? It all happened and that was that – I can't change it.

Torn between going home and the unknown I wash my hands and try to avoid my eyes in the mirror. I know they'll look sheepish, guilty. But they don't have to, do they? Not if I galvanise myself, stop prevaricating and finish what I started. I snap my head up from the washbasin and look at the mirror. There's no sign of sheepishness, or guilt – just steely determination. That's better.
The Satnav says I will be at my destination in forty minutes. I look at the clock – 3.02. The air-conditioning is still misbehaving, but I have an unexpected ally: a cool breeze coming off the sea, glimpses of which I had seen tantalisingly to my right as I sped down the A30.

An odd thought strikes me. Perhaps I have always loved the sea because I had been born in Cornwall. Mellyn lived in St Austell originally, not St Ives, according to my birth certificate, but that's on the sea too. Could someone always yearn for the sea because they had been born next to it? Probably not, but I will believe it to be true. I'm looking forward to spending more time just walking on the beach and exploring the town. As a teenager I'd visited

St Ives and remember little winding streets, the lovely gift shops, cafés and, of course, the beautiful harbour and beaches.

At the top of what must be one of the highest hills in Cornwall, I draw my car onto a scrap of a drive and switch off the engine. I rest my hands on my thighs and feel their heat seep through my summer dress; it's a relief to stretch my fingers after so many hours gripping the wheel. A few deep-breathing exercises help me focus and calm my heart and then I look at Seal Cottage through the windscreen. It looks like the kind of place my imagination would draw if I asked it to sketch the perfect cottage by the sea.

Heavy ancient stone walls support a tiled roof upon which white-framed dormer windows look out over the harbour and towards the main beach, Porthminster, if I'd remembered the signs correctly. Two huge palms stand at either side of a shiny red door. I half expect a bewhiskered fisherman in a striped jumper carrying a lobster pot to come out of it. A stone seal sits to one side of the door and a sign hanging from a chain around its neck reads Welcome to Seal Cottage.

After a few moments fingers of doubt stretch through me and then a twist in my stomach prods me into action. The longer I sit here, the more I'll feel nervous, and the more I feel nervous, the more I'll sit, and so it would go on. I step out of the car and my senses come alive. Salt air sharpens a honeysuckle breeze, sunlight dances on waves; at the door, the touch of the stone seal's head feels rough and warm under my fingers and tumbling from an open bedroom window comes the voice of a woman singing 'Summertime'.

The singing stops as I bunch my fist to knock, but the door opens before I can. The world has become suddenly silent, holding its breath as Mellyn and I look at each other. We are almost the same height, she perhaps marginally taller. She has long straight hair like mine, but chestnut to my black; we have the same straight nose and similar shaped mouths, though her lips are thinner, and her eyes a light blue to my green. Nevertheless, though sixteen years separate us, it is obvious that we're related.

For me, a completely new experience. My heart's thumping in my chest, my legs feel weak. I am now looking at someone who is part of me, has the same blood, knows my origins.

The world stops holding its breath and Mellyn holds out her arms, her eyes moist, her lips pressed together as if trying to prevent a cry escaping. I hesitate for a second as I picture her holding a baby in those same arms before she gave it away, and then I step into her embrace.

'Oh, Lu. If you only knew how many years I've waited for this moment,' she says, a tremor in her voice.

I open my mouth, but unexpected anger shocks me into silence. I want to say, 'Then why did you give me away in the first place?' What was wrong with me? Make her tell me everything right there and then. But that would be cruel, and I don't really mean it anyway, do I? Anger still has my tongue. *For God's sake!* This wasn't a scenario I had pictured and I'm not sure what to do. Many of the meetings envisaged had us both hugging, as we were, and me feeling an overwhelming rush of love for her; which I'm not. A wash of confusion rises from my depths and I suck in a deep breath to calm the waters. At last I say, 'I can't believe it's happening, but I'm so glad it is.' At least that's mostly the truth.

Mellyn nods, holds me at arm's length. 'Let me look at you properly,' she whispers, wiping her eyes on the back of her hand. That wasn't a good idea; her hand brushes against her chest and smears mascara across her white linen tunic dress, but she just laughs and shrugs. 'My goodness, we look identical. You're younger and prettier, of course, but you're my daughter alright.'

I think 'identical' is pushing it big time, but under the circumstances I'll not dispute it. 'We do look similar.'

'More than similar. I'll show you some pictures of me at your age and you'll see I'm right.'

Is there a bit of an edge to her voice or is it just nerves? Into an uncomfortable silence I offer, 'I'm sure you are – it's all so surreal, don't you think?'

She raises her hands and an array of bangles clink together as they fall down her arms. 'It's just mad – I feel like I'm dreaming!'

She gives me the biggest smile then, and the tension between us, real or imagined, disappears. I mirror her smile and she slips her arm through mine. A rush of warmth dislodges the discomfort in my chest and at last I start to feel a bit more like I thought I should. 'Now, come in properly and relax, you must be shattered after the drive.'

The inside of the cottage is just as lovely as the outside. Whitewashed stone walls are hung with seascapes, and a ship's wheel and a wooden lighthouse accompanied by a seagull sit in alcoves that face the quaint mullion windows and the sea beyond. A fireplace piled with logs draws the eye to the centre of the room and a real lobster pot is situated to one side of it.

The far wall has a well-stocked bookshelf and wine rack, and on the stripped oak floor a few good quality rugs in reds and deep greens give warmth to the walls. To complete the picture, two plump red leather sofas have pride of place opposite the fire.

It should have looked like a holiday let trying too hard, but it doesn't. Winter in this room would be perfect: me sitting by the roaring fire with a glass of wine, feet up and listening to the wind whistling outside. I tell myself that this is a little bit previous to say the least, and I tell Mellyn how beautiful her home is, and then follow her into the kitchen.

Though small, the kitchen is well equipped and bright. Lemon and white walls complement the ash cupboards and brown granite worktops. Light grey tiles on the floor draw everything together and the window faces a lovely little side garden burgeoning with wild flowers. I think I glimpse a smudge of blue through yellow honeysuckle at the end of the lawn. 'Is that the sea?' I ask Mellyn and point down the garden.

'Yes, just a corner view, and if you stick your head through the flowers and crick your neck you can see the harbour too.' She laughs and points to the kettle. 'Want a drink now, or do you want to see the rest of the place?'

'Oh, I'd love a quick tour before I sit down. My bum's numb from sitting all day.'

'Yes, and my steep steps will give your thighs a good workout,' she says, beckoning me towards the rickety wooden staircase.

For a two-bedroom cottage it feels very spacious. The master bedroom is pale blue and has truly stunning views from the dormer across the rooftops to the harbour and sea. A glance round the door along the hall reveals a modern bathroom with a shower cubicle and a bath, and the second bedroom is decorated in a warm cinnamon. The view from the window shows me the garden to the left and to the front, down the hill towards the town.

I turn from the window and look at Mellyn. 'This house is just perfect. How long have you lived here?'

She puts her head on one side and thinks for a moment. 'It has to be five, no, nearly six years. Let's go back down and have that tea and we can catch up on the last thirty.'

I follow her downstairs and wonder how much of my history would match the fantasies I'd had in my head for the last twenty-three.

Chapter Seven

Oh, to be swimming in the sea instead of sitting behind an old creaky reception counter that smelled of too many full English breakfasts and other people's holiday sweat.

Rosie Green watched yet another happy couple pass by the door in the indecently bright sunlit street, carrying an assortment of beach towels, Frisbees and picnic lunches. Everyone else always seemed to be having a better time than her lately. In fact, more than lately. If she were honest, which she was wont to be – even to the point of destruction – she never seemed to have what you'd call a great time.

Yes, she was an invaluable member of staff here at Pebble House; in fact, the whole place would grind to a halt without her, and her bosses relied on her. Many, many people relied on her: the success of countless holidays that people had scrimped and saved for, longed for all year, depended on her. That was something, wasn't it? More than something. She had her own flat, rented, but a girl had to start somewhere, and she had friends, well, one or two, and her parents and brother loved her, didn't they? What more could she ask for?

'Rosie, did you clean number twelve yet? I told you an hour ago that a guest rang and asked if we had a room at short notice.'

That answered her question. The more she could ask for was not being spoken to like a downtrodden below stairs skivvy in Victorian England. She might be invaluable, but she wasn't valued as a person by Alan and Nadine, the couple that ran the place. Alan darkened the door to the dining room like a Hammer Horror creature, all glary eyes and upside-down smile. The high-pitched strains of a violin stabbing the air and knife slicing through a shower curtain was all that was missing.

'Yes, I did it straight away.' Her flat monotone and folded arms signalled 'Back off, shit face'. Or at least she hoped they did.

'Right,' Alan muttered through tight lips; he strode over and spun the booking register round to face him. Obviously not a great reader of back-off signals. 'And we have another guest in later this evening, don't we? Yes, Lucinda Lacey, a woman on her own.'

'Why ask, if you know? There it is in black and white on the register.'

His eyes narrowed. 'Not sure why you need to be so surly, Rosie. Just checking everything is in order. Her room ready?'

'Of course. I do my job thoroughly, as well you know.' Rosie shifted her gaze from his nasty little face and out into the street again before she gave in to the urge to slap it. 'If you don't think so, then get someone else.'

'Oh dear. I can see you're in a mood again, so I'll leave you to it.' Alan clucked his tongue against the roof of his mouth and marched off.

What did he mean, again? Cheeky swine. She noticed that he didn't tell her to be politer or tell her off though, did he? No, because he would worry that she'd bugger off and then he and Nadine would actually have to do some work. Oh yes, they knew when they were on to a good thing, alright.

Rosie glanced at her watch. Lucinda Lacey had phoned this morning to confirm her booking and said she'd check in around seven. It was now four thirty and Rosie was looking forward to meeting her. There had been something about the woman's voice that she had warmed to. She had an easy manner and they'd shared a joke about the weather and the traffic at this time of year. Was she here on business or for a holiday? That was something she'd find out over the course of the week, she expected.

Rosie walked over to the door that led outside and leaned against the sun-warmed wall to watch the passers-by. How sad was she? Looking forward to meeting a guest she'd only spoken to on the phone, warmed to, just because they'd had a laugh for a few minutes? Perhaps Alan had been right when he said that she was in a mood *again*. Despite what she'd told herself about being useful and responsible, she had to admit that her career – such as it was – wasn't enough.

Lately she'd brushed off feelings of listlessness, loneliness and not belonging. Her head had argued with the daft ideas her heart whispered to it late at night about finding the 'right one', settling down and maybe one day even starting her own business. Just all silly flights of fancy. Finding the right one was a concept peddled by media and romance novels. There was no right one, just people settling for each other and muddling through life the best they could.

As Rosie turned to go back to reception, another young couple walked past, arms about each other's shoulders, laughing and looking into each other's eyes as if they never wanted to look away. She sighed. Perhaps muddling shouldn't be sniffed at.

Chapter Eight

'I baked a cake. Hope you like coffee and walnut,' Mellyn says, placing a tin on the table. She takes the lid off and watches my face carefully.

I peer into the tin. The smell is intense and delicious, and the cake looks to have at least four layers. 'Thanks! Yes, I do – and my goodness, that must have taken some making.'

'It did, but it's not every day that my long-lost daughter comes around for tea, is it?' She laughs, takes the cake to the counter and begins to cut it.

I watch her back and take a swallow of tea. I feel uncomfortable again because of what she'd said. I don't like the flippant way she said it either.

I hadn't been long lost. She had given me away and hadn't tried to find me. I'd found out that in the last ten years or so, natural parents were allowed to search for adoptees through approved agencies or social services. Surely, she must have known this.

I blow across the surface of the tea and release some of the tension building in my gut. I'm angry with myself for feeling like this, picking her up on every little word. The poor woman must feel as nervous and awkward as I do, probably more, as she was the one who put me up for adoption. I give her my warmest smile and take the huge slice of cake she hands me.

She joins me at the table and we both take a big bite. I like the fact that we attack the cake and don't mess about nibbling it out of politeness. Cakes like this need appreciation. 'Oh gosh, this is delicious,' I say, dabbing a napkin to my mouth.

'One of my finest, I have to admit.' Mellyn's eyes hold a hint of pride and a smile. 'So, I'm sure you have lots to ask me – fire away.'

God. That's a tough one. Where to start? I point to my bulging cheeks to give myself thinking time. I decide the best approach is to continue from where we started upstairs. Perhaps the more important questions will come later. 'You were saying that you moved here nearly six years ago. What made you leave St Austell?'

Mellyn twists her mouth and looks at me. 'It is a very sad story, actually.' She pushes her half-eaten cake to one side and looks out of the window. Then she turns back to me, blinks a few times and swallows hard.

Marvellous. I thought I'd start with something straightforward, and now it looks to be the opposite. 'Oh, sorry. Please don't answer if you'd rather not.'

'No, I'll tell you. There'll be some really tough questions I'll have to answer today, so I'd better get used to it.'

'Only if you're sure.'

She nods and says, 'I moved here after my parents died – your grandparents. They died in a car crash on the way to do some Christmas shopping. I was supposed to be going with them, but I went to meet a friend at the last minute, or I wouldn't be here to tell the tale.'

Oh, dear God. I want to stop her. The kitchen's too hot; the walls are closing in – I feel trapped. How could she just spring something like that on me without warning? The cake has become a cloying lump in my mouth, too heavy to swallow. It guts me that my grandparents have died and such a short time ago. I so hoped I would be able to meet them; yet another stupid fantasy shot. I manage to force the cake down but can't find the words to make her stop. She just goes on and on in a faraway detached tone.

'I had to identify them. Not much of a mark on them, which was a blessing. They did have little cuts here and there on their faces from the windscreen, but nothing too gory. After six months I packed up and came here. They'd left a few savings and with their house up for sale I knew I'd have enough money to start again. I couldn't face being there after what had happened. Too many happy memories. I wanted a fresh start and I found it here.'

She runs her hand through her hair and the bangles clank again. She continues to look trance-like through the window.

'I got work in the jewellery shop in town that I now own forty per cent of. The majority owner has since moved up to Nottingham to look after her elderly parents. She didn't want to leave here, but thought it was her duty. I wish I had that worry. My parents were only sixty-three, active, outgoing. I loved them so much and I miss them every day.' Her voice catches, and she looks back at me, silent tears rolling down her face.

Her expression unlocks something inside and the kitchen walls move back to their original position. My eyes fill, and I reach for her hand. 'Oh, I'm so sorry. That must have been such an awful shock … and it's a shame that I'll never meet them now.' I stare at the crumbs on my plate, avoiding the pain in her blue eyes. Why had I added the last bit? It wasn't all about me, was it?

'They would have loved you, even though …' Mellyn shakes her head, lets go of my hand to wipe her tears away and returns to her cake. 'No use in getting hysterical, we've a long way to go.' She finishes the cake, dabbing the napkin to her mouth, has a sip of tea and leans her elbows on the table. 'Okay, so what else would you like to know?'

If she thinks she's being hysterical, she hasn't seen me in full flow, but the way she just switched back to normal again feels a bit odd. I sit back in my chair. Where on earth should I take this next? 'Mellyn—'

'What do you think of my name – Mellyn?'

I try to stop my mouth dropping open at the change of subject but fail. Closing it again I smile, even though I'm totally gobsmacked for a second or two. 'I, err … Well, I think it's a lovely name. It's …'

Obviously, a rhetorical question anyway because she hurries on. 'When I came here I wanted a complete new start and that included my name. I *adore* the name Tamsyn and seriously considered changing it to that. Do you like Tamsyn?'

'Yes, I …'

'Thing is, I was bullied rotten at school because of the name Mellyn. Smelly Melly with the big fat belly they used to call me, even though I wasn't fat, nor smelled.' She gives a brittle laugh. 'Well, I hope I didn't. And then, later on, my husband called me Melon as a term of endearment. No matter how much I asked him not to, he wouldn't stop. Still, what could I expect – he was such a bastard. Anyway, though I loved Tamsyn, in the end I decided that Mellyn I was born, and Mellyn I would stay. I came through the shit storm because of it and I'm much stronger the other end.'

Shock at the revelation about her husband and also at the hatred in her voice as she speaks about him renders me dumb again. Her eyes have become the colour of waves on a stormy day. Eventually I hear myself say, 'Oh, that must have been awful. I did wonder if you had been married, but then you still have your maiden name.' I pause, expecting something back, but all I get are more waves. Then, because I can't stand the awkward silence, I just say the first thing that comes into my head. 'So, you never had more children?'

'No. Thank God! I couldn't have imagined loving any child of his. And let's change the subject please – I don't want to talk about him.' Her mouth draws into a tight pout as though someone had pulled drawstrings at the corners of her lips.

'Sorry. I seem to be always saying the wrong thing today.'

Sunlight shines on the waves and she smiles. 'No. Not at all, it's just a very emotional meeting, that's all. Please, go on.'

I think quickly. Bullying is common ground between us, and hopefully not too contentious. 'I can relate to being bullied at school.' I stop when I realise she would obviously ask why, and then I'd have to tell her, and then she'd feel guilty, and then I'd have to say sorry – again. Not too contentious? What the hell is wrong with me today? It's as if someone has taken out my brain and replaced it with a cupcake.

'That's a shame, why?'

Yep. Just as I had predicted. Then I remember one incident and run with it. 'Because of my name, just like you.' I shoot her a broad smile as if it's some huge achievement and then get a grip. 'Yeah, they said Lucinda sounded posh and the surname Lacey meant that my full name was alliterative. Of course, they didn't say alliterative, but that they both began with an L.' I'm making it up as I go along now but I can't stop. '"Lucinda Lacey," they said, "who does she think she is – the bloody queen?"' I say the last bit to the table in a very small voice.

'Sounds more like a porn star to me,' she says quietly. My head comes up and our eyes lock. I expect her to laugh but her expression is serious. Eventually she winks and laughs. 'Got you there. But to be honest, having Lacey as a surname is a bit unfortunate. You like Lucinda though, yes?'

It is more of a statement than a question. 'Oh yes. As you know, I use Lu mostly, but—'

'Because that was the only thing I gave you that I was told you would keep. Lucinda means light, and she was the Roman goddess of childbirth. I thought it was appropriate, because you certainly brought me light – and hope, at first, until …' She pauses and drains her cup. 'Anyway, you were Lucinda Rowe originally. Much better than Lacey, don't you think?'

What do I say to that? The way she said it makes me think she's disrespecting my parents, not just musing over the sound of the name. 'Um, I suppose I'm used to it, but Rowe is a lovely name.'

She sits back in her chair, folds her arms and stares at me. 'I hope that you will learn to call me Mum. Perhaps it's a bit soon at the moment, though?'

What the fuck! I swallow anger and frustration. Yes, it is, given that the only woman I had ever called Mum was so recently in her grave. I feel my face flush under her direct scrutiny and wish I could rewind time to when she opened the door. At least I would feel more prepared. 'Yes, I think it might be. Let's just see how we go.'

Mellyn puts her hand to her mouth and her eyes grow round. 'Oh, I've upset you. How stupid of me to say that? Your adoptive mother died not long ago. It just slipped my mind with all the excitement of having you back with me, darling.'

Slipped her mind? How the bloody hell could it *just* slip her mind? And 'darling'? I want to get up and leave. This whole meeting is like a train crash and I'm in the last carriage, knowing what's going to happen but unable to stop the inevitable. Luckily, manners come to my rescue and I thank my parents for making me be polite even when I don't want to be. How very British. 'No, you haven't upset me, really. Don't worry. How far is the hotel from here?'

'You're not going yet, surely?' The fingers over her mouth began to tremble.

'I thought I might. It's been a long day and I need to check in and so forth.' That was lame and we both know it.

Mellyn stands. 'Oh, I *have* upset you, haven't I? Look, don't go yet, I was going to make us supper later. I've got lots of yummy stuff in specially – you like seafood, I hope? If not, I can nip down to the shops and—'

'No, don't put yourself out—'

'I'm not. I was looking forward to it. I want to cook for you.' She stops and sighs. 'This isn't going how I imagined at all. I'm so sorry.'

I watch a frown crease her forehead and she blinks a few times. I think she meant what she said and I'm glad, because I know how she feels. Damn it. Time to reach out with the olive branch. 'No. It isn't going how I imagined it either. Look, let me go and check in, hang my clothes up, get changed and stuff and then come back here in an hour or so? Sound like a plan?'

Her mouth tries to smile but doesn't quite make it. Perhaps she's been taking lessons from Adelaide. 'Sounds like a plan. So, see you about six, six thirty? You just follow the road round and Pebble House is the second on your right.'

'Okay. Thanks. See you soon.' She looks as if she's going to hug me again, so I bend down to pick up my handbag. She leads the way outside.

Chapter Nine

How ironic. I'd come to cast away stones and here I am in Pebble House. The B&B is only five minutes away from Seal Cottage but nearly in the town, so the view from the window is of a small car park and the backs of shops. The room itself is nice enough though. I had chosen it because it had lots of five-star reviews for friendliness of staff, food and cleanliness. It certainly has everything I'll need for the next few days, or a week, depending on how things go. Right at this moment as I unpack my suitcase I think it might be the former.

The iron in its box weighs down one of the bags and I remember Adelaide looking at it in surprise as it lay in my boot this morning. I'm already homesick and that isn't a good sign after only a matter of eight hours or so. It also reminds me to ring Dad and tell him I've arrived safely.

Hearing Adelaide's voice on the line makes me wish I was just around the corner. 'Lu! So glad you called, I was going to give it another hour and then ring you.'

'Sorry. I know I said I'd call as soon as I arrived, but—'

'No, don't apologise, I quite understand. Your dad has just gone to the pub with your uncle Graham. He didn't want to, but I persuaded him. I think he's been sitting about wondering how you were getting on, so that will take his mind off things.'

'Dad's actually gone out for a drink? Blimey. Wonders will never cease.' I talk in clichés for a while, wondering what to tell Adelaide about my less than perfect first meeting today.

Adelaide makes my mind up for me by asking, 'So have you met your birth mother yet?'

'Yes.' Before the call I thought I'd just underplay my worries, but my tongue tells her everything.

'I see. So, you're disappointed?'

'Well, yes, a little,' I answer, noting the surprise in Adelaide's voice and wondering if she's not been listening properly. 'Don't you think her behaviour is a bit odd, then?'

'In ordinary circumstances, yes. But she's had thirty years to mull all this over and probably feels guilty. She might be coming over all wrong because she's nervous. And it sounds like she's not had an easy time, what with the bullying, having you so young, her parents dying in that awful way and then her ex-husband being a, you know … what she called him.'

I smile. Adelaide couldn't say the word *bastard*. I'd never heard her say anything worse than 'damn' in all the years I had known her. Perhaps she would spontaneously combust if she did. 'Yes. I suppose that makes sense,' I say. And it does to an extent.

'Give her time. You don't know enough yet. You haven't even broached how she came to give you up, or who your father was, have you?'

'No. That might come up over dinner, I suppose.' God only knows what will happen when we do talk about that. After this afternoon I'm not looking forward to it at all. 'So, you think it's all okay then?' I so wish Adelaide was here; her wise counsel is exactly what I need.

'I think so, yes. As I said, it will take a bit of time.'

'But what do you make of her wanting me to call her Mum so soon, while apparently forgetting that the woman who was my mum has only recently … left us?' I'm sounding like Dad now.

'I don't know. Perhaps she was trying to make up for lost time. Wanted to show you how much she cared. You can't rule out that she was jealous of Hannah either. It was insensitive of her, nevertheless, but she said sorry, didn't she?'

'Yes.' I can almost see Adelaide perched on the edge of the sofa, eyebrows raised, mouth twisted to one side in a tight pucker.

'There you are then.'

'Oh, Adelaide. Thank you. You are so wise, and I miss you already.' I hear a catch in my voice and draw in a deep breath.

'What a nice thing to say, Lu. Now remember, I'm here at the end of a phone day or night, okay?'

I nod and then remember that I'm on the phone. 'Okay. Thank you, Adelaide, I'll be in touch soon.'

Trepidation steps over the threshold of Seal Cottage with me later that evening, but I needn't have worried. Mellyn is in a much better mood and more … normal, somehow. That thought rattles me. How do I know what normal is for a forty-six-year-old woman who has been through whatever it was she's been through? I don't know her, or what her life is like or had been like, so perhaps I should leave labels out of it.

'Would you like dinner outside on the patio?' She touches my arm. 'Though I'm not sure you'll be warm enough in that sleeveless top. How pretty it is too, the dark green really brings out your eyes. Well, not out physically, of course, that would be a bit macabre. But you're wearing jeans, and I have a cardigan that would fit if it gets too nippy.' She stops and takes a breath. 'I'm babbling, aren't I?'

'A little.' I laugh and touch her shoulder. I do it without thinking, a reassuring touch, a caring touch and it felt natural.

She places her hand over mine. 'I just want to get things right this evening. And I was thinking that we should leave the heavy question and answer session. It felt like an interview earlier – not your fault at all – I suggested it, stupidly. I think we should just chat and I promise that as the conversation turns to the past, as it will, I'll try to answer you calmly. Please forgive me for everything I said before. I was trying too hard and it came out all wrong.'

Thinking of what Adelaide had said I step forward and give her a quick hug and that feels natural too. 'It wasn't all you. I felt exactly the same.' I return her smile and pull a bottle of Prosecco from my bag. 'I could use a glass of this, how about you?'

'That was the best seafood salad I have ever had in my entire life,' I say as I clink glasses with Mellyn across the little white table on the garden patio. It's the truth; I haven't had many really, but of the ones I've had, this one was king. I roll up the sleeves of my borrowed cardigan. It had been a bit chilly outside at first, but the Prosecco is warming me up.

'Thank you.' Mellyn tosses back her hair and smiles. 'It had all the finest local ingredients from Bob the crab man. He comes around the houses selling door to door and has a stall in the market too.'

'Do you mean he is an actual crab, or that he sells them?' I ask, remembering her crack about the top bringing my eyes out earlier. I'm a fan of literalist humour too.

She laughs out loud. 'Yes, he's an *actual* crab. He ties his wares on his back and runs sideways up our hill. On his six legs it doesn't take him long!'

'Is it six or eight?'

'Hm. You've got me there. I think it could be eight including the big front pincers. No.' She closes her eyes 'No. It's eight legs and two big pincers – so ten in total.'

'I think you're right, Mr Attenborough,' I say, and divide the last of the Prosecco between our glasses.

'And I think a nice zesty dessert wine is called for, don't you?' Mellyn smiles and gathers the dishes.

'Pudding? Not sure I'll have room after Bob's finest and your lovely homemade bread.'

'Could you try just a little? I made a mess of it though,' she says, her mouth a straight line.

'I'm sure you didn't,' I say brightly, hoping that she wasn't going odd on me again. 'I would *love* to try some. What did you make?'

'Eton Mess!' she says with a giggle. 'Told you I made a mess of it.'

'Ha, you got me there.' I wave a spoon at her, thankful that the nice evening is still on track.

The pudding, like everything else, is delicious and, after I help her clear away, we return outside, just as the fading fingers of sunset cast a handful of stars high into the soft navy sky. The salt-washed breeze that encouraged me to wear the cardigan has quietened, and the honeysuckle hangs sweet in the air like a kiss to the day. Mellyn insists that we have a brandy to go with the chocolates I brought, and I agree, despite having misgivings about the amount of alcohol we've already consumed. We have a bottle of water on the table too, just to be sensible. It isn't as if I'm drunk, of course, just relaxed and happy. We've not talked about anything personal all evening; the conversation has been easy, and we share the same silly sense of humour.

Mellyn swirls the amber liquid in her glass and holds the side of it against a candle in the middle of the table. 'Nothing like a warm brandy,' she says, her eyes sparkling in the flickering light. 'Neil used to drink brandy.' She removes the glass from the flame, swirls the brandy again and takes a sip. 'In fact, he would drink anything he could get his hands on. That was the problem.' She makes a noise in her throat somewhere between a snort and a choke. 'One of the problems, I should say – he had many.'

'Neil was your husband?' I know that this is an unnecessary question, but safer than asking a more leading one.

'Yes. We were married for six years. I knew after the first month that I'd made a big mistake.' She looks at the question in my eyes. 'He used to get drunk and then beat me. Oh, it was the usual story – sweetness personified until I had a ring on my finger and then, wham!' She thumps her hand on the wrought-iron tabletop, making the candle and me jump.

My heart swells with sadness for her, but again I try to keep my questions neutral. 'That must have been terrible for you … how did he take to the divorce?'

Mellyn gives me a sidelong glance, bites her lip and then speaks to the sky. 'We didn't divorce. He died – three months after my parents, actually.'

My mouth wants to fall open, so I put my hand over it and shake my head. The poor, poor woman. She looks at me and drinks some more brandy. I follow suit, glad of the burning sensation in my throat to clear a path through my emotion. 'How did he—'

'Die?'

I nod. She sighs. 'Neil was cleaning the guttering in my parents' house because we were selling it. He'd done odd jobs around the place, getting it ready for viewing, you know? Anyway, I was there too, painting in the downstairs cloakroom, and heard the crash. I ran out the back door. The ladder was on the patio and so was he. Death was instant according to the coroner. Hit his head on a rockery stone, caved one side of it in completely.'

A shiver passes through me and pulls shock after it. How did she cope with something like that? I note that Mellyn's voice has taken on that faraway quality again and she'd spoken to her glass, the sky, the table, anything but me. She seems distant, unreal. It's like watching a monologue in a play. I assume that must be how she copes – removing herself from the pain, being someone else. 'I … I don't know what to say,' I manage.

'Nothing *to* say really.' Mellyn pours us both more brandy before I can put my hand over my glass. 'I wasn't sad he died, just indifferent really. No, that's not true. I did feel relief if I'm honest, no more beatings, and I could do what I liked with the money from the house. Neil had already started dictating what we would use it for. He wanted a new car, holiday, clothes, and of course he would have frittered it on endless bottles of booze. We lived in rented and I told him I wanted to own our own house. He laughed at that, said it was a waste.' She shrugs her shoulders and gives me a smile. 'Anyway, I moved here, bought this place, started a new life.'

'I'm so glad you did. You deserve some happiness after what you've been through.' I sip my brandy and offer her a chocolate. She pops it in her mouth and makes appreciative noises. I want to steer her away from thoughts of Neil and death before the mood gets any more miserable. 'Do you have siblings?'

She pulls a face. 'No. Just me. I was a bit lonely growing up, but at least I was spoiled rotten!'

'Same here,' I say, and then flick my gaze away, hoping that she wouldn't ask about the loneliness.

'You see it would have been all very different if I'd been able to stay with your father, Joe. He was my one true love. Your life would have been different too – we would all still be together now as a family …' Mellyn leans forward in her seat, rests her elbows on her knees, and covers her face with both hands.

At this revelation, the caramel chocolate in my mouth somehow slips half-chewed down my throat and I start to cough. I feel her slapping my back and holding a glass to my lips. I take a sip and cough even more because I'd taken in the fumes from the brandy as I drew a deep breath. I point at the bottle of water and she hands it to me.

Once I've recovered she says, 'I'm not sure we can handle any more history tonight if you're going to conk out on me!'

I hear the hint of laughter in her voice and that sets me off. We both laugh hysterically, though it hadn't been that funny. It's the best medicine and just what we needed. I nod. 'I think it might be best to wait until tomorrow now.'

Mellyn stands and leads the way inside, still giggling. 'Yes, and I've taken the next few days off work. So tomorrow I have a lovely surprise for you.'

'Ooh, interesting,' I say.

We hug on the doorstep, say goodnight, then I set off down the moonlit street wondering what the surprise will be. For the moment, however, I will be happy just getting to know more about Mellyn and my birth father, Joe.

Chapter Ten

The *Sprite*, twenty-three feet of sleek and shiny green motor cruiser, complete with a bathing platform on the stern, four berths, kitchen, and powerful engine turns out to be the surprise … and she's mine. Mellyn, once clear of the harbour, opens the throttle and races towards the far horizon. I wipe salt spray from my face and laugh into the wind. I still can't quite take it all in. I relive the last few hours over again in my head.

This morning I had received a text from Mellyn to meet down at the harbour because we were off on a picnic. I thought it was an odd place to meet, but it all became clear when, through the shimmering haze, I saw her waving at me from the deck of a boat. Dressed for the part in white crop trousers and a stripy T-shirt with a sweater knotted around her neck, and hair twisted up into a clip at the back of her head, I thought she looked more like my age than her own today. She wore a smile as wide as the sky and her eyes reflecting the sparkling water danced with mischief. The breeze clanked a metal tune through the rigging of an armada of moored craft and I was glad I'd opted for trousers too.

Once aboard, I'd received a hug and the news that to celebrate our reunion, this boat was a gift. My mouth had opened and closed itself a few times and then I asked her what on earth she meant. 'Simple, you silly thing. This boat was mine and now it's yours. It's to show you how much you mean to me,' Mellyn had said, happiness clear in her eyes.

'But … but you can't. It must be worth a fortune,' I'd whispered, realising as I said it that I had no idea about boat prices, but this was no old tub.

'I can, and I have. Not a fortune, a few bob, but you are worth far more to me than any possession.'

Overwhelmed, my heart swelled at the enormity of such a gift, but also because of her last words. I thought it safer not to speak and just hugged her tightly. I could sense that she was waiting for me to reciprocate, but although I felt affection, until I could tell her genuinely that I loved her, I would keep those words in reserve. I'd spoken into her sweater. 'I don't know what to say.'

Mellyn had stepped back and run a finger under her lashes. 'Say thanks and let's get going, eh?'

From my plush swivel seat, I watch the seagulls crying overhead. Mellyn sails the boat expertly along the coast, and the wind tugs her hair free of the clip. I laugh again and draw in a few lungfuls of salt air; it's good to be alive and right here today. If only I could take and bottle the exhilaration, happiness and excitement rushing through my heart, I would never have to worry about being low ever again. I'd just take a sip on grey days, and my cloudy skies would turn blue.

The plan is to drop anchor around the other side of the bay in a sheltered cove and go for a swim – Mellyn, ever organised, had bought a swimming costume for me this morning as she'd walked down to the harbour – then afterwards we'll have a picnic aboard the *Sprite*.

From the boat, the perspective of the land is like watching a commercial for the Cornish tourist board. The sun drenches a long white sandy beach decorated with sprinkles of families, brightly coloured windbreaks, sandcastles, and nearby a raft of surfers bob like seals in the cerulean Atlantic. As I watch, a few pick up a wave and glide effortlessly to shore, even though a jolly breeze whips the crests of waves into white meringue peaks.

Around the headland it's a different story. A few tiny beaches inaccessible by foot cling to the roots of cliffs. Yet seabirds are unafraid, and show off, majestically wheeling and gliding the air waves as if copying the surfers. I note after a few minutes that the *Sprite* has slowed her speed and that the water is becoming shallower and clearer. It seems impossible that these turquoise calm waters belong to the ones we have sailed across around the headland. If I didn't know better, I would have said we had been picked up by a water spout and dropped in the Mediterranean.

As I peer down into the blue, Mellyn shuts off the engine and drops anchor. 'Seen any fish?' she asks, looking over my shoulder.

'Not sure – I thought I saw something glint far below.' I stand and secure my hair in a ponytail. 'Wonder if it was a piece of pirate treasure?'

Mellyn narrows her eyes at my half smile. 'More likely to be a shark,' she says and bites her bottom lip.

'Sharks, here? You're joking, right?'

'No, we have quite a few round these parts,' she says in a broad Cornish accent.

I sigh. 'But not the ones that would attack, surely?'

She looks up to the left and ponders. 'Not unless they're really hungry.' She takes in my worried expression. 'And the name's Mellyn, not Shirley.'

I laugh at the old joke and also to make her think that I'm not taken in by the shark thing – though even to my ears the laughter sounded nervous. 'Hm, so you go in first to see if they're hungry.'

Mellyn gives a hearty complacent laugh. 'You're okay, just me joking. I've been swimming round the Cornish coast all my life and never spied even one.' She pauses and holds up her finger. 'Actually, that's a lie. I have seen a few basking sharks – you know, the enormous ones?' I nod. 'But they will just suck you to death – no teeth, see.' She bares her own and snaps them together.

I raise an eyebrow. 'Are we going swimming or what?'

Mellyn appears from below deck in a light blue swimsuit which accentuates her curves and colouring. I'm impressed by her toned physique and hope I'll look as good at her age. I watch her move around the boat. She has confidence wearing so little that many would envy. The emerald green suit she'd bought me is a perfect fit and she compliments me on my figure. 'I was just thinking the same about yours,' I say. 'Do you work out?'

'Not consciously in a gym or anything. I do swim a few times a week and love walking the cliff paths, of course. I'm lucky, though, I don't really have to watch what I eat.' She tugs my ponytail gently. 'Plus having you so young meant my stomach muscles just snapped back into place without me having to think about it.'

My perfect cue to ask more about what happened back then shouts loud and clear from the wings, but before I can say anything, Mellyn climbs over the back seat and dives into the ocean with a splash. I step onto the diving platform and she beckons me in, a big grin on her face. I glance into the water again and it looks very inviting, but a few droplets that had abandoned the ocean as she'd dived chill the sole of my foot. 'How's the water?' I ask, kneeling down.

'Wet!'

I give her a look and dip my hand below the surface. Yes, it's cold, but warmer than I imagined. 'Okay, let me gird my loins.'

'Just jump in, ya big wuss! No good faffing about or you'll never get in.'

I know she's right, but I've always been the same. I can stand to be hot, but cold is something I avoid where possible. Now, if I was standing in front of a heated pool, the story would have been very different. Mellyn swims over and grabs hold of the diving platform. I feel her cold wet fingers on my elbow sending goosebumps along my sun-warmed skin, and then she pretends to pull me in. 'Okay, okay,' I say, standing up. 'I'm going to dive in – stand back.'

She flips onto her back and laughs at the sky. 'I'd have to be pretty tall to stand back at the moment.' Mellyn has a voluptuous laugh. Sometimes the sound of laughter is a straight, hard line. Perhaps it's false. Laughter like that certainly tells you nothing about the reason for its existence. But hers is plump, rounded and curvy, it makes your own laugh want to join it, dance with it, rejoice in levity.

I give her laughter a dancing partner and get into a diving pose. 'I think you'll find you need to swim away a little, or I'll end up sinking you.'

'Hey, perhaps you should jump in if you're not used to the water,' she muses, performing a lazy backstroke.

I sigh and then execute what I know will be a perfect dive, leaving hardly a ripple in my wake. Icy teeth bite into every part of me, my breath catches in my throat, then my head breaks free of the surface into a raft of sunlight and my ears ring with the tail end of Mellyn's whoop. Already I can feel the bite of cold leaving my blood, so to aid the process I exhale into the water and strike out away from the boat, my arms powering through the turquoise water in a strong front crawl.

Patches of ocean run cold and warm as my body moves effortlessly beneath clouds and sun. Adrenalin runs too, through my veins and my heart, spurring me ever faster. It's as if a switch has flicked in my brain making it neutral, allowing sinews, muscle and bone to take control. It has been a long time since I've felt like this, too long. When I swim I can enjoy the ride, let my mind go blank, feel my worries drain away, submerge in my slipstream.

After a time, an ache in my lungs slows my pace and it's then that I'm aware of my name carrying on the breeze. 'Lu! Lucinda! Come back!'

I stop and tread water in a slow circle; my heart lurches at just how far I have swum. I look at the *Sprite* in the distance and at the rocks closer by. The swell of the water is being sucked inexorably towards them until the waves crash into their craggy faces. I can make out Mellyn standing on the diving platform waving her arms as if she's being attacked by a swarm of midges. 'Come away from the … ocks. It's too dan …'

I make the shape of the okay sign with my fingers, unsure if she can see it, and toss a strand of wet hair out of my eyes to look to my left. In the few seconds I have been treading water, the current has pulled me even closer towards the rocks. Prickles of adrenalin course through my veins again, but for different reasons; against the tide, getting back to the boat will be much harder than the outward journey. I draw a breath and swim.

'My God! You gave me one hell of a scare. I wanted to come with the *Sprite* and get you, but you were too near the rocks!' Mellyn kneels down on the platform and holds out her hands to me. I wave them away and just cling to the rail until my heart stops thundering in my ears and my breathing becomes less laboured. 'Are you okay?' she says, her voice wavering.

I clear water from my nose with thumb and forefinger and nod. 'Yes … perfectly. Just … not used … to sea swimming. Loved being back in the water so much … I didn't think about currents.' I take a few long deep breaths and then catch the look of concern in her eyes. 'Hey, I'm fine, honest.'

'Thank God,' she says, holding out her hands again, and this time I take them. 'I had no idea you were used to the water and then you took off like an Olympian!'

With her help, I heave myself onto the platform and she throws a thick towel around my shoulders. 'Not quite an Olympian, but I did swim for my county for a few years.' I rub my body briskly with the towel. 'There was talk of the Olympics actually, but once I'd started work there was little time to practise.'

'Well, let's get a warm drink inside you and then you can tell me all about it.'

The bright morning turns to a mellow afternoon and the conversation to more pertinent areas. Once I'd recovered from my swim we'd had coffee and cake, then later, sandwiches, strawberries and champagne. The champagne is another treat to celebrate our reunion and I recline on the back seat, my feet up, fizz in hand, and gaze up at the sky's mackerel underbelly. I feel like a star on movie set; things like this just don't happen to me.

Mellyn is sitting on a swivel chair opposite me with her feet on an upturned bucket. As the boat rocks gently on the swell, the sunlit water casts dappled patterns along her arm like an ever-changing tattoo. I pluck up the courage to ask if she'd tell me about Joe. Mellyn gives a sad smile. 'Joe. My beautiful Joe.'

'Was he?'

She frowns at me, head on one side, then understands. 'Beautiful, you mean? Oh yes. He was the most handsome boy in the school, taller than most, muscular, eyes the exact same colour as this turquoise water.' She nods overboard towards the shallows. 'But sometimes they looked greener, a bit like yours. And he had the same jet-black hair as you. Bright as a star, a straight-A student – he had it all.'

I watch her eyes dance as she remembers him, a magnet for the blues flecking the deeper ocean. It's good to hear an account of the past not told in her distant voice. Perhaps she only reserves that for upsetting memories. 'Were you in the same classes?'

'Yes, in the younger years, but not later as we chose different options. He was the scientist, I was the arty one.'

'So, when did you start dating and who asked who?'

She smiles and looks into the middle distance as if she's watching memories on a screen. 'He asked me. It was at the Christmas disco when we were fifteen. He'd borrowed his dad's aftershave and overdone it a tad. He came up to me and my friends at the edge of the dance floor when "Hello" by Lionel Richie was playing and, after a few stuttering false starts, asked me to dance. I said yes, of course, because as I told you, he was the most handsome boy alive, but as soon as we'd set foot on the dance floor the music changed to "Karma Chameleon"! No smooches on the dance floor that night.' Mellyn flushes and looks at her hands. 'Though we made up for it on the walk home.'

'How long were you together?' I ask, hoping that this question holds within it the seeds of my existence. I want a response that will present a bouquet of fully formed answers, blooms for my nectar-hungry inquiries.

Mellyn pokes at a bit of dried seaweed on her ankle and shrugs. 'Around a year, I guess. We would still have been together now, as I said, but everyone conspired against us. His parents, my parents, the school, everyone.' The distant faraway tone is back. She licks her finger and rubs at the seaweed.

'I was fifteen and he'd just turned sixteen. His parents had managed to get him into a prestigious college in Plymouth to do A levels in all the sciences. He was going to be a doctor, you see. When he found out about you, he refused to go, said he'd get a job, we'd get married and that he loved me more than any career he might have had.'

She pauses and looks at me, her bottom lip trembling. I fold my arms tight across my chest to keep a ball of emotion from reaching my throat.

'I loved him so much. I knew being a doctor had always been his dream, so to give it all up for me, us, was a testament to how much he cared.'

The next pause becomes large, solid, and heavy with past regrets, and I know she needs a lifeline. 'Did your parents like him?' An almost imperceptible nod makes purchase on the line. 'Then why couldn't they help you make it work?'

'Because I was fifteen, naive, would have had no prospects for the future, and the school had said they would expel me. Mum and Dad said that with no qualifications I would have no chance at all.'

'But Joe had said he'd get a job—'

'I wouldn't let him. I loved him too much. We agreed that he'd go to college, university, and then we'd make a life. We could give you so much more then.' Mellyn shifts in her seat and the bucket rolls across the deck. 'You see, we had agreed that we would keep you. I would get a flat, and social services would help if I was kicked out of my home—'

'They threatened to kick you out?'

'Oh yes. That's not all, they said that I should get a termination at first, go back to school and sweep the "whole mess" under the carpet as if it never happened … as if you never existed.'

Five words – *as if you never existed* – roll into one and swirl in my mind, collecting snippets of thoughts from my past that still hide in corners and behind screens. Recriminations, anger, sadness, worthlessness, abandonment are sucked into the word-tornado and shredded. I had been so close to never existing, but this woman sitting opposite, a defendant before my jury, somehow fought against the odds ... because here I was. Realisation that it didn't matter that I'd been adopted, wasn't rejected, hadn't been at fault, whirls so hard in my head that I think I might pass out. I owe Mellyn my life. Literally.

Mellyn reaches out her hand. 'You look pale. I expect this is all very painful for you.'

I take her hand and wanted to kiss it, tell her I love her, but something stops me. A huge surge of affection seeks acknowledgment, but I'm not sure it's time. I'm not sure what I feel. I squeeze her hand and say, 'Yes, of course, in one way. But in another I feel so lifted, relieved and very, very thankful to you.' A warm smile smooths her frown and she squeezes back my hand and then rights the bucket. 'So, what happened next?' I say.

Mellyn clears her throat and folds her hands on her lap. 'We told our parents of our plan and they rubbished it. Our love, such a wonderful thing, shared between us, and just for us, was put on show and ridiculed – made sordid. We had a meeting at their house with both sets of parents. It was autumn and pouring with rain. As I listened to their objections, through the window I watched leaves float from a tree onto a pond in the garden. Their red and yellow hues muddied as the raindrops pounded them from above and water sucked them from below. Soon they sank, brown, soggy, useless. I realised that our love was just like the leaves. We had no chance.'

She stands, picks up the champagne from the ice bucket and raises an eyebrow at me. I nod. I need something to wash down my anguish. 'They discussed us in the main as if we weren't there and my parents persuaded his that a termination was the best way forward. Joe and I were adamant that wouldn't happen, and they relented – they couldn't force me, after all. My parents said that I would have a roof over my head but on the condition that we had you adopted.'

I want the champagne to go to my head, but it refuses. 'My God. That must have been so hard, given that you both wanted to keep me.'

She makes a noise in her throat and takes a big drink. 'Hard? It was *the* hardest thing I have *ever* done in my life, bar none.' Mellyn looks at me and then away over the ocean. 'Joe went off to college and we kept in touch every day. I told him that I wouldn't give you up and I'd do what I said I'd do before – go to social services. He encouraged me and said I could move down to be near him. I couldn't live with him, though, he was staying with his aunt while he was in Plymouth. It all started to feel a bit hopeless by then to be honest. Social services said I wasn't homeless, so there was nothing they could do. They also said that given my age, it would be extremely difficult to manage without anyone to support me – said it would be best for you to be in a loving home with parents who could give you everything you needed. Joe and I hoped they were right, eventually agreed, and three days after you were born, they took you away.'

The pain in my heart is too much to bear but bear it I must. I have to be strong for her. I hate that distant tone to her voice and the way her body seems to have slumped as if her limbs suddenly weigh too much. 'Oh God, I'm so sorry … but they were right. You had no choice, and I couldn't have wished for better parents.'

She dabs her eyes with the corner of a towel. 'I'm so glad you understand, and I'm so glad you don't hate me.'

I borrow her towel. 'Of course, I don't! I can't imagine what it must have been like for you. You and Joe. Did you keep in touch with him afterwards?'

'Yes, but our phone calls became less frequent. He was so busy, you see, and he'd made other friends of course. I felt out of it, awkward. I was back at school, but we didn't seem to have much in common. In the end I felt I didn't really know him. One day he phoned, and I told my mum to tell him I wasn't in.'

I sense that she's on the edge of breaking down, so I say in the most matter-of-fact voice I could find, 'He became a doctor then?'

'Not sure. But knowing Joe, I think so. Like I said, we lost touch and I couldn't bear to look him up later. The wounds were too raw, still hurt even now.'

That much is obvious. I think about asking more, but both of us have had enough for one day. 'Perhaps we should head back to the harbour now?' I stand and put my arms around her. She stands too, and we study each other's faces. 'It's been a wonderful day and I'm so glad we found each other again,' I say, but then stop; my throat has closed over.

'It has been my absolute pleasure, Lu. I hope we'll have many more wonderful days.' She gives me a quick hug and then holds me at arm's length, just looking at my face as if trying to memorise it. Perhaps she can see a whisper of Joe in the contours. I know she deserves something special and I want to give it to her.

'I'm sure we will.' My heart thumps, my stomach clenches and then an argument for and against is settled in a second. 'And thanks so much again. I know you want me to call you Mum, and after what you have told me ... I feel like I might be able to before long. I feel so much closer to you now.'

'Oh, what a lovely thing to say!' Mellyn's face lights up and she holds me close. My heart sinks as she does, because it might have been my imagination, but I noticed that the warmth of her smile didn't quite reach her eyes.

Chapter Eleven

In the distance, through the margin of grey gauze floating between sky and ocean, I can just make out Godrevy Lighthouse standing sentinel, a white finger pointing skyward as though signposting heaven. I had read a leaflet that I'd picked up in the lobby of Pebble House, which described how the author Virginia Woolf had visited St Ives regularly on holiday as a child and had later written *To The Lighthouse*. Although it was set in Scotland, the lighthouse in it was thought to be based on Godrevy. Though I'm a voracious reader, I've never read it, nor anything of hers. But I've always wondered if she borrowed another 'o' from somewhere to slot into her surname – just to make it look less canine.

Vigour and energy haven't been swilling around my body just waiting to be used up lately; I think it's probably to do with all the upheaval and uncertainty after Mum's death. In my experience, that type of thing tends to make your limbs heavy and your bottom become irresistibly attracted to comfy chairs. But this morning I leapt from my bed like a March Hare with a head full of adventure and excitement, pleased to find that today my feet had become irresistibly attracted to walking through the still-sleeping town of St Ives to see the sun come up over the Island.

The Island, another leaflet had informed me, was not really an island but a peninsula, complete with a tiny one-roomed chapel and a breathtaking view of the town and beaches. Also, if you were lucky, on a clear day you could see the lighthouse. Dew-soaked grass under my feet, I stand watching the ocean, the sky and the lighthouse. Salt fingers tousle my hair and I hear the chatter of a jackdaw on the chapel roof behind me; I know there is no doubt at all that I am lucky. Very lucky indeed.

Since I had plucked up courage to tell Mellyn that I felt close to her yesterday, and that calling her Mum wasn't beyond the bounds of possibility, I've had a light feeling in the centre of my chest. At first, I thought she'd been annoyed because I didn't call her Mum there and then, but I was mistaken. When she'd come out of the hug, I had seen gratitude and satisfaction in her eyes. She hadn't made a big thing of it, I think that would have embarrassed us both, she'd just smiled, said thank you again, and then we'd returned to the harbour. We'd gone for a light supper in town and then both of us decided on an early night after all the excitement of the last few days. I had called her Mum in my head a few times and it had seemed a little awkward, but not uncomfortable.

Nevertheless, when I had thought of her in the middle of the night, it was 'Mellyn' that my mind preferred to use and not 'Mum'. I said Mum out loud in the darkness, but instead of Mellyn, I pictured the only Mum I had ever known. Remembering her face made me sad. It was as if I had rubbished everything she'd ever done for me, giving her well-earned title so quickly to someone else even in my mind – to a stranger really.

An impulse to ask for her forgiveness nudged my vocal cords a few times, but when I tried the words on my tongue, they slid back down my throat. In the end I thought it best, for now, to keep calling the woman that had given birth to me Mellyn. Until it felt natural to call her Mum. There's no rush, is there? Mellyn doesn't seem to mind, so all is good.

Judging by the way that the grey gauze is lifting on the horizon, tantalisingly revealing the hem of the pink and turquoise sky, I can tell it promises to be another glorious summer's day. I draw ozone into the depths of my lungs, stretch my arms out to the side and imagine what it would be like to take off from the cliffs and fly over the ocean, and then I turn my back on the lighthouse and walk towards the town.

Mellyn and I had arranged to meet later and have a look around the town properly; I'm particularly looking forward to the Tate St Ives. My stomach has already become used to the delicious cooked breakfast Pebble House supplies each morning and grumbles that it's time to eat after such an early start. The fresh air encourages its complaints and I quicken my step.

The smell of crisp bacon turns the grumble in my stomach into a roar and I hurry into the dining room and nod to the only other occupant, an older man wearing a sailor's hat and a jaunty air. 'In all my twenty years of coming here I have rarely met another early bird. It's only just gone a quarter past seven,' he says, and winks a blue eye in a brown weather-beaten face.

'I thought Rosie might let me have a coffee until the breakfast is officially served at half past,' I say, smiling. It's hard not to and it would have been like snubbing Captain Birdseye if I hadn't.

'Rosie's a lovely girl. She's only been here about two years, but she's a big improvement on hatchet-face Hilda.' The wink again. 'My name's Frank, by the way.' He waves a few sausage fingers and has a drink from a white mug with Frank printed upon it in blue letters.

'Lu,' I say, and point at his mug. 'That kind of gave you away.' Frank looks as if he's about to say something else but then Rosie comes in with toast rack and a full English.

'Morning, Lu! You're here early today. Is Frank being a nuisance?' Rosie places the food in front of Frank and laughs at his forlorn expression.

I had taken to Rosie immediately upon arrival. She's a few years younger than me, vivacious, blonde, petite, and permanently rushed off her feet. As far as I can tell she does more than her fair share around the place. The owners, Nadine and Alan, are in charge of smiling a lot and swanning past as if they're extras in Rosie's whirlwind production of *A Seaside Hotel*. She often can look quite serious until she smiles. That smile transforms her face from a cold sprout on the side of a Sunday dinner plate to a strawberry and cream delight.

'Was I being a nuisance, Lu?' Frank calls through a mouthful of toast.

'Not at all, Frank.' I attempt a wink and Rosie draws a chair up to my table and sits down opposite. She sets her back to Frank and leans towards me, her elbows on the table.

'Frank's lovely,' she says in a low voice, 'but he does tend to go on. We always serve him breakfast early but don't tell anyone else. He's been coming here for twenty years apparently. His wife died about five years ago, but he still comes just the same. Says that's what she would have wanted, and he feels closer to her when he's here somehow.' Rosie turns her bottom lip down.

'You whispering about me, Rosie?' Frank's reedy voice snakes across the room.

'Me? Never!' Rosie turns in her seat and puts her hand on her chest as though she's shocked that he would suggest such a thing.

I picture Frank's wife as round, jolly, and curly haired. I can't help but feel sorry that she's gone, even though I've never known her. It's both lovely and heartbreaking that Frank still comes on holiday to the same place. I expect he must feel closer to her when he's here because this is a place they would have planned for, looked forward to, dreamed about for the rest of the year. This is a place where they would have laughed the most, been happy.

I sigh. 'Life can be cruel, can't it? I mean, why couldn't fate allow them to be together?'

'That is a question that only the man himself can answer.' Rosie points a finger to the ceiling.

'You mean the boss, Alan? He is privy to the secrets of the universe?'

Rosie's brow furrows and then she catches the mischief in my eye. 'Yes, and Nadine is pretty clever too. I mean, she manages to be in charge of this whole place without doing anything at all.' Her whisper tails into a giggle.

I laugh and nod. 'I *had* noticed that.' Rosie puts her finger to her lips, tips her head to the corridor where Alan can now be heard chatting to someone, and pushes her chair back. 'I was wondering, could I get a coffee until it's time for breakfast, Rosie?'

'Of course, and I'll take your order too. I have noticed the way you keep looking across at Frank's breakfast.'

'I went for an early walk and now I must admit I'm ravenous.'

Rosie jots down my order and then taps the pencil against her teeth. 'I forgot to ask, is everything going well with your birth mother?'

I had briefly mentioned why I was here to her the other day and am pleased that she remembers. 'Brilliant, thanks. We went on a boat trip yesterday and started to get to the bottom of things.' I can tell that she's genuinely interested but notice the way she keeps looking over her shoulder, torn between my news and the call of work.

'That's great! I'd love to hear more about it all later.'

A passing thought hovers, and most unlike me I go with my instinct. 'Sure. We could go for a coffee or a drink some time if you like?' Immediately I regret it. The poor girl must have little free time and she'd not want to spend it with a stranger, would she? Especially not someone like me.

'That would be nice. I'm fascinated by all that long-lost family stuff. We'll arrange something later in the week?' She gives me a warm smile and hurries off.

Being a fairly good judge of character, I realise that she's genuine, and relief pushes doubt to one side. I remind myself that I'm no longer the 'horns in' timid girl I once was. I am changed and changed I'll stay. Intuitively I know that Rosie is someone I could get on with, given half a chance.

I have many favourite words, and 'bustling' is one of them. It describes the harbour area perfectly. The first part of it, 'bus', is like the word 'busy', and then if you removed the 'l' it reads 'busting'. So, the harbour is bustling, busy and busting out all over with tourists, seagulls, boats, street entertainers, cars sucking in their stomachs to squeeze through the tiny streets, and me, dawdling along, my brain absorbing it all like the skin of a chameleon. I would be more than happy if all the vibrant scenes of the area started running across my body for a while, like a magic lantern show. I stop and glance at my watch. Another twenty minutes before I'm due to meet Mellyn, so I let my feet guide me back into town.

Books had been my friends when others hadn't been during my schooldays, and this town has one of the loveliest bookshops I've yet seen. The St Ives Bookseller looks out onto the cobbled street from two large windows and, as you step through the door, it has the kind of atmosphere that wraps around you like a welcome embrace. It's light, friendly, and permeating the air, that divine inky fresh smell of new books that to me is better than any perfume.

Floorboards creak underfoot, poky corners hold shelves full of hidden treasures, and a further search reveals the more interesting and quirky features that only old buildings have. I could happily browse here all day, discovering authors new, fondly reacquainting with old favourites, and then, at the end of a shelf, almost hidden by a display, I see *To The Lighthouse* by Virginia Woolf.

I read the blurb and a brief biography and feel regretful and a bit stupid that I had assumed she was some grand prima donna writer putting an extra 'o' in her name. On the contrary, she was a feminist free thinker who married the writer Leonard Woolf. As part of the Bloomsbury Group they concerned themselves with democratic politics, art and literature, as well as the structure of sexuality. Sadly, she struggled with mental illness most of her life and, at the age of fifty-nine, drowned herself. I feel incredibly moved as I stand there holding her words in my hands. Perhaps it's the fact that I had gazed at that beautiful lighthouse that very morning as the sun rose, just as she must have many years ago. I am struck by the fragility of life and how, for some, it becomes impossible to bear.

I hold the book to my chest with one hand and continue to browse, trailing my fingers over the regimented spines, enjoying the feel of the glossy covers and guessing their contents from the clues the titles give me. I'm not really intending to buy, however. I have made my choice.

I think about how the brain, or my brain at least, assumes things from brief snatches of information and creates a whole impression about something, or someone, just as I had with Virginia Woolf. My brain had told me she was an upper-class privileged gadabout who had affairs and knew nothing about the real world. It might have gathered such gossip from not paying enough attention to half-watched documentaries, sixth form English Lit wafflers, or even a few minutes having to listen to a Radio 4 play when driving home from work because Mum had changed channels.

'A good choice,' the sales assistant says as she hands me my change.

'Thanks. I picked it because she spoke to me,' I say, though feel a bit daft afterwards, but I'm gratified to see that the assistant smiles as if she understood.

'Can't say as I've read any of hers,' Mellyn says as I show her my purchase outside the Tate St Ives. 'Wasn't she an upper-class twonk who went about being tragic?'

I laugh. It wasn't just me then. 'Not quite. I think some people get that impression of her though, if they don't really know about her life.'

She narrows her eyes. 'Do you know about her life?'

'More than I did yesterday. Did you know she used to come here on holiday?'

'No. So are we going in?' She nods to the entrance, I think a little impatiently. 'I've never been in here. If it wasn't for my culture-vulture daughter with her Woolf and Hepworth ideas, I would be looking round the sales and then straight in a pasty shop.'

'Nothing to stop us doing that later. And the Barbra Hepworth Sculpture Garden isn't in here – it's up the road. We could do that another time,' I say.

Mellyn rolls her eyes and places her hand on her chest. 'Oh, be still my beating heart.'

I roll my eyes back at her and look at the sweep of steps and beautiful curves of the entrance and then at the beach beyond. 'Isn't this a stunning building? And what a location.'

Mellyn shrugs. 'As I said, culture vulture.' She walks up the steps.

I smile and follow her inside. I'm hardly a culture vulture, but it's nice that she thinks I am. I appreciate art and literature, but it's okay with me if Mellyn isn't that bothered. So far, I have found we are similar in some respects and very different in others; it makes things interesting. On the boat yesterday, she gave me the choice of what to do today and she promised she wouldn't moan when I'd made it.

'You mean that this guy thought it would be okay to make a display from electric lights and call it art?' Mellyn says aghast and not so quietly a little while later.

A middle-aged couple glare from under frowns and move away from us. Heat creeps along my neck. 'It's all to do with the interpretation of the geography and history of this area and … minimalism,' I say, reading a sign on the wall but not truly getting it myself.

'Yes, I see that now,' Mellyn says, nodding and stroking her chin.

'You do?'

'No. I think it is the biggest pile of crap and an insult to my intelligence. Let's go.'

I think she will smile, but her face remains fixed and stony. I follow her into the next gallery and she tuts at each display and strides right through, her whole-body rigid as though she's had an electric shock. She stops in the next room and glares at the wall.

'Are they having a laugh?'

'Who?' I wish she'd keep her voice down.

'This lot, charging us to get in here, just to look at something a four year old could do.' She jabs her finger at the massive canvas in front of us. 'In fact, that's an insult to four year old's.'

People are glancing over again, and I look at my feet. 'We could give it a bit of a chance,' I say quietly. 'Let's read the sign to see what the artist—'

'Artist?' She flings her arms up. 'Artists are people like Rembrandt and Constable. These people are … well, I don't know what they are, but I'm off.'

She stalks towards the exit and I stand watching her with my mouth open. 'But—'

Mellyn turns and glares at me from the door. 'But nothing. You stay if you want, but I can't look at this shit a moment longer.' Her face is puffed and erupting in red blotches, as though just under its surface a volcano of embarrassment and indignation are wrestling with anger.

I stare at the canvas and listen to her footsteps growing fainter on the stairs. How could such a colourful pattern of whirls incite such anger in person? I realise that this thought is superfluous, placed there by the logical part of my mind as it valiantly tries to douse the raw shock of her words. Following Mellyn outside seems the right thing to do, but I haven't the faintest idea what I will say when I find her.

A wall separating road from sand curves up the hill to the left of the building and, leaning against it staring out to sea, shoulders hunched, legs rigid, is Mellyn. Long streamers of chestnut hair twirl like batons in the breeze and, as I draw near, I think I hear her say 'ruined it' and swear under her breath. I stand a stride away from her, lean my arms on the wall and follow her gaze. The beach looks much as it had yesterday and, on the horizon, a huge ship glides silently by.

'I was just cursing myself for acting that way in there just now. You must have thought I'd gone nuts,' she says to the ship.

'I didn't know what to think.' I look sidelong at her profile and see her mouth turn up at the edge.

'My daughter has impeccable manners. If the boot was on the other foot I'd be demanding answers and not very politely.'

I shrug and speak to the wall. 'You must have your reasons.'

'I must have, mustn't I?' She sidles along and nudges my elbow. 'Don't ask me to give you a coherent explanation though.' She looks into my eyes, and in hers I think I can detect a mixture of humour and despair.

'Okay, I won't.'

'Since Neil and my parents died, I have trouble controlling my temper. Only sometimes, don't worry.' She winks and nudges me again.

I force a smile but say nothing.

'I saw a shrink and he said that given the shock of it all – their deaths being unexpected – and all the stuff in my past'—she pauses and gives me a meaningful look— 'it wasn't surprising that the grief and abandonment I felt came out in the shape of anger and frustration. He also said that a lot of it was because I was blaming myself for events, and when I lashed out, I was really lashing out at myself.' We both watch her fingernail flick at a patch of sand on the top of the wall. Then she takes a deep breath and continues.

'He taught me some calming techniques and it helped for a while – so did the happy pills. Then after I stopped taking them it became more difficult. I'm normally able to handle it now though.'

I watch her expression struggling with feelings under the surface again and wonder what she blames herself for. 'You mean you felt guilty about giving me up?' Mellyn nods and looks at a family playing on the beach. 'I can see that, I guess, but how can you blame yourself for the deaths of Neil and your parents?'

'I don't really, not deep down. But you see, grief has no logic, according to Doctor Henver. I knew I could have done absolutely nothing to prevent them dying, but there are little voices that whisper in your ear in the wee small hours. "What if?" and, "If only I had done this, that, or the other." Oh, and not forgetting, "It was your fault he was on the ladder – you should have paid for a man to do it." This one really gets to me, even though Neil insisted we weren't spending good money on getting someone in, when he was just as capable.'

I can understand what she means about grief. 'It must have been hard. My friend and neighbour, Adelaide, helped me when Mum died. She told me that grief has no set pattern or master. I felt guilty because I couldn't cry, didn't know how to behave, how to feel even.'

Mellyn puts her arm around me and I rest my head on her shoulder. 'Oh dear, Lu. I'm sorry for being so insensitive, that's another one of my failings. I know it's not been so long since she died. I'm just too self-centered.'

'I've not noticed that. It's only natural that you focus on your own problems when you've just been …' I pause and think about how to describe what happened in the gallery, '… a bit upset.' It's all I can come up with.

'Going batshit crazy you mean,' she says with a little laugh. She scrubs her fist on her nose as if she has an itch. 'I just looked at that stuff and thought what a cop out, you know? All those people like me and you working their arses off to earn a crust, and they … they just vomit on a canvas and call it a masterpiece. Or switch a few light bulbs on and get shed loads of dosh. My dad thought the same about modern art. I could hear him saying it just then inside, and then all the sadness and loss kicked me in the gut … set me off.' She turns to face the gallery and folds her arms. 'The outside of the building is so much more beautiful than its contents.' She catches my look and removes the haughty tone. 'Look. I'm really sorry, must have ruined your day and freaked you out.'

I agree but can hardly say so. She does look sorry though and the explanation has made her behaviour a little easier to understand. 'I don't share your view on modern art, but you've told me what happened, so let's put it behind us. The day isn't halfway through yet. How about we go and grab that pasty for lunch and then look round the sales?'

She slips her arm through mine. 'That sounds more like it,' she says, a huge smile on her face, her eyes sparkling with excitement. I'm rocked on my feet. The weight of her sorrow lifted so quickly that I can't help but wonder if it had been genuine at all. 'Now, I know the exact place! It has the best pasties in Cornwall and it's right opposite a lovely clothes shop. Come on, best foot forward.' Mellyn squeezes my arm close into her side and hurries us down the street.

As I walk along beside her listening to her gunfire narrative on the best shops, eateries, pubs and entertainment in the area, all I can think about is the way she often seems to change her personality. It's as if someone has flipped a switch in her head. I noticed it the first day when she'd been so upset telling me about my grandparents' death, and then minutes later everything was okay again. She admitted just now that she had struggled with her emotions at the time, but that she was normally okay. But I worry that Mellyn might have a skewed view on what normal behaviour was. I also worry about how I'm supposed to respond to it. Today has been an eye-opener and if I'm going to be of any help to my mother I'll have to keep both permanently wide open and watch for the signs.

Chapter Twelve

'If I hear the words, "Of course you need an extra pair of hands, but just hang on while things pick up" once more, I *swear* I'm out of here, Nadine.' Rosie kept her voice calm, but she knew there would be no mistaking the quiet anger running through it, or the way her knuckles paled as her fingers gripped the broom handle.

Two high spots of colour appeared on her boss's pale cheeks as if crayoned there by an invisible child. An invisible child who had a very set idea of what a clown looked like, or possibly an eighteenth-century actress. Nadine had no pompadour wig, but her platinum hair, styled in a high bouffant bob, did a good impression. Rosie watched her plump red lips ruche into a pout and her brown eyes darken in a glower. 'I hardly think that's the right approach, Rosie.' Nadine nodded a warning towards the open dining room door. 'And this is *certainly* not the place for open discussion.'

Rosie swallowed a curse as her boss picked an imaginary bit off fluff from her black skirt and then walked towards the kitchen. *Incredible. If she thinks this is over, then she can damned well think again.* She followed in Nadine's wake, heart thumping, the broom held across her body in both hands like some pretend rifle. It was a good job it was just pretend, given the way she was feeling right now.

Nadine's round behind rudely presented itself as she bent over the dishwasher. Dear God. Rosie put down the broom and covered a smile with the back of her hand; Nadine must have been so worried about her threat to leave she was prepared to risk chipping a nail. 'What are you doing?' she asked, yet the answer was blatantly obvious. It would be great to make sure she wasn't having an hallucination though.

Nadine straightened up, her two red cheek spots spreading to the rest of her face. She placed dishes on the counter and blew down her nostrils. 'What does it look like? Giving you a hand, as I do most days ... though I don't think you notice.'

The gall of the woman. 'Really? You empty the dishwasher most days?'

'No. But I do all sorts of bits and bobs.' Nadine bent over the dishwasher again. 'You know – just to make your job easier?'

'What bits and bobs, exactly?' There was no way she was getting away with this.

Nadine whirled round, eyes like coals. 'God, I don't know! Stuff! I thought I would help out here after you just threatened to flounce out, and all I get is twenty sodding questions!'

'You unloading the dishwasher isn't enough. This place needs another pair of hands, even if it's part-time. I can't keep working flat out like this. I'm twenty-seven and when I get home I just fall asleep in front of the telly.' Rosie felt her shoulders go back and she stuck her chin out for good measure. 'And by the way, I *never* do that.'

'Never do what?'

'Flounce.'

Nadine narrowed her eyes. 'If you say so.' She shut the dishwasher and leaned her bottom against it. 'There just isn't the money for part-time staff. We have a chef, a cleaner and you. We are a boutique hotel, not The Ritz.'

Was this woman for real? 'A chef who cooks breakfast and that's it. He leaves all the ordering to me and the kitchen like a bomb site, which I then have to clean. A cleaner who works three jobs and cuts corners because you pay her pennies, and no, it's not The Ritz, but we have room for thirty guests and they need some bloody looking after!'

'I am aware that you work hard, Rosie, but you make it sound as if you do it all. Alan and I—'

'Alan and you sit on reception for half an hour now and then, while I'm running around the place like a blue-arsed fly. The rest of the time you're missing, usually off out lunching God knows where, or playing golf.' Rosie's heart raced, and she couldn't stop her words from matching it. 'I take the bookings, sit on reception, serve breakfast, talk to guests about the area and offer advice as if I'm a mini tourist information service, talk to folk like old Frank when they need an ear, clean up after the cleaner, order the food, organise the clean linen, strip and change the beds, and so many more things …' She could tell by the shutters slowly coming down across Nadine's face that her words were falling on deaf ears.

'Look. For one thing I don't appreciate you ranting at me, and for another, I've told you we don't have money for a part-time—'

'Okay.' Rosie undid her apron even though her fingers felt like somebody else's; she had no control over them. They flung the apron on the counter and then she heard herself say, 'I'm handing over everything to you right now. Watch carefully as I leave the kitchen, Nadine, not a flounce in sight.'

The question 'What have you done?' repeated inside her skull with every step she took as she hurried away, but the answer came back: 'I don't care. It was about time I stood up to that supercilious, lazy, good for nothing piece of—'

'Rosie!' Nadine yelled, and footsteps echoed along the corridor behind her.

'What?' If that woman was going to try and wheedle her way out of trouble yet again she wouldn't answer for the consequences.

'Stop and listen before I have a heart attack.'

'I've stopped and I'm listening.' Rosie looked at Nadine's heaving bosom and mad pompadour hair.

'Okay, you win. Get a part-time helper but I need to vet them first.' She patted her hair and looked beyond Rosie's shoulder. 'Now I'm off for a lie down. I feel quite giddy.'

Once she had the corridor to herself Rosie leaned her head against the cool wall and took a few calming breaths. She allowed herself a little smile. At last she'd got her way, and hell, did it feel good.

Seated at reception, Alan shook out his newspaper and held it shield-like in front of his face as though he was trying to block out Rosie's. This was his response to her telling him she'd be gone an hour and he should expect Mr and Mrs Barrow before three. He was normally borderline rude, but because of her showdown with Nadine, had obviously crossed the border. Well tough. If he was determined to act like a spoiled brat, perhaps she'd take another fifteen minutes, just to make a point.

Oh good, Lu was seated by the window with a nice view of the harbour. Such a pretty woman but she needed to smile more. Rosie crossed the road and hurried into the café. It made a change to get out and meet someone for coffee, in fact she couldn't remember the last time she had actually gone out for anything, let alone coffee with a friend. Microwave supper, wine, and falling asleep in front of the TV was a routine that she needed to break free of.

'Hi, Lu. You got a good table.'

Lu smiled and her face lit up. That was a cliché, but hers really did. Her green eyes shone with genuine warmth and her wide smile encouraged whoever she was with to copy it.

'I was lucky. Just as I came in a couple were leaving and I grabbed the table before anyone else could,' she said moving her bag from the second chair at the table. 'How are you?'

'Better than I have been in a while actually. I stood my ground with Nadine and eventually got what I was after. Well, I hope I have. I wouldn't put it past her to try and wriggle out of it.'

'Sounds intriguing. Let me get you a coffee and then you can tell me all about it.'

Rosie wondered if she'd said something to upset Lu. After she'd told her about the morning's altercation with Madame Pompadour, as she liked to think of her, Lu's expression had become wistful as she sipped her coffee. Occasionally a frown furrowed her brow and then smoothed again, as if tugged by the tide in the harbour.

'Are you okay? You've gone bit quiet.' Rosie knew what a companionable silence felt like, and this wasn't it. Had she been too gushy and chatty? She hoped she hadn't put Lu off with her eagerness to become friends.

Lu looked away from the window and at Rosie, a half smile on her face. 'I think I am, yes. I was just pondering on something … an idea, but I'm not sure if it's a good one.'

'You can run it by me if it helps?'

Lu placed her cup carefully on the saucer and cleared her throat. 'It does concern you actually. Okay, I was thinking of extending my stay here. I want more time to get to know my natural mother, but mainly I think I should stay longer because I think she's struggling a bit.'

'In what way? Financially, or—'

'No, with her …' Lu shrugged and her neck grew red. 'I don't really want to go into huge detail. It wouldn't be fair telling you …' Rosie watched the colour rise into her cheeks. 'I mean, I don't know you very well, and—'

'Please don't feel you have to – I do understand.' Rosie took a sip of coffee and wondered if she had froth on her top lip. Lu certainly seemed to think so the way she was looking at her face, or was it just a glazed 'deep in thought' stare? She wiped a napkin across her mouth and said, 'So you said it concerned me?'

'Hm? Oh yes, sorry.' Lu's eyes focused and she treated Rosie to the wide smile again. 'If I was to stay here, I would need some kind of a job. I was wondering if this part-time help you mentioned would need experience … and what exactly this person would be doing.'

Two good things in one day. Marvellous. 'You'd be interested? It would be *great* if you were, it's so important to find someone who I'd get along with and I'm sure we would work well together, and it would mean I wouldn't be searching for ages to find someone and—'

Lu held up her hands and laughed. 'Hold on, no more *ands*. I have to know more about it first.'

Rosie laughed too and tried to calm her excitement. 'Sorry, course you do, and I'll warn you the pay won't be great.'

'It doesn't have to be. I have some savings, but I do need something coming in.'

'Okay. You would just be helping me, doing everything I do. So, reception, bookings, serving breakfast, ordering food, sorting the laundry, changing beds ...'

'You certainly earn your money,' Lu said. 'I have A levels in English, Sociology and History. I had experience in my last job dealing with customers, and orders. I'm no stranger to a dishwasher and I'm sure I could get the hang of serving breakfast. I mean, how difficult could it ...' She stopped at Rosie's raised eyebrow. 'I mean, not that I wouldn't welcome your guidance in all of it. I'm sure there's more to it than meets the eye.'

Lu's voice went unnaturally high at the end of that sentence and Rosie thought she'd put her out of her misery. Her comments *had* rankled a little, however. 'No, there's not that much really – mostly just hard work. I never did A levels, so I can't complain if I ended up in a job that requires little skill.' She leaned back and folded her arms. 'So, what were you, then, a manager of something?'

Lu looked at the table and said in a small voice, 'No. I wasted my education. Ended up as an office worker in a small firm that makes windows.'

Although feeling less awkward about her own perceived lowly occupation after hearing this, Rosie could see that Lu was upset. 'No education is ever wasted.'

Lu nodded. 'But I could have done so much more. The problem was that I never felt confident enough to go for my goals. It all stemmed from being adopted. I never felt good enough, because I imagined there must have been something wrong with me somehow, even though my adoptive parents were the best in the world and never gave me cause to feel like that. Silly now I know the truth. Relationships with guys have been a disaster too.' She looked at Rosie and shook her head. 'Anyway, because of all that, I recently decided to change, be a more confident person.

I tried to big myself up to you, chucked in my qualifications – qualifications that I never used – I'm sorry.'

Rosie patted Lu's hand, then removed it for fear of seeming too familiar. This poor woman had a lot of baggage, but she liked her. Lu had such honesty and the guts to tell it like it was: very refreshing. 'No need to be sorry. You were selling yourself to me, so of course you would highlight your successes. It's only natural.'

'I don't think I've had many of those,' Lu said with a wry smile.

'Ah, but it depends how you look at it.' Rosie knew she was good at pep talks and looking at things in a different way. One thing she had in abundance was people skills; she suddenly realised that she was bloody proud of what she'd achieved. 'For example. This morning I got one over on Madame Pomp – I mean Nadine. It might not seem much on the surface, but it was a success.' She put her head on one side and wagged a finger at Lu. 'And as everyone knows, small successes lead to big triumphs.'

'Is that a saying?'

'Yes, I said it.'

Lu laughed, and her face did the lighting up thing. 'No, I mean is it a real saying?'

'No. I made it up just now, but it sounded good and, more importantly, it's true.'

'I guess it is. So, what happens about me going for this job? Do I have to approach Nadine?'

'No, you have to approach me.' Rosie wrinkled her nose and twisted her mouth to the side. 'Which actually you just have, and I say yes. Yes, come and work with me, and we'll have a ball. Well, perhaps not a ball, but we should have a laugh now and then.'

'What, just like that?'

'Yes. I tell Nadine and she vets you, but she'll say yes, or I'll have a flounce or two. What, do you want a three-day interview in which you have to present PowerPoints and convince the board of directors why you're the best in the UK?'

Lu laughed again. 'You're hilarious. Thanks for accepting me – I'm so looking forward to working with you.' Then a cloud passed over her eyes. 'Ah. There might be a problem.'

Rosie frowned. 'What?'

'Nadine will want references. I left my last job without one because I wrote a letter of resignation and was going to give them a month's notice. I never went back though.'

'Why?'

'The day I handed my resignation in was the day I returned home to find that my adoptive mum had … had been killed in a road accident.'

Rosie wanted to reach out and give Lu a hug, but something told her that wouldn't be wise. Lu's eyes flitted from window to table like a couple of wary birds and she continually moved her saucer slowly round and round with her two forefingers.

'God, Lu, I'm so sorry. You have been through it, haven't you? So, your boss didn't give you a reference. Didn't he or she know the circumstances?'

Lu glanced up and her green eyes flashed, cat-like. 'Oh, *he* knew all right. He was just being a bastard because I'd been rude to him that day. Just as well that he didn't give me a reference, he would have said I was insubordinate or crap at my job just to get back at me, I expect.'

'Sounds like you were right to leave. And don't worry, if Nadine asks, I'll tell her that because you were grief stricken you just left without a word and your boss was a stickler for rules or something like that. It will be cool.'

'No, I resigned before I found out about—'

'I know that, but she doesn't.' Rosie tapped the side of her nose and thought a change of subject might be welcome. 'So where is your birth mum today?'

'She's just up the road from the hotel. She part owns the jewellery shop – the Seaside Silver Company. She's had cover the past few days, but she's gone back in for the rest of the week now.'

'Oh, right. I've been past there, but just window shopping. I think my mum knew yours – can't be sure – but I seem to think they were friends a while back. Ask her if she remembers Val Green.'

'Oh really? Yeah, I'll ask. Does she live here too?'

'Did. She and Dad used to run a bar in town, but Mum decided she wanted to move to Spain. We used to go there on holiday when me and my brother Jake were kids. Business dipped a bit here about five years ago, so they decided that having a bar in Spain would be cheaper to run and more profitable in the tourist season. They said I could come and work for them, but my heart is here. In an odd way I feel a bit abandoned …' Rosie paused; that was probably a stupid thing to say. 'Not in the same way as you did when you were younger, I hasten to add. But I do miss my parents – Mum especially.'

Lu nodded and looked at her watch. 'Speaking of which, I must go and see my birth mother. I said I'd let her give me the grand tour.'

'When will you be able start work, do you think?' Rosie wanted to be sure that Lu was up for it.

'Tomorrow if you like?'

'Brilliant. I'll have a word with Nadine and speak to you later.' Rosie waved to Lu as she turned the corner and then hurried back to Pebble House. In her mind she tried to organise a few counter-responses to potential arguments from Nadine, and doubt settled in her chest. Then she thought about everything Lu had been through and how she'd handled it all with honest words and quiet strength. Rosie's smile grew as her doubt shrank. Whatever the arguments from Nadine, she'd win them, because today she had stood her ground and achieved her goal, and once lovely Lu was working alongside her, there'd be two of them to reckon with.

Chapter Thirteen

'At last! I thought you'd decided to go back to Sheffield,' Mellyn says as I walk through the door of Seaside Silver Company. Her voice is light and jokey, but her eyes say otherwise. My eyes slide to my watch – five minutes late, that's all. Here we go again. What the hell is her problem? I don't respond, just look at the display of jewellery in front of the till counter upon which she leans, surveying me with those eyes, the colour of waves on a dull day.

'My goodness, what a totally beautiful collection you have here,' I say, and mean it. I turn in a slow circle and look at the other cabinets around the shop. All manner of silver jewellery nestled on trays of pebbles, and strings of beads mixed with silver shells and precious stones dangle from driftwood and fishing net.

'Thanks, I think so. And thankfully so do the tourists. This is the quietest we've been all morning.' Mellyn allows one side of her mouth to turn up and her eyes become a little warmer.

I let a strand of beads run over the back of my hand, enjoying their cool silky touch on my skin. 'I wouldn't know where to start. There's so much choice.'

'Anything you'd like, it's yours. Take ten items – my gift to you.'

Heat floods my cheeks. 'Oh, I didn't mean that to sound like I was ask—'

'I know. I was going to say it anyway.' Mellyn nods towards an earring display on a driftwood log. 'Those jade earrings would look fantastic with your eye colour and dark hair. Try them on.'

'Only if you let me pay for them,' I begin, but the look on Mellyn's face freezes my words. It's the same expression of tumult that she'd worn at the art gallery. I look away and back at the beads.

'What's the matter with you? Can't you let me do something nice for once without always questioning it?'

Her tone makes me think of a schoolteacher chastising a naughty child. I cast around my memory trying to think of how I'd questioned her. Could it have been about the boat? It must have been, but that *was* an extreme present; it would be normal to be a bit shocked, wouldn't it? I risk a sideways glance and wish I hadn't. No longer grey waves, her eyes have become charcoal storm clouds, and her mouth has turned down at both corners like some nightmare clown's.

'Just think how many birthdays, Christmases, and just-because-you're-my-daughter presents I've missed. Can't you *see* I love you and want to make things, right?'

Mellyn's voice wobbles on the last few words and I look over again. The clown mouth quivers and, as I watch, the entire mask of anger fractures, slips away along with the tears running silently over the contours of her face. She said she loves me. My God, how do I feel about that? Good, I think, but I know I can't say it back.

I hurry over and reach for her hand across the counter. 'Mellyn, Mel ... please don't cry. I'm sorry. I just didn't want you to think I was trying to take advantage of—'

Mellyn releases my hand. 'Mel now, is it? For one moment there I thought you were going to call me Mum ... thought you were going to say it the other day on the boat too after I'd told you all about what happened in the past. You can't bring yourself to, though, can you?'

There's a mixture of sorrow and ice in her expression and I don't know what to say to make it go away. I had been right when I'd noticed her smile not reaching her eyes that day. She *was* disappointed, after all. 'I ... I did tell you that I felt closer to you now and—'

'You did. Ignore me, I'm being silly.' Her smile is too bright, her eyes too sparkly. 'And as regards to me thinking that you're taking advantage, you'll soon know me well enough to realise that nobody *makes* me think anything. I think things because I want to. I am *not* easily led, not even by you. I have had to be tough, independent and savvy. Now please. Make me happy and choose some jewellery?'

I look at her tearful eyes and hopeful smile and nod. I don't want to risk saying the wrong thing. 'Well, thank you. I do so appreciate it.'

'Okay, now go and choose. I can't wait to see what you'll pick!' She claps her hands and makes a noise in her throat that sounds almost like a giggle. A huge fake smile banishes all signs of sadness.

To hide my surprise, I turn my back and look unseeing at the display of earrings. How the hell can I cope with all this? It will certainly take some time for me to accept her almost magical switch from one emotion to another, one mood to another. In a way, her mood hopping from sad to happy reminds me of a storm clearing away oppressive heavy feelings on a humid day. But that doesn't happen instantly, does it? And it leaves people feeling refreshed and pleased that the day is once more light and hopeful. The change in Mellyn has the opposite effect. I can't feel light and hopeful now she's smiling, because I know without doubt there will soon be another storm building in a corner of her sky.

'Don't let me catch you looking at the prices either.' Her voice just behind startles me. I'd not heard her leave the counter. 'Pick with the eye, not with the head.'

An hour later I look in a mirror in the storeroom of the shop and have to admit that the jade earrings reflect my eyes and look great against my suntanned skin and dark hair. A beautiful mother-of-pearl bead shell and silver necklace nestles in the hollow of my throat, and two rings and two bracelets of a similar style complete the gift session. Mellyn had tried to force more on me, but I explained that it would feel too over the top. I normally only wear a watch and a ring. She'd frowned at this, particularly when she'd learned that the ring had been my adoptive mother's but had let it go nonetheless.

I hear the bell on the shop door tinkle indicating a customer had left the shop. Mellyn comes in behind me, places her hands on my shoulders and looks into my eyes through the mirror. 'Absolutely stunning, dahling!'

Despite her previous mood and the hurtful things, she said, my smile is genuine. When Mellyn's on form it's infectious. 'Why thank you. I really love them all.'

'Not surprised. You have a good eye for the most expensive pieces,' she says with a wink.

My reflection looks like a waxwork as the smile fixes itself on my lips, though inside my head I'm screaming with anger. Damn her! After all she said about picking anything and not looking at the price tag! Now she's trying to make me feel like a sponger. My breathing quickens and it's all I can do to keep smiling and my anger buried. Through gritted teeth I manage, 'Really? I have never owned expensive jewellery.'

'Well you do now.' She kisses me on the cheek and breezes back into the shop, tossing over her shoulder, 'Shall we go out for dinner this evening, so you can show off in all your finery?'

At that moment I really don't feel like going anywhere with her, apart from to see a psychiatrist, but then remind myself that she needs my help; that's why I've arranged to extend my stay, after all. If I can't hack her odd behaviour, then I should pack up and go home. Then a thought strikes me, and I wish it hadn't. Sometimes there were similarities between my old school bully Megan and Mellyn. Though Megan had been a blatant bully and hadn't the subtly or finesse that Mellyn had when setting out to get her own way, they both had that similar cold, even predatory look in their eye when they were doing it.

I look at my frowny face in the mirror and lift my chin, practise a determined no-nonsense stare instead. No. Mellyn isn't a bully – well, not like Megan anyway. And even if she is, I need to face up to her and make this work. Mellyn needs me and I need her. I am the new me, the strong me, the confident me. I will stay here, look after her. My birth mum needs me. The fact that she's had a tough life needs to be remembered. The fact that she fought to keep me needs to be bloody remembered. Without her determination I would never have existed in the first place. I would have been terminated … ended. So, if she's a bit fucked up in the head, I need to learn to deal with it. We would go out. It will be a lovely surprise to tell her I'll be staying in St Ives for a while over dinner – well, if Nadine has said yes, of course.

'Lu?'

'Yes?'

'So, what do you think!' Mellyn calls from the shop. 'About dinner?'

'I think that would be a lovely idea!'

A stain in the shape of a map of Italy looks down on me from a corner of the hotel room ceiling. When I say Italy, I mean the boot bit. I wonder how many people have laid on this bed looking at it and remembering past holidays, or even planning to go there. Perhaps it had inspired some to go to the pizza place in town. Maybe it hadn't. I would bet that I'm the only one whose brain has turned a wiggly stain on a ceiling into anything at all, let alone a map. Ponderings such as these indicate that it's time for a nap.

I yawn and turn my head on the pillow, noticing a trail of sandy footprints from the carpet by the door to the bathroom. I expect that I could soon be vacuuming similar prints from all the carpets in Pebble House and cross my fingers under the pillow. When I'd got back an hour or so ago Rosie wasn't around, and Alan sat on reception with a sour expression on his haughty features. I'd smiled and received a curt nod in response. This wasn't unusual, however, so I shouldn't read too much into it.

A knock on the door drags me back from sleep just as I'm drifting into it and I pull a pillow over my head. The knock comes again a few seconds later, so reluctantly I slip from the bed and open the door.

'You okay?' Rosie says, looking at my hair.

I reach up and realise it's stuck up at the front because of the pillow. I pat it down. 'Yes, good. Just been trying to have a little snooze.'

'Oh, sorry to disturb you, but I wanted to tell you what happened with Nadine.'

'Come in, come in.' I pull out the chair from the desk for her and I sit on the bed. Everything I want to do rests on the next few minutes and I watch Rosie's face carefully. It doesn't look particularly hopeful.

Rosie sits down and puts her head on one side. She isn't smiling. 'I talked to Nadine and as I expected she tried to backtrack on what she'd said this morning … and would you believe that she said no to hiring you?'

I tell myself that it doesn't matter, even as a heavy weight squashes hopeful excitement flat in my chest. I'll just have to get another job elsewhere. 'Never mind. Thanks for doing you best, Rosie.' I see a flicker of a smile in her eyes and fold my arms. What's so funny?

'I asked you if you believed it, and you haven't answered me,' she says, the flicker of a smile now a flame and a giggle enters her voice.

'I'm not sure what you mean. Yes, of course I believe it.'

'Well that's where you'd be wrong, because she said yes!' Rosie throws her arms up and bursts into laughter. 'Your face is a picture!'

I watch her, trying to see the funny side of my heart falling into my boots because of what she'd said at first. She points at my expression and sets off giggling again. I see my Neanderthal frown in the mirror and I laugh too. 'That was very cruel, Rosie, but I'm glad she said yes.'

Placing her hand on her ribcage she takes a few calming breaths and nods. 'It's true that she didn't like the idea of someone I obviously get on with working here, but I soon persuaded her by threatening to flounce out again.'

I picture Rosie flouncing and Nadine's expression. 'Thanks. And when do I start?'

'Tomorrow.'

'Excellent.' As I say that, it occurs to me that I won't be able to stay at the hotel indefinitely. I've been so caught up in everything to do with Mellyn that I hadn't thought it through. My face must register my concern.

'You okay?' Rosie asks.

'Fine. No, I was just thinking that I'd need to get flat hunting pretty quickly.'

'Oh. I assumed that you'd stay with your birth mother.'

It's then that I realise that's the only bit I *had* thought through. In the shop this morning as I witnessed yet another of Mellyn's storms, any idea of staying at Seal Cottage had been sucked out and shredded in the gale. I want to stay and help her, but instinctively I know that living together would be disastrous. 'I think it's a bit soon for that. I'll see how it all goes.'

Rosie picks what looks like dried jam from her overall and speaks to her shoes. 'You could always stay at mine. I have two bedrooms. The second one is very small, but you're welcome to it and I could use the rent.'

Living *and* working with Rosie … how would that be? I do like the woman, really like her, but did I want to become that close? If I was to keep Mellyn happy and her moods a secret, it wouldn't work. Rosie is just so sweet, open and friendly, I'd be crying on her shoulder in no time. I don't want to say no outright, but I can't say yes either. I stand and straighten the duvet, so she can't see my face. 'Er, can I think about that? I'm not really sure what I want to do yet.'

'No problem. I'm not sure that I could stand living and working with myself either, if I had a choice.'

She's nothing if not perceptive. I turn around and hope my face looks honest. 'It's not that. I think you're lovely. I just need to decide if I want to live by myself for a while. I'm thirty and have never tried it. Can you imagine?' I raise my arms and the two bracelets that I'd got that morning clink together.

'I totally understand,' she says, reaching out to touch the bracelets. 'These are gorgeous – new?'

I nod and show her the rest, which I'd put in a drawer. 'A present from Mellyn.'

'Mellyn?' Rosie says, and then realisation dawned. 'Oh yes, your birth mum. Wow, they are stunning.'

'They are. The trouble is, I'm not used to wearing lots of jewellery. It just isn't me. I will wear them often though because Mellyn … Mum, will think I don't really like them if I don't. She's quite sensitive.'

'Do you call her Mellyn or Mum?'

'Mellyn at the moment. I don't feel right calling her Mum yet. She wants to be called Mum, but I feel it would be betraying the only Mum I ever knew until recently …'

'You should do what makes you feel comfortable. No good pandering to people if you don't feel it's the right thing inside, is it?' Rosie stands up, twists her hair up into a ponytail and secures it with a blue velvet band that matches her eyes perfectly.

She's right, but it's not as simple as that. Mellyn desperately wants the title of Mum to affirm her importance in my life. To signal that she means something to me, to the world. I shrug and put the jewellery back in the drawer. Perhaps my brain will poke me awake again tonight with this dilemma. I fold my arms and look at Rosie. 'I see my adoptive mother as my mum still. I see Mellyn as my other mother, so for now I'm calling her Mellyn or Mel. I might try Mum in a week or so.'

'Sounds like a plan. Right, I must be off.' She pauses in the doorway. 'I'll see you tomorrow at six thirty in the kitchen, okay?'

'Okay. What shall I wear?'

'Black trousers or a skirt, comfy shoes and a smartish shirt of some kind? You'll be helping me serve breakfast. Then later, anything comfy really, because you'll be cleaning and running about like an insect with a blue bum.'

I can forget my snooze. A pair of black trousers or a skirt needs to be bought. 'Great, thanks. See you then … and Rosie?'

Already a few steps down the corridor she turns and looks at me. 'Yeah?'

'Your skirt's tucked into your knickers.'

Rosie grabs at her bottom with both hands while twisting her neck to try and see. 'No it's not ... is it?' One look at my face and she sighs. 'Payback, huh? Very funny, Lu. In fact, hi-lar-ious!' She flicks a duster at me and disappears down the stairs.

Before going out shopping I brush my hair and retouch my eye make-up. I tell my reflection that if somebody had said a few months ago that I would be looking forward to starting work at stupid o'clock, doing menial tasks for low pay, I would never have believed them. It's true though. I am in control of my life and my future for the first time ever, and I'm determined to make a difference to Mellyn's. I'm so looking forward to going out for dinner with her this evening and springing my big surprise. At least I know that there will be no storm brewing, because Mellyn will be over the moon.

Chapter Fourteen

An exotic insect preserved in amber. That's what it's like to be at the centre table, alone, overdressed – ridiculously so – bathed in the orange glow from the lamp in front of me and painfully aware of surreptitious glances and more blatant stares from other diners. Decorated with fishing net and strewn with lobsterpots, Jack's Crab Shack is not the kind of place Mellyn had led me to believe. I did wonder when she'd said the name of it on the phone, but her hushed tones and reverent description of Jack's as the best place for seafood in the area had convinced me that dressing up was appropriate.

'You need to come done up, and wear all your new jewellery,' Mellyn had said. 'You never know, the Cornish paparazzi might be there!'

The place is packed with holiday makers in shorts and sandals. A few children race around pretending to be aeroplanes, men laugh raucously and down pints of cider, and then there's me in high heels, a low-cut green figure-hugging dress, made up to the nines, hair curled and pinned at each side with sparkly clips and dripping in jewellery. I look at the clock. Where the hell is sodding Mellyn? The cool evening air sneaks in with a customer and I'm reminded of the night of my thirtieth birthday. My escape is just through the closing door …

The closing door is now flung back again and slammed to announce Mellyn's arrival. My embarrassment is complete as all heads turn in her direction and then back in mine as she says at a theatrical pitch, 'Darling! How absolutely divine you look tonight!' Dressed in jeans and a T-shirt she hurries towards me, arms outstretched.

She kisses me on both my heated cheeks and then pulls her phone from a pocket and demands that I smile. 'Mellyn. Everyone is looking at me. Just sit down and—'

'And so, they should! You look wonderful tonight!'

Her finger clicks a few times regardless of my stunned expression and the flash leaves white spots in front of my eyes. I look down at the table, but she still clicks away. What the fuck is wrong with her? 'Stop that and sit down, or I'm leaving.' Quiet fury accentuates my every word.

Still looking at the table I hear her chair scrape back and see the phone tossed on the table in front of me. After a few seconds she says, 'So what's your problem this time? Is it because I'm a few minutes late?'

Incredible. Has she really no idea? And a few minutes late – more like fifteen. I want to raise my head and look at her, but I need more time to get my racing heartbeat under control. I fiddle with a fork. 'No. It's because I have been sitting here in the middle of the room like an overdressed idiot. Overdressed, I might add, because *you* said I should. People have been staring at me.'

I pause and take a breath to try and remove the tremor from my voice. I look up and into her eyes; her expression is neutral. She appears to be listening as if we were just having a normal conversation. I want to yell, but that would draw even more attention. Through gritted teeth I finish, 'Then you came in and started taking bloody photos of me. I am embarrassed beyond belief.'

'Well it's about time you showed some spark. You've been too passive so far,' Mellyn says and laughs. 'Can we get a menu over here, Jack?' She waves at a rotund man behind the bar.

I look at her grin and picture myself slapping it from her face. 'Did you set me up to see how I would react?'

'No.' She looks up to the left and twists her mouth. 'Well, kind of. I wanted to show the town what a stunning daughter I have, and you normally look *so* dowdy.'

I have no reply that's anywhere near suitable. My eyes moisten, and I don't know if I'm more furious with myself for letting her get to me, or her for being such a complete cow. I blink and decide she's won the toss. 'Look. I know you have had a shit life and have issues, but please don't dump it all on me. It's really not fair. And I was so looking forward to tonight because I had a surprise for you, but now I'm not sure it's a good idea, Mellyn.'

I feel the tremor in my voice but I'm relieved that it sounds strong, determined. I can see that the continued show of strength and no-nonsense approach has wounded. She deflates in front of me, all her show and bluster disappearing along with her manic grin. Good.

Her hand creeps across the table towards mine. 'Surely you don't think I wanted to hurt you?'

I fold my arms and lean back in my chair. 'No. Of course not. I mean, you just did what any loving mother would do, didn't you? Humiliate, insult ... oh, and make me the laughing stock of the restaurant. How could anyone be hurt by that?'

Mellyn puts her hand over her mouth and shakes her head. Tears well and she dabs at them with her napkin. 'I ...' She takes a few deep breaths. 'I am so sorry. I honestly thought you would like to be the centre of attention. And when I said dowdy, I meant that you hide your beauty under ordinary clothes. You're an exotic butterfly, my darling, and you should spread those wings.' She looks down at her hands and sniffs.

Either she's a bloody good actress or she's deluded enough to think that setting me up like this will make me happy. Either way it isn't great. I'm torn between getting up and walking out and trying to comfort her. She looks so vulnerable and clearly distraught. Thankfully Jack comes over and saves me.

'Hello, Mellyn, what can I get for you?' He talks to her, but his eyes sweep me up and down, linger on my chest. 'Great jewellery ... er?'

'Meet my beautiful daughter Lu,' Mellyn says, her face once more miraculously transformed into sweetness and light.

Jack draws in the fleshy folds on his bald forehead, which welds his almost mono-brow together. 'You never said you had a daughter?'

'That's because we are only just reunited.' Mellyn takes my hand across the table. I allow it. She gives me a grateful smile. 'Yes, I foolishly gave her up for adoption many years ago.'

'You didn't have much option as I understood it,' I say, taking my hand back.

Mellyn nods and opens her mouth to say something, but Jack gets there first. 'That's nice for you both.' He stands back, looks at us, and rubs his hands absently over the stained white apron straining across his belly. 'You look similar, most attractive.' He takes a pencil from behind his ear and poises it over his notepad. 'So, what can I get my favourite customer tonight?'

'My usual lobster special, Jack. I suggest you have the same, Lu – it's to die for.'

Jack appears to smile but his lips just stretch as if they're under duress – on their best behaviour. His dark eyes twinkle but with something akin to contempt rather than humour. Mellyn looks at me, head on one side, oblivious. 'Yep. Sounds good,' I say. I can't give a stuff what I eat at the moment.

Jack nods, takes our drinks order and leaves. Mellyn leans forward and whispers, 'Did you see his face when we ordered the lobster? God, he was fuming.'

'I noticed he looked disgruntled, what was wrong with him? You'd think he'd be pleased that we ordered the most expensive thing on the menu.' While I was waiting for her to arrive, I'd had ample time to study the large blackboard at the end of the room. The lobster special was at the top of it, along with the price.

She giggles and says in a low voice, 'Yes, but it's on the house. It always is when I come here. Jack's a sly one and Neil was another. We all know what happened to him though – got what he deserved – the bastard.' She flaps her hand at my expression of distaste and whispers, 'Anyway … I'll tell you why I get free food here later. You never know who's listening.'

Jack comes back with our wine and we sip it a silence that grows deeper and more awkward with each swallow. I try to rationalise her behaviour yet again and wonder if I have the strength to keep riding the rough with the smooth. The rough is dominating our fledgling relationship; perhaps it can never take flight into the happy blue yonder.

'So, what was the surprise you had? I do hope I haven't ruined it. Please accept my apology and know that I would never, ever do anything to hurt you. I'm just not very good at being a mum, am I?' Mellyn has her earnest face back on.

Should I tell her, or make something up and go home at the end of the week as I had planned? I have never wanted to see Dad and Adelaide as much as I do right now. I think about the brief chat I had with Dad yesterday. The relief in his voice was palpable when I'd told him I was fine and that Mellyn was nice; I hadn't mentioned her mood swings. He'd worry if he knew it all. Adelaide did know some of it, and also that I was thinking of staying here for a while, but I'd sworn her to secrecy. Her wise words had fluttered down the line like little sugar fairies, their wands magically waving away my doubt and strengthening my resolve.

'Okay,' I say, picturing Adelaide in my head along with a dozen sugar fairies. 'I can see you're sorry. The surprise is that I have a job at Pebble House. I want to stay here longer so we can get to know each other properly. I hope that's what you want too.' I blurt my words out in a rush before I have time to overanalyse them.

Both Mellyn's hands fly to her mouth and she makes a noise in her throat that sounds like a cross between a giggle and a sob. 'Oh, Lu! That is the best news I have *ever* heard!' She half rises as if she's about to fling her arms around me, then notices my cringe and sits back down. 'We must order champagne to celebrate,' she gushes, casting excited eyes about for Jack.

'No. This wine is fine. I really have had enough of people staring at me this evening – an ice bucket would be the living end.'

'Whatever you say, my dear.' Mellyn takes a gulp of wine. 'And I promise I'll be on my best behaviour from now on. Anything you don't like, just tell me and I'll zip this big gob of mine. I want to make you happy.' She raises a forefinger and holds my gaze. 'You know what half my trouble is? I haven't had the practice of being a mum. It's only really occurred to me I suppose. But I will get better, you can be sure of that.'

'Well, now I'm staying for a while you'll have plenty of practice.' I smile, and she returns it, but I note a flicker of what might have been annoyance in her eyes. Perhaps she wanted me to say she doesn't need improvement. Well, she can piss right off.

Jack arrives and places two huge plates on the table, each groaning with a lobster and all the trimmings. 'Bon appetite,' he says through a small mouth.

'You're such a magician with food, Jack,' Mellyn purrs. He gives a brief nod and just as he turned away she says in a condescending manner, 'And could you send a bottle of your finest wine over when you have a minute? There's a love.'

'I'll pay for the wine,' I say. It's clear that Jack is well and truly fuming as he stomps towards the bar.

'Nonsense. As I said, everything is on the house here.' Mellyn's eyes sparkle with mischief as she looks at me over the rim of her glass.

I don't think I want to find out the reason why. Gut instinct tells me I won't like it. In case she decides to divulge it now, I crack a claw and take a mouthful of the succulent meat. 'This is absolutely gorgeous.'

'It is. When I said Jack's had the finest seafood I wasn't joking.' Mellyn waves a fork at me. 'Now, did you like the decor in my spare room? Because if not, we can go shopping for paint and wallpaper at the weekend. I want everything to be just how you like it, Lu.'

Bollocks. She thinks I'll stay at Seal Cottage. Not an unexpected assumption, but one that I can really do without at the moment. 'I had thought I'd find a bedsit or something for now,' I say brightly, trying to shutter my eyes to the disappointment in hers.

'When we've got to know each other a little more we can think again, but thanks for making such a generous offer.'

Watching Mellyn's face try to control her feelings I wait for the familiar eruption from the emotional volcano. All the signs are there, the red blotches on her face and neck, the quickening breath, the frustration behind the eyes revealed as if on two mini cinema screens. She dabs each corner of her mouth with her napkin and says, 'If that's what you want, Lu, that's fine. As I said earlier, I want to do whatever makes you happy.'

So, she *can* control it after all. This is a real positive as far as I'm concerned. I give her a wide smile and pat her hand across the table. Despite her erratic behaviour this evening, it's clear that having me stay in St Ives is going to help her, and I'll do all I can to makes sure she feels loved, respected and appreciated. God knows she's had little of all three in her life so far.

I note the grateful look in her eyes and then she applies herself to her meal. In a way it seemed like the roles have been reversed between us. I'm the mother helping to socialise the wayward child. For the first time in my life, I realise that someone depends on me, needs me, and furthermore, that I like it.

Chapter Fifteen

A fresh wind whips my hair into streamers as I stand up to my ankles in foamy breakers. Deep cleansing breaths of salt air replace the scent of bacon, eggs, toilet cleaner and furniture polish that my new job has ingrained into my clothes and pores. I relax my shoulders and wiggle my toes deeper into the wet sand, then turn my head at the squeal of a small child a little way to my left. 'Mummy! Look, a jolly fish!' I smile to myself as I picture a jelly fish sitting on the sand having a good old laugh. A few feet away from the breakers, the child squats and pokes at something with a yellow spade. I watch the mother scoop up the child and hurry away up the beach.

Unbidden, a memory of my mum doing the same brings unexpected emotion and I'm glad of the sea spray on my face. I remember the smell of the old red beach towel that we always took on holiday: peanuts and a trace of vinegar. Why it smelled of those I have no idea – it was always cleaned. Closing my eyes, I can feel its scratchy warmth and see Mum wrapping it around me after I'd done my usual trick of staying in the sea until my skin turned blue.

I open my eyes and looked up at the scudding white clouds edged with grey. Not a typical summer's day, but no less beautiful for all that. I think about Mum and the unfairness of life bringing her early death. I also think about all the happy times we'd had and told the far horizon how much I had loved her.

On my way back up the beach towards the town, thoughts of Mellyn and how much we've grown together over the last few weeks puts a spring in my step. I am so lucky to have had a wonderful woman who brought me up, and now I have a chance at building a happy future with a second mum. Since that day two weeks ago at the Crab Shack, we've had neither a cross word, nor have I worried that she'd been on the edge of one of her meltdowns, as I thought of them. When I wasn't working, we'd done touristy things, visiting areas as far as Tintagel in the north of the county and Land's End in the south. We've laughed a lot, been out on the *Sprite*, and chatted about the past, both hers and mine, once until the early hours of the morning.

On that occasion, I had stayed over at Seal Cottage, and though she hasn't mentioned it again, I know that Mellyn would love me to move in. Having no luck on the accommodation front, the rent being too high or the bedsit too much of a dump, I have begun to seriously consider that possibility. The hotel room is eating into my savings pretty quickly, even though Nadine has grudgingly allowed a discount. I'll run it all past Rosie later, but now I'm late back from lunch and if Nadine's on reception she'll have a few choice words lined up on her acid tongue.

From his stool on reception, Alan extends a bony forefinger and beckons me over. He reminds me of a vulture eyeing injured prey. Tall, gangly, hunched-shouldered and hook nosed, he points at his watch and raises a bushy eyebrow. A polite smile on my face, I wait expectantly holding his cold grey stare. I'd be damned if I'll speak first. If he wants an explanation for why I'm seven minutes late, he can open his beak and ask for it.

'Forgot the time, somehow?' he asks, tucking both hands under his armpits as if he's getting ready to roost.

'No. I called in at the butcher to make sure he knows we need extra bacon for the weekend, but he was busy with a customer.'

'Extra bacon?'

'Yes. Extra bacon.'

'What do we want extra bacon for?'

'To eat,' I say, and hide a smile. I see a flash of anger behind his eyes and watch a movement in his cheek as he clenches his jaw.

'I realise that,' he snaps. 'But who do we need extra bacon for at the weekend?'

'Oh, I thought you knew. We've had to accommodate six cancellations at the last moment due to a death in the family at Golden Sands Guest House.'

'No, it's the first I've heard.'

I know it's the first he's heard, because Rosie only took the call just before I left for lunch. The owner's sister died unexpectedly this morning and he was grief stricken, couldn't cope, so he asked if we had room for his weekend guests. I had gone to the butcher on the way to the beach, so I'd told Alan a half truth. I was late for no reason in particular. 'Right, well, if there's nothing else I have to get on with cleaning the rooms.'

'Who's died then?'

'Ask Nadine. I really must get going,' I say over my shoulder as the double doors swing closed behind me. It's unlikely Nadine will know. Alan was stuck on reception. This means that his wife probably sneaked off before the phone call for a facial, or to the hairdresser, and left him in the lurch. I laugh to myself as I collect clean linen from the airing cupboard, thinking of Alan's bemused expression when he asked about the bacon. This place really is run by Rosie and, to an extent, me, nowadays.

'Laughing on the job, young lady? That will never do!' Rosie says close behind me.

'God, you nearly made me drop all these towels!' I turn and shove them into her arms. 'Here, make yourself useful and carry these up to room fifteen while I get the sheets.'

'Bossing me about already and you've only been on the job for a fortnight. Okay, I'll help you, because as it happens I'm on top of all my jobs, unlike some latecomers.'

'Don't you start! I've just had Alan the Vulture have a go.'

'Alan the Vulture?'

'Yes. That's what I was laughing at ... well, about bacon actually.' I glance at her puzzled expression as I unlock the door to number fifteen.

'You been at the gin?' Rosie giggles and follows me inside.

Half an hour later the room is transformed. Sour sweat, and other more unmentionable aromas have been removed with gloved hands from bathroom and bed. Also removed as a result of my explanation was the puzzled expression from the face of my co-worker. 'I wish you hadn't told me you call him Alan the Vulture. I won't be able to look him in the beak now without seeing one.' Rosie laughs and sits on the side of the bath.

I laugh too and perch on the loo. 'We'll have to think of one for Nadine.'

'Oh, I already have one – Madame Pompadour, or just the Pomp sometimes.'

'Because of her hair?'

'Yes!'

Laughter grips us both for a few seconds and I have to take a few deep breaths to stop myself getting hysterical. 'Okay, change of subject.' I force a sober expression and look at Rosie who's fanning her face and dabbing at tears of laughter on her cheeks.

'Good, because I might pee myself if we carry on and you're on the toilet!'

'Stop!' I say through the laughter bubbling in my throat. 'I need you to be serious for a minute. Though you do look less like a cold sprout when you're laughing.'

'A cold sprout! How rude. Same goes for you though. Your face lights up when you smile … Truth be told I was thinking of asking for your hand in marriage.'

'Rosie, hush now!' I had an odd feeling in my belly when she said that, and I feel heat rise up my neck. What the hell's wrong with me?

'Righty-ho.' Rosie swallows and folds her arms. 'What is it?'

I draw a breath and concentrate. 'Well, as you know, I've been having trouble finding a decent place to live and I can't keep forking out to stay here.'

'You want to stay at mine?'

Oh dear. Her face is shining with delight. What now? 'Um. No, though thanks for offering again. No, I was wondering about staying with Mellyn.'

Rosie shrugs and purses her lips as if in thought, but I have a good idea that she's trying to hide her disappointment. 'It's up to you, but I thought you said that might not be such a good idea? How is she with you now? I don't like to pry.'

I have told her bits about Mellyn's mood swings, but not the detail. 'Much better now. We're growing really close and I'm feeling like we're working towards the wonderful mother–daughter relationship I always dreamed we'd have. I'm even ready to call her Mum … I think.'

'I think you've answered your own question there then, Lu.' Rosie stands and puts the cleaning products into a bucket.

'Yes, I think I have. I just don't want to move in together to jeopardise what we already have … you know, living in each other's pockets?'

'But you see each other loads anyway, and you're both out at work all day otherwise. Give it a chance. You could tell her it's temporary … like a trial?'

'Now why didn't I think of that?'

'Because you're just not brainy like me, obvious really.' Rosie gives me a friendly push and walks out of the bathroom.

'Thanks, Rosie. Running it past you really helped.' I follow her and scoop up the bag of dirty linen. 'And you know what? I reckon if we did the rooms together like this, we'd finish much quicker.'

'When we can, yes. But today I would have been on reception if the Pomp hadn't done a runner before Alan the Vulture had a chance to!'

That sets us both off again, and after she leaves I have to check my mascara in the mirror before going out into the corridor.

Honeysuckle fronds frame the fading sunset and beyond it hangs the crescent of the moon; an ethereal pendant on a chain of stars. The light breeze brings with it the heady sent of honeysuckle and ocean, and from my position on the garden recliner, my imagination makes pictures from the wisps of high dark cloud. Replete after another wonderful meal cooked by Mellyn, a tickle of excitement rises in my chest at the thought of springing the Seal

Cottage moving-in surprise. She's inside making coffee and I listen to her pure clear voice drifting through the open kitchen window. I can't be certain what the song's called, but it's the old one about being amongst the leaves so green-o.

'You have a lovely voice, Mel.' I put the recliner into a sitting position and take a coffee mug from the tray in her hands.

'Oh, thank you. I sing when I'm happy.' She smiles at me and depresses the plunger on the cafetière. 'Before you came back into my life there wasn't much to sing about.'

'That's a lovely thing to say.' I think about that and laugh. 'I didn't mean to say that it was lovely that you were unhappy before I came!'

'I know that!' Mellyn laughs too and then from her jeans pocket she pulls out an envelope, a very old and yellowing envelope, and puts it on the table between us. 'Have a look in there,' she says, her eyes shining.

Lifting the flap, I take out two much-handled photos, one dog eared, and place them next to each other on top of the envelope. A smile grows in my heart as I realise that both are of me as a baby. One is me as a newborn in a white knitted outfit and hat, asleep in a cradle, and one's me about two months old, wearing green dungarees and propped up on a cushion. I know the baby is me, because in each photo is Bluey Bear. Bluey is the bear I've had forever. He's the bear that after Dad had told me who had given him to me, was shoved in a box and put in the attic. 'It's me,' I say in a small voice.

'It is.' Mellyn picks up the newborn one and traces her finger across it. 'This was taken the day before they took you ...' She stops and swallows some coffee. 'The other is the one your parents sent me to let me know how you were doing. Did they tell you the bear was from me?'

An image of me aged seven kicking the bear at the wall and stuffing him in a box comes back as if it were yesterday, along with the feeling of betrayal and disbelief. It was the day of the adoption revelation and Bluey took the brunt of my fury. I look at Mellyn's hopeful face and swallow. 'Yes, they did. I always treasured Bluey. I put him in the attic when I grew up, but he's safe.' I wonder if a half truth will result in the moon falling from the sky and squashing my lying little head flat.

'Joe … your dad picked it. He said it would protect you, when we …' Mellyn blew out a long breath through her mouth and composed herself. 'When we couldn't.'

My eyes fill, so I blink and look to the heavens. The moon doesn't look like it's about to fall, but it should have. What a stupid little idiot I'd been back then. I had two sets of parents who loved me. I watch a moth alight on the highest honeysuckle flower and try to calm my breathing. This is no good. I realise that I need to clear my mind of guilt and blame. After all, I was only seven at the time and terribly hurt. That little girl grew up to be me and I need to show her some love in order to be able to move forward.

'I hope you aren't too upset, love,' Mellyn says, and I feel her warm hand cover mine. 'I know we have been parted most of our lives, but I wanted you to see that me and your dad always loved you.'

I lower my gaze from the stars and nod. 'I know. I just wish things could have been different for all of us.' She sighs and nods too. I drink some of my coffee and when I'm sure my voice is strong enough I say, 'I have a surprise for you.'

'You do?' she asks, her head to one side, a half smile forming on her lips.

'I do. How would you feel about having me live here on a trial basis?'

Her smile grows wide and lights up her eyes with joy. 'Oh, that's fantastic! But why a trial?'

'Because we should see if living together is a good idea. I don't want to jeopardise this lovely relationship we have at the moment in any way. I don't think it will, but we need to be sure. Also, I want to be straight with you from the off. Honesty is so important if we're going to move forward.'

'Oh, Lu. What a very wise young woman you are.' Mellyn leans and kisses me on both cheeks. 'I'm overjoyed with your decision and so proud that you can speak your mind so eloquently.' She sits back, rests her chin on interlinked fingers and looks at me, respect in her eyes.

I'm proud of me too. I had no clue how to phrase the trial basis thing, but it just came out naturally. Of course, the worry of it triggering a meltdown for Mellyn had been there like a shadow in the wings, but I just stuck to my guns and said it. Before I quit my job, Mum dying, and then finding Mellyn, I would have become tongue-tied, flustered, and pulled my horns in. So much had changed in such a short time, both bad and good, and it had taken me along with it. I had changed for the good, and it would be for good. There was no going back now. It's the right time for something else too. I smile at Mellyn and say, 'Thanks for saying you're proud of me. It means a lot … Mum.'

Predictably, the much-longed-for title of 'Mum' reduces Mellyn to a blubbering wreck and it's a long time before I can get any sense out of her. I will still call her Mellyn in my mind, but she deserves Mum now. She promises that she will do everything in her power to make me happy and that she'll behave herself perfectly for the rest of her life. We laugh at that.

Later, after Mellyn and I have celebrated with a bit too much brandy, we chat in her doorway just before I'm ready to leave for the hotel for the last time. Then I suddenly remember something. 'Oh, I saw Jack from the Crab Shack today in the market. He waved but we didn't speak. You never did tell me why your meals are free when you go there.' As soon as I'd asked I wish I hadn't. The lovely evening and the brandy made my tongue loose and a wicked glint in Mellyn's eye confirms my mistake.

'I slept with him for a few months,' Mellyn says, a giggle in her throat. 'We got on really well. He isn't an oil painting to look at, but he's a good laugh.' Her eyes harden to grey chips. 'And then he went all sanctimonious on me and said we had to stop as he loved his wife too much to hurt her. Said he thought I was getting too serious.' Mellyn throws her arms up so violently that all her bangles smash into each other. 'Me, too serious! He was the one with the armfuls of flowers and chocolates sneaking round here under the cover of darkness like some randy hound dog!'

A landing light comes on in the house across the way and I notice a shape slip past the curtain. 'Mum, shh. I think someone over there is snooping,' I whisper.

'Oh, that'll be the nosy old crone Freda. She's always getting off on other's gossip.' Mellyn doesn't lower her voice.

'Right, thanks for another lovely evening. I'll be off. I have to be up at six thirty.' I kiss her on the cheek and make to leave, but she catches hold of my elbow.

'I haven't finished telling you my story.' This time she has the grace to whisper. 'So, I told him that if he didn't want the love of his life to know what we had been doing every Tuesday and Thursday in my bed, in graphic detail, I would dine out for free whenever I saw fit.' She draws herself up to her full height, sticks out her chin, defiance in her eyes and the pride in her voice large in the still night air.

I don't want to look her in the eye again. How I wish she'd kept this particularly sordid little skeleton locked away in its cupboard. Does she hope I'd condone her crowing over blackmail like that? I feel the air prickle with static and the silence shifts from expectant to uncomfortable. I pretend to brush something off my trousers and say, 'I see. No wonder he looked furious that night when there were two of us to feed.' And then before she has time to say anything else I give her a quick hug and set off down the street. 'See you tomorrow. I'll give you a call!'

Mellyn's voice follows me. 'I can tell you think I'm in the wrong, but he bloody deserved it!'

I picture every landing light in the street flicking on in synchronicity and turn back, putting a finger to my lips. 'Shh! Look, it's none of my business, we'll talk tomorrow.'

'Yes, okay. You'll understand when I give you more of the background. As you know, I've been used and abused by men before and this one was going to sodding pay ...' Her voice comes after me, low and menacing, 'Just like Neil did.' Then she tosses her head and gives a bark of what's supposed to be laughter, but to my ears sounds like a release of anger. A cold finger traces the length of my spine even as I wave and hurry away. What the hell did she mean by that – just like Neil did?

Later, I assess the evening as I lie in bed in my hotel room. Even though Mellyn was on the edge at the very end, up to then she had shown a huge improvement. There's a warm feeling in my heart when I think of her expression after I'd called her Mum for the first time. I hate the sordid little game of blackmail she's playing with Jack, and that thing she said about Neil … did she mean he got his comeuppance because he fell to his death? I suppose she must have. I remember that she'd said he got what he deserved the night at the restaurant too. That whole thing made me feel uncomfortable, but then it was probably just a coping mechanism. Of course, it isn't nice to gloat over someone's untimely death, no matter who they were. But who am I to judge? I'd not been beaten and hurt by a man who was supposed to be in love with me, had I?

I punch my pillow and turn over. Perhaps we could talk through it together and she'll see it's best to let the bad memories of the past go – exorcise them and move on. I should know that better than most. I'm helping Mellyn, supporting her through the bad times – even though it's not always easy – by sticking by her and not allowing the ghost of Megan, that I sometimes glimpse watching me from behind her eyes, take possession. We'll make it in the end; our future is bright and this time tomorrow my new address will be Seal Cottage. I'm happier than I have been for a very long time.

Just before I drift off to sleep, Dad's worried face pops into my mind and I know I ought to give him another ring to tell him I'm staying even longer. Adelaide will help smooth the waters, thank God. Adelaide deserves sainthood – St Adelaide, Patron Saint of Eyebrows.

Chapter Sixteen

'At the harbour, Lu? You sound like you're in the next room!' Adelaide's familiar throaty laughter down the line brings with it images of home. 'No matter how long I live I will never stop marvelling at things we take for granted like the mobile telephone, the jet plane, and the Internet. Now *that* really does boggle my mind! I couldn't tell you how it actually works.'

'It isn't that easy to understand for me either!' I laugh, and half listen to her talking about the moon landings while I watch fingers of late-afternoon shadows stretch along the harbour wall and dip into the bay. Boats large and small jostle on their moorings as if gearing up for a race, and the clank, clank, clank of metal on mast sounds less like a tune today and more as if they're having a conversation about their nautical adventures.

'Your dad mentioned you'd phoned this morning. He told me about you moving in with Mellyn.'

My half listening switches to full. Though Adelaide's voice sounds neutral I can't help wondering which layers of emotive words remain unsaid whilst these innocuous ones had been selected.

'Yes. I decided it was time to tell him – and that I was staying longer too. He seemed okay about it, but I think he's hurting underneath. You know what he's like about keeping it all in.'

'Your dad just wants to make you happy. Of course, he misses you … terribly, but as I said to him, you haven't gone to the other side of the world and you will see him again.'

Again, I half listen to Adelaide telling me about her sister's friend's daughter who went to Australia while I do a quick analysis of her words. It doesn't look good. Dad is obviously in bits.

The pause before 'terribly' and the fact that he must have told her he was worried I wouldn't see him again kicks me hard in the gut. My intuition that he was hurting when I had spoken to him this morning was obviously right.

'Of course, I'll see him again. He's my dad, the man who brought me up, loves me, and …' My words stick in my throat, so I take a breath and watch a seagull swoop down and try to grab a sandwich from the hand of the man on the next bench.

'He knows that, love. Don't upset yourself.'

'How can I not be?' I push my hair out of my eyes only to have an offshore breeze push it back again. 'Look. Do you think I should come back this weekend? I'm sure Mellyn would understand.'

'That depends. Do you want to?'

I blow down my nostrils and twist my hair into a clip while I think about that. 'Not really. I've just got my relationship on an even keel with Mellyn and we were supposed to go to Truro shopping on Saturday.'

'An even keel?' Adelaide says quietly. 'I thought you two were fine after the first few hiccups?'

Bugger. I wish I hadn't let that slip out. Without even trying, Adelaide has that knack of drawing things out into the open that I'd rather keep hidden. 'Yes, they are … it just came out wrong, I guess.' I'm glad she can't see the blush on my cheeks. 'I think in a way that Dad should try to understand more. I haven't spent any time at all with her over the last thirty years for goodness' sake!'

'Okay, love. No need to get angry.'

'Oh, Adelaide, I'm sorry. I'm not angry with you – or Dad really. I just feel so torn.'

'I expect you do. And really, I think you're more frustrated than angry, aren't you? Also, your dad hasn't mentioned that he wants you home, has he?'

'Not to me, no …' I expect he had to her though.

'Well, there you are, then. There is one thing I wondered about the other day – how are you for clothes and everything? Most of your stuff is here.'

'I've been buying what I need. And I'm not sure that would go down very well with Dad, me rolling up to take all my stuff away.' I force a laugh and wish I hadn't.

Adelaide laughs too and hers sounds more genuine, though it's strange to hear her laugh. 'Well, how's this for an idea? I've been well overdue a holiday for a few years and I was chatting to my sister Evelyn the other day, and she said—'

'You're coming down here on holiday? That's brilliant!'

'Yes, with Evelyn! How did you guess? I hadn't finished ...'

'You always do go around the houses, Adelaide. That would be fantastic. You could bring a few things down for me and we could have a proper catch up.' I miss her, and until now, I hadn't realised how much.

'Yes. It will be lovely to meet Mellyn too.'

Would it? Doubt crept into my mind. But I say, 'Yes, I'm sure she'd be delighted to meet you too.'

The last of my clothes in the wardrobe and drawers and my toiletries in the bathroom cabinet, I sit on the bed in my lovely new room, the Cinnamon Room as I think of it, and look out across the rooftops of St Ives. Tomorrow is the first of September. I think back to the New Year's Eve party at Ellie's that Sally had dragged me along to, me a little worse for wear, sitting at the bottom of the stairs under a sprig of mistletoe that had seen better days and fending off a kiss from Ellie's cousin, who'd also had seen better days.

I'd escaped to the garden and as my breath hung in the cold January air like little puffs of smoke, I made a wish on the brightest star in the black deep sky. I wished that the coming year would be different to all the others – exciting, challenging, and most of all, I wished for happiness. Little did I know that my wish would be granted in its entirety. It's certainly different, because here I am for the first time living away from home with a new job in a new town. Exciting because my life has changed almost completely; I've managed to shake off the humdrum and predictable. Challenging? God yes. My dear mum was taken so cruelly and unexpectedly. Nevertheless, even though I've tragically lost one mother, I've become reunited with another, and though there are still problems, I can honestly say I'm happy.

I go to the window and look down to my left at the garden. Two jackdaws alight, fold their wings, and chatter for a while like old friends on the rose arbor next to the rampant honeysuckle. Rosie's a good friend. There are lots of firsts in my life at the moment, and for the first time, I know I have a genuine friend in Rosie; I've never felt so close to anyone apart from family. Since school, when Gill told that vile bully Megan about my adoption, I had never completely trusted anyone outside the family ever again. I count Adelaide as family, of course.

I think about what might have happened if I had picked another B&B to stay in. I would never have met Rosie, might not have found a job, and that would have made staying here far more difficult. I have a lot to thank her for. Yes, the job is hard, sometimes dirty, knackering always, but it's good honest work. Straightforward, with no complications like a sinister boss, and Rosie and I have so much fun. We're very alike, share the same humour, and direct it in liberal doses at the Pomp and the Vulture, as Alan had now been shortened to. We said that sounded like a crazy name for a pub and pretend that we'll open one in the future.

With my head and shoulders out of the window and my neck craned to its full extent, I can just see a strip of blue Atlantic. An ear-to-ear grin stretches my cheeks and I draw in a deep lungful of fresh air. Sea on my doorstep. This is a far cry from rainy grey streets and old squashed together buildings ingrained with years of industrial grime burgeoning across the seven hills of Sheffield. I had lived there for the first thirty years of my life and I'm surprised to realise that I don't miss it at all.

'Bangers and mash seem a bit tame after your culinary delights,' I say over my shoulder to Mellyn, who's sitting at the kitchen table. At the sink I attempt potatoes, the unfamiliar peeler awkward in my hand.

'I don't eat like that all the time. I was doing it to impress you!'

'That's a relief. I got these sausages from the local butcher. They looked really good – outdoor-reared pork too of course.'

'Of course. I'm sure they will be lovely, but as I said, there was no need to cook. We could have gone out to celebrate you moving in.'

I turn to face her; the peeler drips brown water onto the floor tiles. 'I'd like to stay in. Let's just be normal for a bit. No more impressing me and fancy meals out – costs a fortune.' I wipe up the water and turn my attention back to the potatoes.

'We could have gone to Jack's,' she says quietly.

Oh, for goodness' sake, why can't she let that lie? It must be obvious I don't approve. 'I won't be going back there, and please let's not discuss it tonight, Mum. I think we should, at some point, but not now.'

'Suits me.' Her voice sounds neutral, but I can't see her expression. I hear her push back her chair and open a cupboard. 'Now, which wine would go down well with your sausages?' She stands next to me and places two bottles of red on the drainer.

'It's only bangers and mash. Why don't we have a soft drink?'

'Nonsense! Pick one.'

Drinking every night doesn't go well with early mornings. But to please her I say, 'I think the Merlot.'

'You don't like the cabby savvy?' Mellyn frowns and sticks out her bottom lip.

'Yes, but—'

Mellyn laughs and pats me on the head. 'Just messing about. You are *so* easy to wind up.'

'Where did you learn to make onion gravy like that? It's phenomenal, and the mash is as creamy as the creamiest thing invented.' Mellyn loads her fork with a combination of both and stuffs it into her mouth.

'My ... other mum. She was a brilliant cook.' I glance across at Mellyn and note a shadow flit across her eyes.

'As good as me?' She gives a little laugh.

'Yes, but in a different way. You cook more fancy stuff. She was more of a meat and two veg kind of gal.'

Mellyn chases a hunk of sausage around her plate and stabs it. Hard. 'I told you, I don't normally cook like that.'

'It wasn't a criticism. I love your food.'

She takes two long swallows of wine and tops up her glass. I put my hand over mine – I've had two already. She shrugs and puts the bottle down. 'You could seriously do something with your talent. Why not go on a cookery course? You're wasted in that job.'

Though I hadn't planned on staying at the B&B forever, her words annoy me, and I can't put my finger on why. I think it's because I don't think she has the right to comment, having left my upbringing to others. 'One day, perhaps.'

'That's been your trouble. You've bobbed around like flotsam at sea. It's about time you took the bull by the horns and—' She stops as she catches the annoyance in my eyes.

'I'm fine for now. And to be honest I have done quite a bit of bull horning these past few months.'

'Bull horning!' She lets out a hoot of laughter and a spot of gravy lands on her chin. I look at it and can't keep a straight face. 'What the bloody hell is bull horning?'

'Okay, it sounded good at the time.' I laugh and put my plate to one side. 'Want pudding? It's only shop bought sticky toffee pudding and clotted cream.'

'You trying to give me heart failure with all this comfort food?' She draws her mouth into a straight line and furrows her brow. Then she smiles. 'Of course! Bring it on.'

Rain keeps us in after dinner, and so in pyjamas we make ourselves comfy with wine, chocolate and fluffy blankets on a sofa each next to the log fire. 'I bet that fire looks really cosy in winter,' I say through a mouthful of chocolate whirl.

'Only when it's lit.' Mellyn slides me a mischievous look over the rim of her glass.

'Oh, ha ha.' I throw a chocolate at her which she catches deftly.

Stretching out my legs I think about the first day I saw this room and pictured myself in it at Christmas. I imagined that I was jumping the gun then, but it looks like that's a real possibility now. But then there's Dad …

'Penny for them.'

I tell her but leave Dad out.

'That would be fabulous if you could stay here! I usually spend it alone.'

'But that's terrible. Have you no family at all – aunts, uncles?'

'Nope. Mum and Dad were only children and the only real friends I have are all in St Austell.'

'Couldn't you invite them here, or you go there?'

'They all have families, Lu. Nobody wants a woman on her own at Christmas.' She winks. 'Especially the ones with wayward husbands.'

If I was wondering whether to go back to Sheffield for Christmas before, I'm not now. Poor Mellyn. My heart swells with sympathy for her. Okay, there's the femme fatale drawback, but nobody should be alone at that time of year. Perhaps Dad could come here, or I could take Mellyn there? We must be able to work something out.

'We always make a big thing of Christmas,' I say, and take a sip of wine. 'Mum always makes … made, her own pudding, cake and …' Without warning my words run out. I realise that this will be the first year without her.

Mellyn speaks into her glass. 'Must hurt, eh? I remember the first year without my parents. Unbearable. They died just a few weeks before Christmas Day.'

I want to change the subject before I start to cry. Something pushes at the edges of my memory … something Rosie had mentioned. Ah yes. 'Talking of friends, I've been meaning to ask you, do you remember someone called Val?'

Mellyn twists her mouth to the side and frowns. 'Don't think so. Val who?'

'Green. She's the mother of my friend Rosie, you know, the one I work with?'

'I didn't know Rosie's surname was Green, thought it was something else.' Mellyn puts her glass down, yawns and stretches her arms above her head.

Am I boring her?

'So anyway, her mum Val and her dad moved to Spain and opened a bar a few years back. Rosie thought you and her mum were friends. Val used to run a bar here, but—'

'Nope, never heard of her. Wanna 'nother drink?' She avoids my puzzled look, gets up and goes to the kitchen.

'No. I'd better not, thanks,' I say. Why has she gone all weird?

She comes back in with a bowl of peanuts and a huge glass of red. 'Can you believe I'm peckish after that heart attack on a plate you fed me?'

Her eyes look too bright and red blotches on her skin spread upward from her neck. 'Must be all the wine – it can give you an appetite.'

She narrows her eyes and with her cheeks full of nuts I'm reminded of an angry squirrel. 'You think I drink too much, don't you?'

'I wouldn't say too much—'

'What would you say then?'

I want to tell her to calm down and stop cutting off my sentences, but the look on her face tells me that would be a bad idea. Instinct makes me stand my ground, however. 'Perhaps a bit more than is good for you, I guess.'

'I think you're right,' she says, and drains half the glass. 'But then if you'd had my life, you'd drink. Neil drank and when he'd had enough, he beat me. Did I not tell you that?' She leans forward, her mouth tight, her eyes bright with defiance.

The last time she'd looked like this was the day at the shop ages ago when she'd been angry that I didn't want to pick the jewellery. I don't need this now. 'Yes … you know you did. Let's change the subject, Mum.'

'Yes, let's. What news from your end?' She stretches her mouth into what's supposed to be a smile, exposing her wine-stained teeth and bottom lip.

The only news I have is Adelaide's and I've no time to consider if sharing it will make things better or worse. I need to get Mellyn off this track, so I tell her.

The rest of her wine goes the same way as the last bottle and a half. She places the empty glass gently on the side table, but her knuckles are white as she grasps the stem.

'So, let me get this right. Your neighbour is coming to visit you in a few weeks?' Her voice is calm, but I'm not fooled.

'Adelaide's much more than a neighbour. I don't know how I would have coped with everything if she hadn't been there for me,' I say and look her in the eye.

'But I haven't had you to myself for five minutes. Is *he* coming too?'

'Who?'

'Your dad,' she spits, as if she's got something nasty in her mouth.

'No. Why?'

'You said *they* are coming.'

'Adelaide and her sister.'

'Sounds like the title of a film. A boring one.'

Before I can stop myself, I snap, 'How rude! What's the matter with you? Just because a dear friend is coming here on holiday and thought she'd visit me, doesn't mean I think any less of you. She was actually looking forward to meeting my mum. Ha! Like that's going to happen now.' I go into the kitchen to put space between us and to avoid looking at her shocked white face.

I lean against the sink and watch a droplet of water form, grow fat and then plop from the end of the tap into the washing-up bowl. I watch another and then another. The detergent bubbles raft together around the clear water the droplets leave behind, and I realise I'm the bubbles to Mellyn's droplets. Always reacting rather than acting. Pacifying her moods, trying to protect her. Until just now and that time at the restaurant, I've always kept my temper. It might not be a good idea to lash out, given what I'm trying to achieve by being here, but I'm only human after all.

Her voice drifts in from the sitting room. 'Please come back in, Lu. I behaved badly when I said I wouldn't the other night … and I am so, so sorry.'

I turn the tap and the droplets stop. I go back into the sitting room and find Mellyn where I left her … with another full glass of wine. A bottle is open on the dining table. I glance at it and wish I knew what to say next.

Unbelievably she misinterprets my look at the wine. 'Would you like another glass? I forgot I had this one – it was at the back of the cabinet.'

'No. In fact I think it's time I went to bed.'

'Oh please, not yet, not when we've had a falling out.' She slurs her last few words and I watch her bottom lip trembling. 'Can you forgive me?'

I look at her big blue eyes pooling with tears and know that I can. I have to. 'Yes, Mum, I forgive you. I just wish Neil wasn't dead, so I could bloody kill him myself for what he's done to you.' I close the gap between us and wrap her in a hug.

Mellyn rests her head on my shoulder and her sobs shudder through my body. 'Too late. I … I got there before you.'

What's she on about now? 'Got where, Mum?' I hold her at arm's length and wipe the streaks of mascara from her face with a tissue.

'Told you the other night that I made him pay.' Her legs buckle, and she drops heavily onto the settee. I sit opposite, my brain trying to block the implications of her words while I watch her pick up her glass from the table and down half of it in one. I go to take the rest away from her, but then freeze when she says, 'I … killed him. I killed Neil.'

Chapter Seventeen

Grey dawn light slips under the curtains and onto a lopsided dog's head peering from a heap of clothes on the bedroom floor. I rub my eyes and look again. The dog turns into a pillow that I had punched, folded and then flung across the room during a sleepless night. I sit up and check the time on my phone. Five o'clock. Two hours sleep then. That doesn't bode well for a long day's work at Pebble House. Would Rosie manage without me just for today? Probably, but then I would have to face Mellyn, and her terrible confession hanging in the air like a vile curse on an innocent tongue.

I lie back down and pull the duvet up around my chin and think about the whole stomach-churning mess once more. Mellyn had switched, as I thought of her moods, after I'd mentioned Val, Rosie's mum. That was when she'd really started drinking in earnest, but why? I sit up again and draw my hands down my face. Did that actually matter? The real problem was that she had got very drunk and decided to share the fact that she had murdered her husband. Murdered him in cold blood and then asked me not to tell anyone.

I stare at the birds of paradise patterning the beige curtain, but instead see the whole surreal scene again. Mellyn's tortured eyes staring across at me from the sofa, her ghostly face, the words, 'I killed Neil,' in my ears, but my brain refusing to process.

After what seemed like a very long time I'd said, 'What do you mean?'

Mellyn let out a long sigh as if she'd been holding her breath and shrugged. 'He had hurt me badly the day before – said I had been ogling the postman – my wrist and hand ended up in a sling.

Neil had been working in the shed and had a wooden mallet in his hand the moment he saw the postman leave. He came in with it behind his back, smiled sweetly at me and then smacked it down on my wrist and hand as I gripped the banister to go upstairs for something.'

I remember that I had put my hand over my mouth to stifle a cry but Mellyn didn't notice. She'd had that trance-like stare on her face and the distant sing-song voice was back.

'So, the next day, the day I killed him, we were round at my parents'. I told you before that he was doing the guttering, so we could get the house ready for sale. I was painting in the downstairs loo with my one good hand, and then I went upstairs to use the bathroom …' She stopped and shoved her hands through her hair a few times and then wiped her mouth on the back of her sleeve. 'Didn't want to get trousers on my paint as I remember.' She laughed and shook her head. 'No … I meant paint on my trousers.'

I hadn't wanted to hear the rest. I knew it was inevitable, but I wished she would stop. A desperate part of my mind pretended that maybe she was so drunk she was just making the whole thing up. I wished with all my heart that I could believe it. Mellyn began speaking again.

'On my way back, I caught a glimpse of Neil on the ladder through one of the bedroom windows. My wrist was really sore after the struggle to get my knickers down and up in the loo – I'd banged it on the wall. I remember looking at the bandage and thinking you poor pathetic cow. How did you let it come to this? The next minute I was at the window, the window was open … and then I grabbed the ladder with my good hand and shoved with all my might. Neil went down so fast … so fast. I heard his skull crack on the patio like—'

'Oh my God!' I jumped up and wrapped my arms around myself. I just stood there staring at her, a hundred words in my mouth but not one able to break free. She stared back, her expression blank, her eyes dead. I swallowed down a roll of nausea and said, 'What … why? I don't know what to say … I …'

'Say nothing. It happened and that was it. I thought I owed it to you to be honest. If you know, then you will really understand why I'm … why I fly off the handle, and you'll be able to … help me. Help me!' she wailed. Leaning forward she put her elbows on her knees and covered her face with both hands. An animalistic howl left her lips and then she curled up on the sofa in the foetal position, heart-rending sobs shaking her whole body.

I had comforted her, of course. What else could I have done? I gave a curt nod in answer to her plea that I wouldn't tell a soul and helped her up the rickety stairs to bed. She was out cold before I could undress her, so I just covered her with the duvet.

In the bathroom I splash cold water on my face; my eyes feel like they've been taken out, rolled in sand and glued back in. The mirror tells me that's not far from the truth. Red and green as a colour combination normally works – except when it's applied to eyes. Even my skin looks tired, pale and lined. I stroke the furrow in my brow just above the bridge of my nose. It wasn't as deep as that a week ago, was it?

Hot water needles bring back some semblance of normality to my tired body, so I tip my head into the full force of the shower in the hope that it will do the same for my brain. In my mind's eye I see Mellyn's pleading face again. How can I not tell anyone? How can I calmly go about my business knowing that my mother is a murderer? Wouldn't that make me as bad – an accomplice? And her cry for help. How can I? I've been kidding myself that I would be able to help since that day at the art gallery, pretending I was some sort of natural counsellor, when all I really am is a daughter who loves her mum.

I shut the shower off and into the silent steam I exhale the impact of that thought, tendrils of truth lost in a fine mist. Did I love her, really? I saw an image of a determined sixteen-year-old, successful in her fight to preserve life, but unable to hold on to it afterwards. Even though Mellyn had brought me into the world and had been desperate to keep me, the walls of life had been just too high to scale.

Wrapped in a fluffy towel, I sit on the edge of the bed. Emotion swells in my throat and for the first time I admit to myself that perhaps the fondness in my heart is turning to love, even though she has myriad faults, problems, psychological issues and a streak of stubbornness as long as the Nile. If it hadn't been for the stubborn streak, I might not be sitting here in this fluffy towel deciding whether or not to repay her fighting for my life by taking hers. Because that's what would happen if I confessed to the police, wouldn't it? I would in effect be taking away her life.

From the kitchen door I watch an early honey bee dip into the heart of a rose. I imagine there would be bees on Mum's rose bush back home, all the tight buds would be open, and the air would be heavy with its perfume. I wonder if Dad is up yet and if he's looking out of the kitchen window at the roses. My heart decides that's too painful to witness, so I put it out of my head and look at a crack in a patio slab.

I take a few swallows of strong hot coffee and feel it burn an arabica path to my gullet. What would Mum have done in my shoes? I look at my bare feet and wiggle my toes. She would have said put your shoes on for a start; Mum was always practical. She might have suggested that perhaps Mellyn was just being dramatic for effect; she did confess in her sing-song voice after all. Then she would have decided that something so dramatic was unlikely to be for effect. She would have said trust my gut. My gut agrees with her decision.

On the bedside table next to Mellyn's snoring form, I place a plate of toast and a pint of water. The only visible part of her is a tangle of chestnut hair and a foot. It's even clearer to me that our roles are reversed, but, unlike the last time I realised this, I don't like it. Now my responsibility has taken on life or death status. I hold her terrible secret in my care and must protect it and her from exposure. Mellyn's like a fragile but precious ornament, and it's up to me to keep her from breaking.

'Are you sure you're okay?' Rosie says, closing the dishwasher door with her hip and frowning across at me. 'You don't look well, and you've hardly said more than a few words all morning.'

'Yes, I told you, I'm fine.' I wipe down the countertop and fold a clean napkin. I can feel her eyes hot on the back of my neck and know I haven't fooled her.

'Look,' I say turning to face her, and feel a smile hovering valiantly at the corners of my mouth. 'I'm just tired. I was up chatting to Mum until late last night and then I couldn't sleep straight away. Lots of things in my head – you know how it is sometimes.' I turn back to my folding.

'Yes. Sounds like it was a successful chat – you just called her Mum. That's a first.' Rosie walks across the kitchen, hops up on the counter beside me and tucks her hands under her legs.

'Yes, I did, didn't I?' And it is a first. At least something good had come out of the disaster. 'Called her Mum to her face the other day too for the first time.'

'Ri-ght. So, if things are good, why do you look so bloody miserable?' Rosie grabs a napkin, shakes it out and flicks it at me like a duster.

'I just folded that!' I snatch it from her and sigh at her crestfallen expression. 'Oh, for goodness' sake, I can see I'll get no peace until I tell you. Adelaide is coming down for a visit soon and I don't think Mum was keen. I think she felt jealous, you know, the old life muscling in on the new … her new.' I look up at Rosie and she looks back, nodding like one of those dogs on the back shelves of cars.

'I can understand where she's coming from. She just gets you all to herself and then wham!' Rosie slaps her hand on the counter. 'Up pops Adelaide – Adelaide who means the world to you, no less.'

My eyebrows shoot up. Perhaps Mellyn hadn't been acting so weirdly if Rosie understood her feelings. 'Do you think I should tell Adelaide not to come?'

'Nah. Mellyn will have to get used to it. No use pandering to her every whim, if you start that, it will never end. My mum is similar – give her an inch and all that.'

'Funny you should mention your mum,' I say, wiping down the cooker. 'My mum had never heard of her – guess you must have got it wrong.'

129

'Really?' Rosie jumps down from the counter and fills the kettle. 'I wasn't absolutely certain, as I said, but something rang a bell about your mum's shop. Perhaps Mum was friends with the woman who part owns it, the one who lives up country now?'

'Could be. You'll have to ask your mum next time you speak. Also, it's about time you popped round and met mine.' I push the coffee pot towards Rosie. 'Make it nice and strong, otherwise I'll not last the day and the Pomp and Vulture will be on my back.'

She laughs and returns to her task. 'Yes, they'll be on mine too. Thanks for the invite – I'd like to meet Mellyn.'

Good. I've managed to pacify her curiosity without cracking up. I must be a better actress than I thought. Out in the corridor I open the cleaning cupboard and clank out the mop and bucket. I notice my hand holding the mop handle. It has short fingernails, rough red skin and a tremble in its grip: a sign of emotional exhaustion? Perhaps, but I'm tough, determined, responsible – oh yes, and a good actress apparently. Losing Mum and finding another, along with her deadly secret, has changed me irrevocably. The old me of six months ago wouldn't recognise the new. On balance this is a good thing, but why did the change have to come at such a terrible price?

Chapter Eighteen

It made a nice change to be able to enjoy a soak and a glass of wine; normally her chin would be on her chest after a meal for one in front of the telly. Rosie had Lu to thank for that, an extra pair of hands made all the difference. Looking round her little flat earlier though she'd had to concede that she was glad her friend had turned down her offer to move in. For one thing, she was probably the messiest person she knew, for another, her tiny living space wouldn't accommodate her mess and another human being, and the last thing … well, she didn't really want to think about that one.

An errant bubble threatened to land in the wine glass. A puff of air from her lips sent the orb tumbling towards the tap and with a silent pop, it was no more. Rosie needed to do something with her life before her own bubble became no more. Though the Pomp and Vulture pub she and Lu joked about opening was just that, a joke, would it be such a bad idea? They worked well together, were both competent women – hell, Rosie had practically run the B&B single-handedly for two years. It didn't have to be a pub, neither had experience in that field, but perhaps it could be a coffee shop instead, maybe serving light meals; it could even be licensed. The phone rang in the hallway. Damn. That would be Mum.

'Mum! Yes, sorry … I know I said I'd ring at seven, just forgot.' Rosie struggled to belt her robe whilst mopping the drips from the bath with a towel under her foot.

'Easy to forget, eh? That's nice for a mother to hear I'm sure!' Val laughed, but her daughter wasn't fooled.

'How could I forget you, Mum? You're in my every waking thought.'

'Hm … So how have you been then?'

'Good, thanks. I was just thinking in the bath how much better my life is with Lu working alongside. We are similar fish really, though different in some ways. We are alike in the fact that we're underachievers … have battleaxes for mothers—'

'Watch it, madam. I might be in Spain, but I can be there by late morning tomorrow. You're not too big for a clip round the ear 'ole!' Val laughed and this time it was genuine.

'Yeah, right. You never laid a finger on me and you know it. I was thinking that in the future it might be a good idea to set up some sort of business with Lu.'

Val snorted down the line and Rosie clenched her jaw. Here we go.

'You can't *just* decide to start *some* sort of business, love. It's a damn sight harder than that. You have to research your market, spend time planning, then—'

'Yes, Mum, I *do* know. I was just floating an idea, that's all. I haven't even mentioned it to Lu. It would be nice to do something with my life that I could be proud of before much longer, you know?'

'Of course. You're wasted in that job – you're a talented young woman – and I'd help with whatever venture you decided on. I have experience in business, after all.'

Rosie smiled. The pride in Val's voice was both for herself and her daughter. 'You do. Speaking of which, how's it going?'

'Busy! We've had the most hectic summer so far. Once this month is over it will start tailing off a bit. Your dad is grumbling as usual. He grumbles when we're slack, grumbles when we're busy.' Val sighed. 'The truth is we both miss you and Jake something awful. Miss Cornwall too. We were only saying the other night: if we have another year out here we might have enough savings to come home, buy a nice little cottage and retire.'

A lump formed in Rosie's throat. 'Oh, Mum, that would be brilliant! Seeing you twice a year isn't enough, and if you come home you could really help Lu and me get on our feet business wise.'

Truthfully, she would like to do it with the minimum interference, but if it encouraged her parents to return then she'd say almost anything.

'That's settled then, Rosie Posy,' Val said, a tremor in her voice. 'And is this Lu not getting on with her birth mum? You said she was a battleaxe like me.'

'I think they have their moments, but overall they're very happy to be together again. It's funny, but I could have sworn you and her mum were friends a while back. I kept meaning to mention it to you but forgot. Lu told me today that her mum didn't know you after all though. She's invited me round to meet her, so that'll be nice.'

'What's her name?'

'Mellyn, don't know her surname, runs the jewellery shop on the high street.' Rosie poked a blemish on her chin and wiped steam from the mirror with the cuff of her robe to check it wasn't as big as it felt. 'Mum? Have you nodded off?' The spot wasn't the largest, but it looked pretty angry. There was still no reply from Val. 'Hello? You still there?'

'Er, yes. I was just trying to shoo a fly out of the window.'

There was something wrong with Mum's voice, she thought … it sounded as if she was upset but pretending not to be. 'So, did you know her? I had wondered if you'd been friends with her business partner instead. She went to live up country to—'

'Be with her aged parents, yes. It was her I was friends with, not Mellyn. I spoke to her once or twice, but we weren't friends. Think she was a bit odd – not sure you'd want to meet her. Now, have you decided what you want for your birthday? You always leave it 'til the last minute and we end up just sending money. I'd like to get something nice this time,' Val said, her words running into each other, her voice up a few octaves.

'My birthday isn't for three months, Mum.' There was definitely something wrong. 'Your voice sounds a bit odd, and you seem on … on edge I suppose you'd call it.'

A too-shrill burst of laughter down the phone confirmed Rosie's worries. 'Don't be daft, there's nothing wrong with me at all.

Just rushed off my feet as usual. Oh, I think your dad could do with a hand in the bar. I'll ring next week, love you!'

The disconnect tone was the perfect soundtrack to Rosie's disquiet.

Disquiet had settled for 'wait and see' after a good night's sleep. Mum could be odd too at times, despite what she'd said about Mellyn. Nearing Pebble House, Rosie inhaled the early morning air and detected a hint of smoky autumn twirling around a salt breeze. Autumn was one of her favourite seasons: the turning leaves, the smell of wood smoke – she opened the door and walked through to the dining room – the country paths ready to be explored, the … Bloody hell, what was up with Lu?

Lu turned her back and began laying another table even though she hadn't finished the first one. Rosie followed and placed a hand on her shoulder. 'Too late, I already saw your crumply face and tears in your eyes. What's wrong?'

A sniff. 'Nothing you can put right. You've done enough as it is.'

'How do you know until you tell me what it is?' Rosie moved to the other side of the table and watched Lu's face closely. The tears that threatened to spill never got the chance under Lu's fierce napkin attack across the eyes.

'I'm being dramatic,' Lu said, but the attempt at a smile turned the corners of her mouth down instead of up and added a chin wobble. 'It's just that I have so loved working here …' She looked at the napkin and took a deep breath. 'Pomp just told me that the main holiday season will be over soon, and they can't afford to keep me on beyond the end of next week.'

'She did what?' A fire ignited anger under her ribs. 'We'll see about that!'

Lu grabbed her arm as she made for the door. 'No! Look, she's right in a way. It will get slack now leading up to winter, and—'

'It does tail off, yes, but this is St Ives!' Rosie threw her arms up. 'We get tourists year-round and if they would get off their arses and promote the business, offer an evening meal for example, update the ancient bloody website, think of new ways of attracting people instead of just doing sweet FA, then you wouldn't have to lose your job.'

Lu nodded. 'But we both know they won't do all that. There's no point in sticking your neck out on my behalf, and you certainly shouldn't go and see her now while you're fuming.'

'I will be calm but firm, don't worry.'

Calm but firm only achieved a compromise. Perhaps fuming would have been better. Rosie looked through the glass double doors of the dining room. A middle-aged honeymoon couple had requested an early breakfast as they were off on a day trip and the woman whispered something in Lu's ear as she set a coffee pot on the table. She laughed, and a flush crept up her neck. Rosie swallowed. She wouldn't be laughing in a few minutes.

Lu came through the door and the smile faded as she scanned Rosie's face. 'Don't worry. You tried your best.'

'I managed to keep you for two days a week – that's if you want them. I wouldn't be offended if you said no. I can appreciate that you need more hours than that—'

'Really? That's amazing. Of course, I want them, but how did you manage it?'

'I threatened to walk out right now. Calmly and firmly, I might add,' Rosie said, and smiled at Lu's obvious relief. The compromise went down much better than she could have hoped.

'I don't know how to thank you.' Lu's eyes became pools again. 'I have never had a friend who ... well, who was a *true* friend before.'

'Okay, that's enough emotional stuff. Go and help chef while I grab myself a quick coffee and a bite. I missed breakfast.'

On her way to the kitchen Rosie glanced at the reception and was surprised to see a tall attractive woman leaning against the desk while scrolling down her phone. It was a bit early for enquiries and she didn't recognise her as a guest.

'Can I help you?' Rosie slipped around the desk and added her best welcome smile.

The woman tossed her thick chestnut hair and mustered a half smile that didn't even attempt to reach the striking blue eyes. 'Yes. I've just popped in to see Lu, but as there's been *nobody* on reception for the last five minutes to ask, I thought I'd ring her and tell her I'm here.'

Rosie imagined neither the look of reproach nor the rude manner of her speech. Must she be calm and firm a second time today? She looked pointedly at her watch and said. 'It *is* only seven fifty, madam. We don't normally expect people to call so early.'

The blue eyes narrowed and through a tight mouth the woman said, 'I am not people. I am Lu's mother.' She put her head to one side and looked Rosie up and down as if she'd found something unpleasant in her path.

Great, seems like Mum's analysis was right. 'Oh, I see. How nice to meet you?' Rosie offered her hand and a smile. 'I'm Rosie.'

Mellyn encased her hand in a cold limp shake. 'You too.' She inclined her head briefly but did not smile. 'Lu went out without her watch this morning, so I thought I'd bring it in.'

'Mum! What are you doing here?' Lu stood at the dining room door, a full English in each hand.

'Don't get your knickers in a twist. Just dropping your watch off to your lovely friend here.' Mellyn held the watch aloft and beamed a smile so wide that Rosie imagined the top of her head might fall off.

'Hang on, I'll just serve these, and I'll be back.'

Mellyn's smile disappeared with her daughter. Rosie stepped back and folded her arms. How could she switch so quickly; this woman wasn't just cold, she was freezing. Mellyn drummed her nails on the counter. 'Lu tells me that you thought me, and your mum were friends. I can't recollect her at all—'

'Yes. Funnily enough I asked Mum last night on the phone. She said I was mistaken, and that she was friends with your partner, though she did speak to you once or twice.'

Mellyn's frosty outlook immediately changed to fair with a chance of sunshine. 'Ah, I see. I thought it must be something like that.'

'You needn't have worried about the watch, Mum,' Lu said, hurrying over and giving Mellyn a quick hug. 'But I'm glad you have, because you've met each other at last.'

'We have! And you must come over for dinner one night, Rosie. We were only talking about that the other day, weren't we, Lu?'

Rosie looked at the warm light in Mellyn's eyes and couldn't believe how quickly she'd changed again. The chance of sunshine had morphed into a heatwave. 'I'd love to ...'

'What about Friday?' Mellyn placed a hand on Rosie's arm.

Rosie glanced at Lu. 'Yes, that's great thanks.'

The two women said goodbye to Mellyn and watched her walk away up the cobbled street. 'You seem to have made a good impression in such a short time,' Lu said. 'And up until now she's seemed wary of any friends or family encroaching on our relationship. Must be because you're such a wonderful person.'

'Yes, must be that.'

Lu laughed and went back to work.

Alone once more, Rosie continued to stare at the street long after Mellyn had gone.

Chapter Nineteen

'We can't just go back to Cornwall on a whim, Val. Who's going to run this place?'

Val looked across the bar at her husband and wondered when he'd stopped actually listening to her. Perhaps he'd never listened and she'd just realised. No, that couldn't be the case, because there had been times when he'd been clearly detached from a conversation and she'd added things like: 'And then, would you believe it, an alien landed and asked directions to Malaga?' Sometimes he'd nodded and other times he'd raised an eyebrow and tutted at her silliness. They should be silly more often.

'I didn't say *we* should go, Rob. I said *I* should go. Kelly could use a few extra hours.'

'On your own … why? You've been a right Moody Judy since you spoke to Rosie last week, and now you want to go and see her?' Rob folded his arms across his paunch. 'Has something happened that you're not telling me about?'

'Moody Judy and Rosie, sounds like a sitcom,' Val said and laughed, more at the fact that her husband looked like a grumpy overweight leprechaun in his green Ireland shirt than at her almost joke.

'It's not funny, Val. Has anything bad happened?' A hiss punctuated the silence as Rob pulled a pint and took a long swallow.

That was his answer to everything. No wonder he'd got such a beer belly. When he turned sideways he looked like a capital D. Peter Kay had come up with that one, or was it the Liverpudlian comic with the teeth? Rob snorted and banged the glass down, obviously exasperated that she was just standing there, staring.

'Eh? No … nothing bad has happened. I just think she could do with a bit of mother–daughter time. I told you she was over the moon when I said we'd try and move back home soon.' Val watched Rob rub his hands through his thinning grey hair and then over his cheeks. God, he was overdoing the drama thing just a bit.

'I don't know, love,' he said, shaking his head. 'It seems a bit drastic. How long would you be gone for?'

'Drastic? I plan to go over for a few days, five at the most, to see our daughter, perhaps even Jake if he's not too busy. It's not as if I'm emigrating to bloody Australia!'

'Okay, no need to go bananas.' Rob thrust the palms of his hands towards her. 'Go if you really must. It will be expensive employing Kelly for all that time, but I suppose we'll manage. But most of all, I'll miss you.'

Right then he looked exactly like the shy young lad she'd fallen in love with. There he was peeping out from behind lines and wrinkles, eyes full of passion and ready to take on the world. A rush of love pushed her towards him and she slipped behind the bar and into his arms.

'I'll miss you too,' she said, nestling her head on his shoulder. 'I love you so much but don't tell you enough.' Shit. Where'd that come from? Perhaps the same place as an ocean of tears pressing against the back of her eyes.

'Oh, Val. That's nice. And you know I feel the same. Guess we're just too busy to turn around, let alone tell each other how we feel. Still, once we move back home we'll have a new lease of life, eh?'

A soft kiss on the neck and a travelling hand wouldn't do in the middle of the bar. Val stepped back. 'There'll be time for that later if you're lucky. But now I have to sort out a flight.'

***

Adelaide raised an eyebrow at her reflection. Did this brown cardigan say, 'smart travel wear' or 'dowdy old woman'? She'd ask her sister's opinion when she arrived; Evelyn was more with it. Adelaide had never been with it, though if that meant jeans and shouty colours then she'd much rather be without it. She smoothed a cuff and looked at the pale liver-spotted hand against the gravy brown. If it turned out that the cardigan said 'dowdy old woman' then it would be true, wouldn't it? The face in the mirror confirmed it. Perhaps not dowdy – could a face be dowdy? – but yes, old. Seventy-seven was six months ahead and she seemed to be hurtling towards it quicker with every passing day.

A photo of her last husband looked at her from the dressing table and she smiled at it. Christopher had left her when he was just sixty-three, so she should be damned well grateful that she was going to be seventy-seven, God willing. Adelaide fastened the clasp on her beads and settled their coolness in the hollow of her neck. From her bedroom window she saw Steve Lacey hurry down the path and drive off to work. Poor lonely Steve. Here she was bemoaning her age when his lovely Hannah had been taken from him at fifty-nine. Senseless. What was God thinking on that rainy spring morning? Still, they had a raised a lovely daughter. A light feeling lifted in her stomach and pushed the weight of sadness away. Soon she'd see Lu again.

'So, the taxi will be here in half an hour. Just time for a cuppa.' Evelyn paused with her hand on the kettle and looked at Adelaide. 'But then I don't fancy those little toilets on the coach – I always think the door is going to fly open and everyone will see me with my knickers round my ankles!'

Adelaide laughed along with her sister. The sound surprised her. She didn't laugh nearly enough, didn't find things that funny really. But she had so missed Evelyn's ready humour and hectic approach to life. Nottingham wasn't so far away, but Evelyn had a husband, children and grandchildren to keep her busy. There seemed precious little time for visits. 'I wonder if I should learn to drive?' Adelaide looked at her sister, her head on one side.

'Drive? We've just established that you're a dowdy old woman and made you change your cardi, and now you're on about driving!'

'You're seventy-one and *you* drive.' Adelaide folded her arms and pretended to be hurt.

'Yes, but I've been driving for fifty-two of them.'

'Never too old to try summat new, our dad used to say.'

Evelyn gave her sister a withering look and sat down opposite her at the kitchen table. 'He meant a pint of cider down the Angel instead of bitter.'

Adelaide laughed again. 'I miss those times, when we were kids. It all seems so long ago...' She looked out of the window at the lavender and remembered her dad telling her all the names of the flowers.

'That's because it *was* so long ago. Now, stop being so bloody maudlin and tell me what the heck you're so worried about that I had to drop everything and agree to come to the back of sodding beyond with you,' Evelyn said in a rush, her double chin mottled and wobbling.

'I told you already. I can't put my finger on it, but I know that little Lu needs help.'

'Because of her wicked birth mum, yes, you said. You didn't say how we could help though.'

'I didn't say she was wicked either ... just not quite right somehow. I get the feeling that Lu isn't telling me everything.' Adelaide watched her sister's face, noting the sceptically raised eyebrow. Evelyn always put too much eyebrow pencil on; perhaps she'd have a casual word if she could think of how to introduce it into conversation. 'Anyway, Steve is worried sick, and I know it will put his mind at rest if we go and check on her.'

'But why did you want me to come?'

'Because, strange as it might seem, I would like to spend some time with my only sister, and because it would look odd if I went on my own – more obvious that I was going to check up on her—'

'But you are.'

'I know, but—' Adelaide stopped when she saw the twinkle in Evelyn's eye. 'Dear Lord. Poor Lu won't know what's hit her when she meets you.'

A grin stretched Evelyn's round face. 'I expect you'll solve all her problems – everything – in half an hour with the usual sage Adelaide advice?'

That rankled. 'I seem to remember you coming to me for advice pretty often over the years, and no, of course I don't expect to solve everything.'

'Hey, no need to get on your high horse. I was teasing. You do give pretty sound advice as it goes.' Evelyn looked at her watch. 'Right, let's make a move. The taxi will be here before you've managed to tie your trainers.'

'Trainers? I wouldn't be seen d—' Adelaide caught the twinkle again and allowed the corners of her lips to turn up briefly.

Chapter Twenty

Minds are wonderful things – full of compartments, hidden drawers and deeply recessed, securely locked strongboxes. The terrible secret I've been living with for the past week or so has been put in the strongest of these, and so far, it hasn't discovered how to pick the lock. This, I realise, is due to the continued support of my best friend Rosie, the imminent arrival of Adelaide and her sister, but mainly because of Mellyn's return to normal. Better than normal, in fact pretty damned near perfect. A nagging worry that this can't last rattles at me from inside a hidden drawer from time to time but stops when it realises I'm not listening.

It probably helped that when I returned from work the day I'd left toast and water by her cocooned form, she hadn't mentioned the events of the night before, except to say, 'Things will be different from now on. I am so sorry.'

Things have been different. Mel is back to laughing and joking, taking me out sailing, even said she was looking forward to meeting Adelaide. Last night she suggested that to supplement my income, I should help out in the shop a few days a week. When I said I'd think about it, her face had remained untroubled and she agreed that perhaps I should have a trial day to see if I'd like it.

I look at the prawns on the drainer that I'm supposed to prepare as a starter. They're dead, of course they are, but if I almost close one eye and glance a little to my left, I'd swear that one of them just wiggled its front legs. I poke another one with the chef knife and the others look at me reproachfully with their beady, black … dead eyes. My finger gets as far as the first prawn, but the cold hard shell may as well be a force field.

I watch water from the cold tap streaming across the affected finger and shudder. Why had I said that I'd start dinner as Mum was working late? Rosie's coming over in an hour and it needs to be done properly. She'd been unable to make last Friday in the end as she'd fallen prey to a migraine, as she'd put it. I cover the staring shellfish with a sheet of kitchen roll and wonder about the migraine thing again. Had she just said it to make an excuse? Mel had put her on the spot and she'd been quiet for the rest of that day. Rosie has been fine since, though, so there's no use worrying about things that have already happened, or not in the case of the made-up migraine scenario.

Sensible advice reminds me of Adelaide. I dry my hands and hug myself. I'm so looking forward to seeing her arched eyebrows and non-smile. She and Evelyn would be arriving in Newquay round about now, and then in a couple of days they'll make their way to Pebble House for another few days. Would she be pleased that I've cast away stones to her exacting standard, or will she feel there are still a few more to be unearthed?

I look out of the kitchen window just in time to see a cloud throw a shadow over the garden and tuck the sun away under its folds. Who am I kidding? Yes, of course there are more stones to cast, and some that should have remained buried deep. A corner of the strongbox appears so I replace it with a picture of the prawns. I lift the kitchen roll, let it fall again and open the fridge instead. We're having a throwback 1970s evening and three steaks sit on a plate on the middle shelf. I take them out. If I can't bring myself to handle the prawns, I'll make a salad and marinate the steaks.

'This prawn cocktail is utterly scrumptious,' Rosie says to Mellyn as she passes a basket of warm rolls across the table.

'Thanks,' she says and then winks at me. 'It's a good job I came home a bit earlier or you wouldn't have got it.'

'Okay, don't rub it in,' I say and butter a roll. 'I haven't prepared shellfish before, Rosie, and I couldn't bring myself to do it tonight either. I just felt so guilty.' I glance up in time to see a look of amusement pass between her and Mel. 'I know it sounds daft, but the poor little things were just looking at me, blaming me for killing them.' I point the butter knife at Rosie. 'Which I didn't, I might add.'

Mel takes a mouthful of wine and her eyes bulge, goldfish-like. She presses her napkin to lips and makes a noise between a cough and a sneeze, clearly trying to suppress laughter and avoid spitting out her wine. 'Oh, you are funny, Lu!' she manages, once she gets her breath back.

Rosie laughs too and nods. 'Yup. A total nut job.'

I have to agree and join my laughter to theirs. I look at them both, two of my most favourite people in the world, and wish we could preserve this moment forever, press the scene between the pages of a book like a fragrant rose petal. Years into the future we could gather round, open the page and remember the room, the smells, the tastes and the way we felt exactly at this instant. Happy moments are so precious, yet often so hard to recapture once time has left them behind.

'So, tell me about your family, Rosie,' Mel says pushing her plate to one side and resting her chin on interlocked fingers.

'Well, Mum and Dad run a bar in Spain – I think Lu told you that.' Mel nods. 'Before that they ran the Cockle Shell Bar just down the coast from here, but they lived around the corner from where I do now, here in St Ives. My brother Jake is—'

'Ha!' Mel slaps a hand on the table, making us both jump. 'My dad sometimes used to sing a song called that. How funny.'

Rosie and I look at each other. 'Called what?' Rosie asked.

'There was a song in the seventies called "My Brother Jake".' Mel looks at our blank faces and smiles. 'I don't expect you two to have heard of it. Anyway, sorry, carry on.'

'So, Jake is an estate agent in Penzance. He's two years younger than me. We get on now but when we were little we fought like cat and dog.' Rosie laughs and pops the last bit of bread in her mouth.

'I wish I'd had a sibling to fight with. Beats being an only child,' Mel said, gathering the plates and taking them into the kitchen.

I was going to agree but then thought that might upset her. 'I wish I had a brother or sister,' I whisper to Rosie. 'It was lonely at times growing up.'

'Well, you have me now, don't you?' Rosie gives me a big smile.

The silence at the start of the main course is a little unnerving. 'Steak okay – not too rare?' I ask.

Both Mum and Rosie make appreciative noises and shake their heads.

Rosie says, 'No, I'm just savouring it, truly delicious, Lu. What's the marinade?'

'A bit of this, a little of that, a pinch of the other. I can't tell you my culinary secrets or I'd have to kill you afterwards.'

'Worth dying for,' Mel says, her cheek pouched with food. 'It's cooked to perfection.' She washes the mouthful down with a swallow of wine and tops up our glasses. 'Tell me, do you have boyfriend, Rosie?'

I watch Rosie's eyes grow round at the abrupt change of conversation and a deep crimson wave splash up her neck. 'Er … no, not at the moment,' she says in a voice so quiet I have to strain my ears to hear above the scrape of metal on crockery.

'A gorgeous creature like you? Madness!' Mel says, the candlelight catching a spark of mischief in her eyes.

Though desperate to rescue my friend, I can't think of anything to say that won't obviously be changing the subject. Rosie hadn't been very forthcoming talking about past relationships with me, let alone Mel.

'Thanks for the compliment, Mellyn. But I don't really do long-term relationships. They've not worked and I'm much happier on my own.'

'Yes, same here,' I pitch in without stopping to think.

'But that's preposterous! Two lovely young women without a man to warm their bed? I know you said you'd once had a bad experience with a married man, Lu, but it's time you found someone.' Mel points a loaded fork at Rosie. 'You too, madam. I can see I have much work to do here.'

Rosie and I share a glance. Mine says 'don't mind her, she's very outspoken.' Hers says 'please God let her shut the fuck up.'

'Mum, we can't all be lucky enough to find someone like my dad. It will happen one day, or it won't,' I say, and wink at Rosie.

She looks a little less lobster-like now and manages a weak smile.

'That's so true,' Mel says, adding more butter to her jacket potato. She bites the corner of her lip and looks at us, and for one horrible moment I think she's going to cry. 'He was my one and only true love. I still miss him so.'

Rosie dabs at her mouth with her napkin and clears her throat. 'It's a shame you never found anyone else to make you happy, I—'

'Oh, but I did, love!' In seconds, Mel's face leaves 'on the verge of tears' and arrives at 'insanely happy', complete with sparkling eyes and a huge grin. 'My Neil wasn't Joe, sadly, but he was a hard-working, thoughtful man whose only mission in life was to make me happy.'

My mouthful of steak suddenly becomes tough and I want to spit it out, along with a few choice words of incredulity, but Rosie speaks before I can.

'Oh, that's nice. But why didn't you marry him in the end?'

Mel looks at her in bewilderment. 'I did marry him. Only been married once, Rosie. He was so caring and attentive. I didn't know how I'd cope when he died. In a way it was like being left by Joe all over again ...' She brought the napkin up to her face and dabbed at the corners of her eyes.

Rosie looks at me, a frown deepening, and I try to warn her with a flash of my eyes not to say more. I'd told Rosie briefly about Mel's abusive marriage and that she'd lived in fear for most of it and then ... and then Mel sits there and tells her such a *huge* whopping lie. *Why?*

I push the steak to the side of my mouth with my tongue, feel my cheeks flush, and my heart picks up a pace. I want to avoid Rosie's eyes but, if I do, she might just press Mel for an explanation. Damn it! Mel wouldn't be happy that I'd told Rosie and, if she's cornered, there's a good chance she'll go into meltdown.

Rosie puts her cutlery down, turns to Mel and opens her mouth. 'Not sure I understand, Mellyn—'

'More wine, anyone?' I ask, picking up the bottle. I rest the neck on the rim of my glass and then watch it overturn, the red liquid seeping onto the white tablecloth like a bloodstain at a murder scene. 'Oh, bloody hell!' I say through the meat in my mouth. 'So sorry!'

Mel and Rosie leap up and apply their napkins to the tablecloth while I run to the kitchen for a damp cloth and to spit the damned steak out at last. I send my voice into the other room. 'Rosie, can you come and get this cloth while I wet another?' Rosie immediately hurries in. I grab her arm and whisper in her ear. 'Don't say anything about the abusive husband – Mum doesn't know that you know about Neil. I'll explain later.'

A light of recognition dawns. 'Right, okay, no probs,' she says and rushes back into the dining room.

I swirl another two cloths in cold water. Explain everything later? That should be interesting.

'Out of the way, Lu,' Mel says, coming up behind me. 'No point in trying to bring the mountain to Mohammed.' She plunges the tablecloth bundled in her arms into the cold water in the sink.

'Ah, yes, good thinking. I didn't think – just panicked when I saw the stain.'

She looks at me, her eyes steely. 'Not like you to be clumsy.'

I want to say, 'Not like you to blatantly lie for no reason.' But then for all I know it's exactly like her. The more I get to know my mother, the more I realise I don't actually know her at all.

Rosie comes in before I can think of a reply with the near empty wine bottle in her hand. 'I could run down to the off licence and get another if you like?' she says to Mel.

'No need, love, there's plenty more where that came from.'

The Black Forest gateau and heavy double cream conversely engender a light conversation about the busy tourist season, the weather, and jokes about the Pomp and Vulture.

'Well, you have the offer of a few days in the shop. At least you won't have to worry with me as your boss.' Mel pokes me in the arm and grins.

Rosie raises her eyebrows and I can see her mind ticking over. I hadn't had chance to discuss working at the shop with her yet. 'Yes, that's true.' I smile, even though it isn't, and gather the dishes quickly, ceramic on ceramic hopefully drowning out anything Rosie might be tempted to say. 'Who's for coffee?'

'That's great, Lu,' Rosie says, smiling at Mel and me. 'No job-hunting worries and you'll not have to get your hands dirty.'

Mel holds her hands up, a half smile on her lips. 'Lu's not decided yet, Rosie. I don't want to put pressure on her.'

'Coffee?' I offer again into the awkward silence. They both accept, and I leave them talking about why silver-backed earrings don't cause a skin rash.

Mel and I wave from the door until Rosie turns the corner and disappears into the soft night.

'What a lovely girl,' Mel says, slipping an arm through mine and leading me inside. 'Nightcap?'

'No thanks. I'm tired out … in fact I might go up to bed.' I can't face a big scene. There's an empty well in the centre of my chest drained of anger and frustration, yet slowly filling with disappointment. Everything had been going so great lately, such a damned shame.

At the foot of the stairs Mel puts her hand on my arm. 'You're upset with me, aren't you, for mentioning that you could work with me in front of Rosie? I just didn't think.'

I look into her eyes for any hint of amusement or artifice. There's none. Only honesty floats on their blue seas. Concerned wrinkles on her forehead, a woebegone downturn of the mouth and an air of expected forgiveness bring anger and frustration pouring back into the well. 'For goodness' sake, Mum. Do you really think I'm upset about that? Yes, it would have been nice to tell Rosie myself, but that's the least of it!'

Mel lowers herself to the foot of the rickety stairs and shows me a bewildered face, the lamplight on her hair in the otherwise dark kitchen creating a halo of innocence. 'I'm at a loss then,' she says, her bottom lip trembling. 'Was I asking her too personal questions? I did notice she went a bit red at one point—'

'Yes, that too, but most of all I'm upset about your barefaced lies!' I don't intend to yell, but the well has flooded.

A hand flutters to her mouth. 'Lies?'

I blow slowly through my mouth, close my eyes and lean my hot forehead against the stone wall. 'Lies about Neil, Mum. Lies that you and he were happy, that you were devastated when he died, that his only mission in life was to make you happy. Nothing about him being a bastard, who you hated, who beat the crap out of you.'

'But surely you realised why I said all that?'

I open my eyes and look at her relieved ear-to-ear grin. 'No. No, I didn't. *That's* why I'm struggling here,' I say, trying to calm my breathing.

'To put her off the scent of course.'

I want to slide down the wall and disappear into the floorboards. 'What on earth do you mean? You're making no sense whatsoever.'

Mel laughs and waves her arms expansively. 'If she knew the truth about my marriage she might put two and two together and realise that I killed him, silly. You can't be too careful, you know.' She stands and switches the spotlights on. 'Now, how about I make you a nice cup of cocoa? I'll join you. See how good I'm being – no nightcap.' She gives me another huge smile.

She begins to sing 'Shake, Rattle and Roll' and I watch her move round the kitchen opening cupboards, taking out a saucepan, cocoa, opening the fridge for milk, and I want to scream but I can't. I feel like a spider trapped under a glass. I can see what's happening around me but there's nothing I can do to escape my fate. The higher I crawl up the smooth sides, the harder I fall. I can't get a foothold on the way forward … and the way back is blocked.

Chapter Twenty-One

I can't remember if the yo-yo I had as a child was red and yellow, or yellow and green. Advanced moves such as Walk the Dog were beyond me, but I did master a steady up and down, even the occasional out and in; I could keep it going for ages too. It is now my considered opinion that instead of a spider under a glass, I have become a yo-yo.

Up and down, high and low, my moods and life are directed and dictated by Mel.

It's less than twenty-four hours since she'd lied, and I wonder what on earth to do about it – everything is back to normal. Over cocoa last night, Mel explained in a rational manner that she knew it was wrong to lie to Rosie, but she had done so because the shame of what she'd done could be safely hidden under it. She could almost believe the lie to be true if she tried hard enough. I had told her that I understood, and I kind of did, but not really. Then this morning we had breakfast at a lovely café in town and afterwards we had worked side by side in the shop all day, and I'd really had a great time. Not a pretend for show great time, a really great time.

I listen to Mel chatting to a customer while I string black and white pearls, their perfect simplicity fascinating and incredible – pick up a bead, feel the cool smoothness between finger and thumb, and then whoosh, watch it slide and tap, slide and tap – so therapeutic. Even more so than playing with a yellow and green or yellow and red yo-yo. Yes. Things are back to normal.

Grey clouds push away at the edges of positivity. Normal? But for how long? Perhaps it's me that's mad and not her at all. Mad? Is that what I think Mel is? The customer – a round, middle-aged lady in too-large spectacles and a gingham shirt – doesn't think she's mad, hanging on to her every word, real interest in her eyes as Mel tells her about the source of the turquoise in a pendant around her neck.

Mel doesn't *look* mad either, dressed in a green velvet shift dress and low stylish heels, her glossy hair in a ponytail, her make-up expertly applied. The smile that she tips me and the warmth in her eyes are not those of a mad woman as she wraps the pendant for the woman and takes her payment.

I thread more beads. Dad always said I was too dramatic, that I overreact. In my head I hear his voice of reason: 'She's odd, certainly. Eccentric, yes, prone to mood swings, of course, but mad?' I listen to him. I want to very much believe him, but then my rational voice, indignant and spiky, pokes holes through the calm reason. *Cold-blooded murderer*, it said. 'Don't forget that, Dad.'

Mel says goodbye to the lady and is about to come over to where I'm sat at the entrance to the back room, but the shop doorbell jingles the arrival of a tall gangly young man whose arms are too long for his jacket. His Adam's apple bobs alarmingly as he asks if she has anything suitable for a second wedding anniversary, and his skin flares, joining up the dots on his pimply face. Moments later he's regained his sago and jam complexion as Mel puts him at ease, showing him this necklace, that pair of earrings, and what about this bracelet, while all the time avoiding prolonged eye contact and smiling a lot.

Mad people don't have those kinds of skills, do they? Or do they? Perhaps the accepted term is psychosis nowadays, and anyway, whatever I want to call her condition, I haven't the first real clue of what kinds of behaviour define it, or the experience to deal with it.

But she's your mum. You have to stand by her and find a way to help. This is why you're here. Yo-yo. *How many times have you said the same thing though?* Pendulum. *You had a choice. You couldn't turn her in; she gave you life, so you can't take hers. It wasn't cold blood – he beat her for years and years and … so you've made your decision, now stick to it.* Rock.

Rocks are so much more reliable than yo-yos or pendulums and are uncrushable, unlike spiders. Rocks are steadfast, strong and stalwart. I have never been anyone's rock before, but if anyone needs one, my mum does. I'm not Megan's victim any more, I'm a strong woman with the guts to change my life. To make Mel's better too. Perhaps I can find the number of this Doctor Henver she's seen in the past and try and get help there.

The man's face becomes serious as he stands at the window and holds a bracelet in one hand and a necklace in the other, up to the daylight. Is he picturing his wife wearing them? He clenches his jaw, purses his lips, all the time looking from bracelet to necklace and back again. It must be nice to have someone to care so much. The man stops being serious and a look of triumph passes over his face as he turns and presents his choice: the necklace.

'I didn't want to sway you one way or the other,' Mel says, placing the item in a gift box. 'But I would have gone for this, too – so pretty.'

The man bobs his head and joins the dots again. 'Just like its soon-to-be owner.'

'I'm sure she'll love it.' Mel flashes him a smile. 'And if she doesn't, she can come in and exchange it for something else.'

'I'm sure it will be perfect,' the man says, handing over his card. 'We will certainly be back at some point though. This is a lovely shop and you've been so helpful.'

As the door closes behind him Mel turns to me and says, 'I do love my job sometimes. Did you see his little face when he brought the necklace over?'

'I did. He seemed a sweet man, and you were brilliant with him.'

A huge grin stretches her face. 'Thanks, Lu. I must admit I am a people person and, without bragging, good at my job.'

I think about that and have to agree. It's just as well I'm staying put, however, just in case there comes a time when she might not be.

Adelaide filters into my first waking moments. I open my eyes and a smile in my heart lifts me out of bed and to the window. I draw back the curtains: sunny, blue sky, slight breeze – perfect. A sunny Sunday and Adelaide; everything I could wish for.

Hunched shoulders, moist eyes and a fake smile wait for me downstairs. I focus on the smile and the words 'let sleeping dogs lie.'

'Will you be back for dinner?' she says in a too-bright voice.

'Not sure, Mum. Best not to make anything for me, and then if I am back, I'll sort myself out.' I pick up my bag from the back of a kitchen chair.

She follows me to the front door and watches me take sandals out of the shoe box next to it. 'I'll still make roast beef, it's always nice cold in a sandwich the next day.'

'Yep.' I slip the sandals on and avoid her gaze.

'So, you're meeting for breakfast at the Singing Kettle, the café we went to yesterday?'

She makes it sound like a betrayal. 'That's right. You're so clever finding such a great place.' I land a light kiss on her cheek and open the door.

Her cheery voice follows me down the path. 'Have a lovely time, Lu.' Then it forgets to be cheery and ends in a wobbly, 'Love you.'

I don't turn, but reply, 'You too.' And I suspect that it must be true, because if it isn't, I'd be hundreds of miles away.

Two ladies with exactly the same eyebrows sit at a window table in the Singing Kettle. They haven't noticed me standing just inside the doorway and are sharing a joke. The sight of Adelaide actually laughing is like seeing Santa on a surfboard – most unusual and a little unsettling. A contrast to Adelaide's slight and grey sits Evelyn's round and auburn, but their features made sisters of them, and those twin eyebrows wiggle away any doubts anyone might have of their familial provenance.

'Lu!' Adelaide stands and flaps her hands. Dressed as she is in black trousers, a white blouse and black sleeveless cardigan I'm reminded of an excited penguin. 'Lu, over here!' she calls, even though I'm already walking towards her. 'Evelyn, it's Lu!' she prods her sister's shoulder and flaps again.

Evelyn nods and smiles. 'I had grasped that, you daft ha'porth.'

I walk into a hug and home. Though our embrace is quick, Adelaide, stiff as a board, is already awumah-ing and patting my back as if she wants to get my wind up. I figure out that awumha must be a cross between aw, um and ah. Poor Adelaide is hopeless with displays of affection. The familiar smell of her perfume, the sound of her voice, places me in our kitchen and envelops me in warmth and safety. Safe is something I haven't felt for a while now, I realise. This is an odd adjective for my thoughts to throw at me. Perhaps it's the fact that I never know what to expect from life any more.

'My goodness, you look well,' Adelaide says, holding me at arm's length, all brows and dark searching eyes that miss nothing. 'This Cornish air must be doing you good.'

'It is lovely here, Adelaide, but I feel all the better for seeing you again.'

'And I you, my dear.' She gives a real smile and nods at her sister. 'I expect you've guessed this is Evelyn?'

Evelyn stands up and sticks out a hand from a whirlwind flurry of pink and green chiffon and an exploding bosom. 'Pleased to meet you, love. You're much prettier than Adelaide described you.'

'Oh thanks. And what a pretty blouse that is.'

'Pretty if you like big and bold, but then that's me to a T, isn't it, Adelaide?'

'It is. We're like chalk and cheese considering we're sisters.'

'But there are a few obvious similarities,' I say and then stop. Instinctively I know that any mention of eyebrows would not be a good idea … not after my birthday night when Adelaide had rubbed hers off and caught me laughing. 'Your eyes are very alike,' I add.

'Noses and chins too,' Adelaide says.

'I have a few more than you though, eh?' Evelyn chuckles and sits down.

'What, noses?' I ask, and then wish I hadn't as their twin eyebrows attempt to knit themselves into frowns.

'No, chins,' Evelyn says and shoots her sister a look.

I sit down and clear my throat.

Adelaide does a three-second curl of the lips. 'I'd forgotten Lu's daft sense of humour. Now, we've already ordered a pot of tea. What do we fancy for breakfast?'

'Second breakfast in my case,' Evelyn says and pats her ample belly. 'I couldn't bear to turn down a full English seeing as how we'd paid for it.'

'How are you liking Pebble House?' I ask, scanning the menu. 'Be careful what you say – I work my fingers to the bone in that place.'

'It's lovely. We met your friend Rosie this morning, and she made us laugh telling us what you and her call the owners,' Adelaide says. 'It's a shame you had your hours cut though, love.'

'It is. Still, Mum has offered me a few days in her shop. I did my first day there yesterday and really enjoyed it.' I watch a cloud pass over Adelaide's face. 'What's up?'

'Nothing really … it's just strange hearing you say Mum. At first, I … oh, don't mind me. I'm a daft old woman. I'm thrilled that you call Mellyn Mum. Honestly I am.'

The air in the café packs the comforting aromas of bacon, coffee and pain au chocolat into my lungs, but I'm not comforted. We discuss our breakfast order, word upon word layering over Adelaide's explanation, but in my head it's still all I can hear. I know where it came from. It came from her still being in my old life, in my old street, with our old neighbours, with my dad … but without Mum. Without the woman who brought me up, the woman who used to be Mum, who was still Mum really, but who was gone … had been taken.

'I haven't forgotten her, you know,' I blurt into a discussion about black pudding. 'I'll never forget her, or what she did for me.'

Adelaide puts a hand to her lips as if she wanted to unsay her earlier words. 'I've upset you, haven't I? I *knew* I had.'

I look at the concern in her eyes and the sympathy in Evelyn's and dredge up a smile. No, she hasn't upset me. I've just become detached from the old life, Dad, the grief, and preoccupied with the new and all its problems. If I'm upset with anyone it's with me.

'Not at all,' I say to the laminated menu. 'I just wanted you to know that even though I've cast away stones, there are some that will forever be my foundations.'

Adelaide's cold thin fingers encircle my wrist and she removes the menu with her other hand. 'Look at me.' I look at her. 'I know that, Lu. And I also know how strong those foundations are … how strong you are.'

I nod and put the menu back up, a barrier against her searching eyes and the raw emotion threatening behind mine.

'Right. Enough of this stuff or I'll be crying into me black pudding!' Evelyn says, attempting a laugh.

Adelaide adds her Santa on a surfboard and relief has me joining him in the waves.

Late afternoon seeps into our day, showing off its muted colours and perfuming the air with a lazy mix of salt and lavender. I can't remember the morning leaving, but I remember what it's like to be normal. This is normal. Sitting in a tea garden watching bees crawl amongst hedgerows threaded through with coastal flowers, spending the morning wandering the harbour, eating ice cream, discovering things in gift shops in the town that we couldn't possibly live without and laughing, without even a thought reserved for the eventuality of a possible meltdown.

Evelyn has gone off to buy postcards after demolishing a Cornish Cream Tea almost as soon as it was placed on the table. This was after two breakfasts, an ice cream and a pasty. Apart from food, the woman had an enormous appetite for laughter, loud clothes and life in general, and I liked her immediately. It's obvious that this quest for postcards had been discussed by the two sisters previously; I saw an almost imperceptible nod pass between them as I spooned jam onto my scone. Evelyn had left us alone to have a heart to heart, but mine doesn't know where to begin.

'I shall be the size of a house at this rate,' Adelaide says, lifting a cream-laden scone.

'I think it would take a while to even get you to the size of a Wendy house,' I say with a twist of my mouth, and then look off over the lawn and to the sea beyond. Part of me wants Adelaide to know everything; the other, and more sensible part, tells me off.

We eat, drink tea, watch seagulls try to snatch a sandwich from an unsuspecting tourist, and talk about how wonderful it is to sit in a cottage garden on the top of a hill, the sun on our skin, watching the world go by in one of the most beautiful parts of England, nay, the world. But all the time, under the day to day, a strong current of tension and uncertainty tugs our lips into a straight line after sentences end, or conversely forces a smile. Eventually Adelaide breaks free.

'Now, tell me, Lu. Are you happy?' She looks at me with those perceptive eyes, head on one side, lips pressed together as if blotting lipstick on an invisible tissue.

I pretend to choke on my tea. 'What a question to ask. I think you'd be hard pushed to define real happiness.'

'That's what you came in search of wasn't it, though, love?' she says to the sky.

'Yes, I suppose. I think it's safe to say that things have been a bit up and down, but I'm certainly finding my feet, getting to know Mum and settling into my new life.'

'It will take a while, of course it will. I for one think you've done a grand job. So, does your dad, though he finds it hard to talk about it all for long.'

'I do know that. I ring Dad every week.' Tension twists my words into a snippy defence when I don't want it to be.

'Of course, you do.' Adelaide pats my wrist and pours more tea. 'I just want you to know he's proud of you because he might not have said it to you directly.'

Dad hadn't. He wouldn't, it's not his way. Our telephone conversations have mostly been about the weather, his work, my work, the latest news. I don't want my wrist to be patted. I'm not a pet dog or some kind of crazy person who has to be soothed. I look up into Adelaide's sympathetic eyes. No. I'm not crazy. That's Mel, not me. I wouldn't be like her.

Would. Not.

'Mum has mental health issues.' The words are out of my mouth before I can net them and drag them back into the strongbox. Not even a meteoric rise of Adelaide's eyebrows can relax the knot of anxiety in my gut. What happened to *I am a rock*?

'Oh, love. What kind of mental health issues?'

I watch her hand move towards mine across the table and I fold my arms. 'As you know, she lost both her parents and husband over a short period of time. As you also know, he was cruel to her, but she still blames herself.' I then tell her about how Neil 'died'.

'Oh dear. Yes, that must all play on her mind.'

'She feels that it was her fault he was up the ladder in the first place, getting the house ready for sale. Anyway, because of all this, she has mood swings and I'm having to learn how to handle them. Just lately though she is trying much harder, and we get on really well. When she's okay we have such fun. We laugh a lot, do mother and daughter things that we never had the chance to do, and I love spending time with her.'

'And when she's not okay?' Adelaide copies my arms folded stance and adds a raised eyebrow.

Damn her. She has this unnatural ability to sledgehammer through my walls and reduce my blather to rubble. 'When she's not okay, I am her rock. I will not abandon her, I will stay strong for her, and we'll get through it.' I give a shrug and say to the floor. 'So that's that.'

'Hardly happiness though, is it?'

I give her a look. 'We can't be happy all the time, Adelaide. I think it will be a good idea if you actually meet her. You'll see how lovely she is.' I wonder if it would be a good idea at all even as I say the words.

'I'm sure I will. We could pop into the shop tomorrow. You did say you were working there on Mondays?'

I nod and swallow misgivings about allowing my old life to crash into Mel's domain without discussing it with her first. 'Yes, that would be cool. We could arrange to meet for dinner too before you go home?'

'Oh yes. I'll look forward to that.' Adelaide's eyes abandon their squinty interrogation and she allows the corners of her mouth to twitch into a brief curl. I'm glad of that. Much more like the Adelaide I know and love.

Evelyn comes back a few minutes later and we order more tea, look at her cards and a plethora of bric-a-brac that had 'spoken to her'. She embroiders a fantastic tale of how she'd haggled and bagged a bargain, and that customers in the shop had cheered and clapped. Adelaide knits her eyebrows and says she wasn't born yesterday, or the day before that, either.

We share an amused look when Evelyn insists it's the truth. Adelaide shakes her head. She's not buying it. Like me, she has a good nose for a fib. Though she had smiled earlier and said she was looking forward to meeting my mother, I'm not sure that she's satisfied by my half-truths and stoic words.

There is one thing that I know with unshakable certainty, however. Adelaide would not like to learn the whole truth.

Chapter Twenty-Two

It's irrational. No, I'm irrational. Mum had been normal when I returned the night before after missing supper because I'd eaten with Adelaide and her sister. She'd been normal when I said they would probably pop into the shop – cheerful, even – and normal this morning at work. So why do I feel like I'm standing on a fault line? There's no sign of a tremor about her, nor shaky ground. I'm the one with clammy hands, a rapid heart rate and my stomach leaps every time the shop bell jangles.

'You were very professional with that customer, Lu. I could see she was just on the edge of snotty about the price of that ring, but when you gave her the provenance she wound her neck in,' Mel says, bringing two mugs of tea in. 'Biscuit?' She pulls a packet of luxury chocolate creams from under her arm and waves them as if she's encouraging me to fetch. There I go again. She's just being nice and I'm being … irrational.

'I didn't notice her being snotty,' I say, and take two biscuits, just to show willing. 'I thought she was just interested in why it was more expensive than the other one.'

'Ah,' she says, a self-satisfied smirk on her lips. 'That's where experience comes in. I've been dealing with customers a lot longer than you, don't forget.'

'Really?' I crunch into a biscuit. 'It had completely slipped my mind.' I make my mouth into a cheeky smile and hope irritation doesn't show behind my eyes.

'Very funny. Now what do you think of these – just came in this morning.' She pulls out a long box from under the counter and takes off the lid. Inside are three incredibly beautiful turquoise and mother-of-pearl necklaces.

I hold one up to the light and marvel at its intricate workmanship and beauty. 'Wow, where are these from?'

'A Navaho workshop in Arizona. I only ordered three for now – they're pretty expensive. I'll probably tag them at three hundred pounds and see if they sell.' Mel takes the other two out of the box and arranges them on a black velvet cloth on the counter. 'I'll polish them up and put them in the window this afternoon.'

'They would look great on the driftwood display. I can do it if you like?' I say. 'They deserve to be centre stage.'

'You certainly have a good eye. And yes, okay, thanks.'

The shop bell jangles a new arrival, but my stomach forgets to leap as I place the third necklace down next to the others. 'Good afternoon, ladies. Is there something I can help you with, or are you just browsing?' Mel asks.

'We're here to see you, actually, and Lu of course.'

I turn around. My stomach goes into a roll, the fault line shakes my legs and my heart gallops up the scale. Luckily my lips have the good sense to smile and my voice to sound bright and cheerful. 'Hello!' I look at Mel and sweep an arm through the air. 'Mum, this is Adelaide and Evelyn. Ladies, Mum.'

Broad smiles are worn, and hands shake all round. 'We can't call you Mum ...' Evelyn says with a little laugh. 'Mellyn, isn't it?'

'It is,' Mel says with what sounds like a genuine and normal laugh. 'I'll pop the kettle back on, shall I?'

'Only if it's no trouble,' Adelaide says. She sounds normal too.

While Mel busies herself in the stockroom, I show Adelaide and Evelyn around the displays, our conversation punctuated with *ooh*s and *aah*s from both, but mainly Evelyn. 'These pieces are speaking to me, Lu,' she says.

'Which ones in particular?'

'All of them,' she replies, rolling her eyes. 'My husband will have heart failure when he sees the bank statement for this holiday.'

Mel comes in then and adds her laughter to Evelyn's. She uses her voluptuous laugh, and everyone seems ... normal. The ground feels firm under my feet and my stomach has settled for a slight swell.

Easy conversation flows with the tea and Adelaide wins immediate favour with my mother when she says that anyone with eyes could tell that she and I are related.

Even Dad is mentioned in passing, and Mel shows compassion for his loss and seems genuinely pleased that he's getting back on his feet work wise. Then she mentions my birth father, Joe, someone I had only glossed over with Adelaide because I didn't want her to mention him to Dad. There's a slight wobble when Evelyn suggests that perhaps I could trace him and try to meet up, something I of course have thought about but haven't spoken aloud. Mel's eyes begin to cloud over but Adelaide blows them away with, 'Early days, yet, Evie. It would be a mistake to rush into anything.'

I watch relief creep across Mel's face and listen to the conversation turn to how wonderful St Ives is and Cornwall in general. I join in now and then, but mostly my thoughts are about Adelaide. Her arrival has put colour into the day and because she always knows the right thing to say and do, a potentially disastrous meeting has become like a gathering of old friends. The day I left Sheffield I had wondered how on earth I would manage without her, and sometimes I still wonder. I catch a twinkle of reassurance in her eye, and not for the first time wish that she didn't live so far away.

I wash up the mugs in the tiny chipped sink after the ladies have gone, then come back into the shop to check the floor for crumbs. I sink to my haunches and gather a few with dustpan and brush. Over my shoulder I say, 'I thought that went well. I could tell you liked them and they liked you too ...' The rest of my sentence sticks in my throat as I look up at Mel's blotchy red face and tight line of a mouth. Her eyes are twin storms; mine look away, seek shelter. Because I'm crouched, her hands are level with my head and I see them make fists so tight that her knuckles become bone.

I know what's coming and it certainly isn't anything to do with normal. I have no idea why she's on the verge of meltdown, but she is, and I'm not being irrational, not this time. I put the dustpan and brush down and push through my calves to a standing position. 'Mum, what's wrong?' I ask, now only a foot away, her fury charging the air between us.

'What's wrong? *What is wrong?*' She smashes both her fists down on the end of the counter, fixes my eyes with a deep indigo blaze, her chest heaving, spittle on her chin. 'I'll tell you what's wrong! That fat bitch stole from me!' Again, the crashing fists. 'Stole from *me*, and right under my nose!'

Her words are like punches; I step back and lean my weight against the counter. My mind struggles to process. 'Evelyn? Evelyn, you mean?'

She jabs a forefinger in my shoulder. 'Of course! Adelaide isn't *fat*, is she?'

I put a hand to my shoulder and my eyes fill and not because it hurt, though it did. Mel's eyes have the same wild look in them as Megan's: the look that can't be reasoned with. I'm back in the schoolyard with the smell of bitumen in my nostrils, the heat of the sun searing my neck, the realisation in my heart that I had been betrayed and was trapped far away from Boris and home. I had thought I would never feel like that again ... until now.

I focus on a display of jewellery instead of a thread on my sock this time, and then up from my gut, riding on a rush of adrenalin, come fighting back. After everything I've tried to do for her, the terrible secret she foisted on me, and now ... and now this. My horns are out. I'm no longer the girl in the playground and I'll be damned if I'll allow her to send me back there. I smash a fist on the counter so hard that a box of silver cleaner jumps to the floor.

'How *dare* you scream in my face and prod me like that?' My face is inches from hers.

Mel's jaw drops and it's her turn to take a step backward. 'I-I—'

'Oh, stop it with the *I*. Everything is always about *you*, isn't it? You never stop to think what your bloody self-obsession does to me, to your daughter!' I watch her deflate, her face drain, her shoulders sag, but I can't stop. 'And now'—I fling my hands up,— 'now you seriously believe that Evelyn, one of the loveliest women I have ever met, is a thief. Even though I've only known her five minutes, I refuse to entertain that ludicrous idea!'

Mel wipes her eyes on her sleeve, backs up to the till and sits down heavily on a stool. 'But ... but I can't think of another explanation.' Fresh tears well and overflow. She lets them run silently down her face, perhaps imagining that I'll feel sorry for her, all mascara smudges and haunted eyes. Instead I just think she looks pathetic. Pathetic, and I've had enough.

'What do you think she stole?' I say through a small mouth.

'Well ... she admired the new Navajo necklaces so much, remember? She said she would love one but that her husband would hit the roof.'

I look at the black velvet cloth with the necklaces on it. Two. Not three. There has to be a simple explanation. The cloth is much closer to the end of the counter than it was earlier and in my mind's eye I see Mel move it along to make way for the tray of tea and biscuits. 'Have you checked behind the counter? One could have slipped off.'

'Of course, ... that's the first thing I did when I noticed one had gone.' Her voice is contrite and soft, but my heart is hard.

I walk over and look on the floor, in boxes under the counter, and even in the offshoot. But it has to be somewhere. It *has* to be. I go back into the shop, drop to my knees and check the cracks in the floorboards. It's an old shop and I'd noticed that one of the knots in the stripped floor was loose the other day; perhaps the necklace had ... I glance up at Mel to ask if she has a screwdriver and the mystery is solved.

She has a tissue out, her back to me, blotting at the smudged mascara in a hand mirror, and there, hanging from the lace on her top, is the missing necklace.

The idea that Evelyn had actually stolen it never once crossed my mind, but the fact that it has been found sends relief rushing up to calm my panic. If it had been lost somehow, there was no way that Mel would listen to reason. Evelyn would have been to blame and that would have been that.

I take a step forward. It's clear to see what's happened. The necklace's clasp is shaped into a silver sun; its hook-like rays must have attached themselves to the lace as she brushed past or leaned against the end of the counter.

'It's stuck to the lace hem on your top behind you,' I say to her eyes through the mirror and pinch my mouth shut.

She turns around and cranes her neck. 'What is?'

I step behind her, unhook the necklace and place it back on the velvet cloth. I say nothing; my eyes do all the work.

'Oh,' she says in a very tiny voice. Scarlet blotches spread across her cheeks and her gaze dances across my face like a butterfly trying to settle on an unfamiliar flower.

'Oh. Is that all you have to say?' I want to rage at her, slap that sheepish little grin to the floor.

The grin slides away as if I have done so and her bottom lip starts to tremble. 'How can you ever forgive me?' Mel shakes her head and puts her hands over her face. Her voice comes through the gaps in her fingers, muffled and raw with emotion. 'I don't know what came over me. I just saw red, and …' She takes her hands away and gives a shuddering sigh. 'Tell me what I can do to make it right.'

'Nothing,' I say, anger afire in my heart. 'Right now, I want to get as far away from you and your pathetic excuses as I possibly can.' I pick up my jacket and bag and hurry to the door.

'Lu, please! I'm so sorry! Stay and we'll talk it through!' she sobs, grabbing my arm as I step into the street.

I shake her off. 'Don't touch me!'

She recoils and leans her weight against the door, tears running into snot, her face a mask of anguish. I couldn't care less. I turn my back and walk away.

Chapter Twenty-Four

It's a clear day, yet unlike the last time I stood in this spot, I can't quite make out the sentinel finger of the lighthouse. The edges are blurry, the white seeping into the blue creating an impressionist watercolour. Blinking doesn't help, nor does taking deep lungfuls of salt air, but a man walking his dog towards me dries up the rest of my angry tears. We mustn't show our emotions in public.

No. That would never do.

For good measure I turn around and pretend to examine the edge of my shoe until he passes, and then a familiar voice calls my name and leadens my heart.

'Lu! Didn't you hear me, love?'

I look up, wishing I hadn't. Adelaide and Evelyn have appeared from the chapel and are fanning their arms at me. They exchange a few words when I don't respond and then hurry towards me. I'm so bloody stupid! I should have gone to Seal Cottage, not come up here. St Ives isn't the largest town in the world and it was likely I might run into them. Well now I have, and Adelaide will want answers.

Adelaide slows her pace as she gets nearer, studies my face and whispers something to her sister puffing along behind her. Evelyn nods and walks back towards the town. I heave a sigh from the bottom of my lungs and wait.

'You've been crying,' she says breathily. 'What on earth is wrong, Lu?' A hand on my shoulder. 'I thought you were working all day. Has something happened with your mum?'

A burst of laughter escapes. 'You could say that.' My mouth tries to turn itself up at the corners, but gravity works against it. Adelaide's concerned face becomes a watercolour.

'Oh dear. Come on, let's go and sit on that bench over there.'

On the bench I find a tissue pushed into my hand and my voice breaks through the knot in my throat after a few moments. I didn't intend to tell Adelaide exactly what had happened, but as usual she drew hidden words up from the safety of my heart and out into the exposure of the day. 'So, anyway ... I'm wondering if I can live like this for much longer, Adelaide,' I say to a dandelion clock a few feet away. I daren't look at her. She didn't say much while I was explaining, and it's what she didn't say that sunk in.

'And I'm wondering if you should try. I am sorry to say it, I know the woman has mental health issues, but I think Mellyn is dangerous.'

That whips my head up. 'Dangerous? What makes you say that?' I know she is, she'd murdered her husband after all, but I'm baffled as to why Adelaide thinks so.

Her eyebrows are caught between a frown and surprise. After a moment she says, 'It was a look she gave me.' She holds a finger up. 'Now don't get me wrong. She was very nice to us, made us feel welcome, and I was relieved that she wasn't as bad as I had imagined. But not long before we left, you were chatting to Evelyn, and she gave me this look.' Adelaide pinches her lips shut and looks up to the left. 'That look was so full of what I can only describe as ... pure hatred. I was rocked on my feet, I can tell you.'

Sadly, I'm not surprised at this but say, 'Are you sure? She can look a bit askance and ...'

'Yes, I'm sure. I knew somehow that she wanted to do me harm. I think she's dangerous and not to be trusted under any circumstances.'

I want to say, 'Well I'm sorry to say you're right. She killed her husband in cold blood. She says he was a drunken bully that beat her, but perhaps he didn't. Perhaps she lied.'

That thought is a new one.

I didn't know that I'd even considered it. It must have slipped from a box in my mind marked 'unknown' and attached itself to the others. 'I don't know about dangerous, but she *can* be jealous sometimes,' I say.

'Jealousy out of hand can lead to worse,' Adelaide says, and I wonder how she knows these things. 'I think you should consider coming home'—she looks up at the sky—'just until you've had time to think about everything.'

My brain latches on to that, but my heart baulks. Going home would be like running away, wouldn't it? Running back to my old life just because the going got tough. The new me doesn't run from things any more.

'I think that might be a bit rash, Adelaide. I came here to meet my birth mother, build a relationship. I can't just dump her because she has a few problems. A mum is forever, not just for Christmas.'

Adelaide looks at the half smile I've fixed but doesn't return it. She doesn't even attempt one of her 'blink and you miss it' ones. 'A few problems is an understatement, love.' She touches my face briefly and I have to look at another blurry dog walker on the path. 'I'm worried for you. Just come home for a while, just until you can think clearly. You can't do that in the middle of it all.'

I don't know what to say. I have a ball of cold spaghetti where my decision-making thoughts should be. Tangled, mixed up ends that are too slippery to grasp. 'I'll have to think about it, Adelaide. I'm so confused right now.'

She twists her mouth to the side and blows down her nostrils. 'Okay. I can see that, I suppose.' Then she turns to me and searches my face with those wise miss-nothing eyes. 'Just don't wait too long to decide. You could even come back with us on the coach. We leave here tomorrow, but we're finishing our trip in Mevagissey. We managed to change the dates of the tickets, so we'll be here for a few more days.'

Smiling at her hopeful face I nod and say, 'Okay. I promise to think about it. Thank you for being here, Adelaide ... I don't know what I would do without you.'

'Nor I you, my dear.' Her voice cracks on the *dear* and she looks in her handbag without really looking. 'I was never blessed with children and, well, you're like a granddaughter, in way.'

I put my hand on hers. We look out at the lighthouse, neither one of us speaking, yet our hearts hear every word.

I notice that the shop has the closed sign on it as I walk past on the way to Seal Cottage. It's only three thirty, so Mel must have been too upset to work. Anger still simmers in the pit of my chest, but it's tempered with sympathy. Mel obviously couldn't help herself and I was floundering. I had gone for a walk after Adelaide had left for the hotel and I had arrived at an idea. As I walk up the path to the cottage I decide it will depend on what my mother has to say to my idea and suggestion as to whether I stay or leave.

The cottage feels empty, a bit like me. No sign of Mel downstairs. As I cross the kitchen to the stairs, through the window I catch sight of chestnut hair lifting on the breeze. I peer outside. She's in the garden with a glass of wine – oh, how marvellous. Eyes that look as if they have seen hell stare at nothing and her mouth worries at a nail. I step through the door and she jumps up.

'Oh, thank God! Thank God you came back! I wasn't sure if you would …' She stretches her arms out to me.

I don't walk into them. 'I wasn't sure if I would either. We need to talk, but first I'm going to take that wine glass away from you.' A flicker of annoyance passes her eyes, but she doesn't comment or resist when I take the glass and put it in the kitchen.

'I can't begin to tell you how sorry I am,' she says as I draw my chair up to the table.

'I think you should try.' I fold my arms and set my mouth.

'I know you're furious, and I don't blame you. It's just that I jump to conclusions sometimes. On the surface I was polite and pleased to see Adelaide and her sister, but underneath I felt insanely jealous. So, when I found the necklace gone, I didn't even consider that Evelyn hadn't taken it.'

'Why were you insanely jealous?'

'Because Adelaide has known you longer than I have. She watched you grow up when I didn't – me, your own flesh and blood.' A sniff. 'Your own mother. Your real mother.'

And whose fault is that? is desperate to join the conversation, but instead I say, 'I left everything behind, came here to find you. Then I chose to stay here … with you. Doesn't that mean *anything*?'

Mel nods emphatically. 'Yes, yes it does. I'm just irrational sometimes. I can't think logically when anger takes over.' Her eyes dart away. 'I am so, so sorry about prodding you on the shoulder. I feel so ashamed.'

'It was the look in your eyes more than the prod,' I begin, and then slam a door shut on more tears. I'm sick of it, quite frankly. 'I had a long walk and a think about what to do next. You need help and I can't give it to you. Therefore, you must go back and see Doctor Henver or someone. You need professional help.'

'I'm not sure that's necessary. I've been improving lately, you said so yourself the other day, and—'

'Improvement punctuated by unpredictable and increasingly worrying behaviours is not good enough, Mum. We need to do something.'

'Everything is shaken up now you're back in my life. It will all settle soon.' She sighs, then probably realises that exasperation isn't a good idea and gives me a bright smile.

'Sorry, but I can't live like this.' My voice has a cold edge that I'm not used to hearing.

'I promise it will be okay. I realise I have a problem, and that's the first hurdle, isn't it? Look, what about inviting Adelaide and Evelyn over tomorrow night? I'll prove to you that I—'

'They'll be gone by then. I said goodbye to her on the Island earlier. And *all* the hurdles have to be jumped to reach the finish line, Mum. You're not even close.'

Mel folds her arms and says through a tight mouth. 'You seem very cold all of a sudden. What happened to compassion?'

'It left earlier today when you jabbed me in the shoulder and turned your eyes into little flames of hate.'

She unfolds her arms and reaches out a hand to me.' I don't hate you. You're the most precious thing in the world to me.' Her voice trembles and her eyes fill … again.

I don't take her hand. 'Then do as I ask, or you'll lose me.'

'You'll leave if I don't see a doctor?' Her voice lends the tremble to the hand hovering over her mouth.

'Yes.' I watch her face closely; her skin, already pale, turns ghostly and down it runs silent mascara tears. It's as if I'm watching a play. She reminds me of a Pierrot doll and I hate myself for feeling so detached, but I can't help it. She either agrees, or that's the end of it.

'Okay. I will see someone. Anything to make you stay,' she says so softly I have to strain my ears.

I can see she means it and I should be relieved, and I am to an extent. I have achieved what I set out to with surprisingly little resistance. There's a little shot of ice water running through my blood though. A little shot of ice that warns of deceit, lies and double crosses. But if I'm staying then I have to trust her – what else can I do?

***

'Adelaide? Oh yes, Adelaide. What a surprise.' Rosie put a smile in her voice but furrowed her brow. Adelaide didn't sound herself at all. Also, she hadn't really expected a call. She'd just given her number in case Adelaide and her sister needed advice about places to eat or the area in general. Rosie cradled the phone under her chin and poured a glass of wine.

'Yes, sorry to ring you when you're at home, but as you know we're off to Mevagissey early tomorrow and I needed to ask you a huge favour. There might not be time in the morning – you'll be run off your feet as usual – and …' Adelaide's gunfire sentences ran out of bullets and Rosie thought she heard a sniff.

'Okay, I'll help if I can.'

'I won't go into detail but suffice to say that Lu has had a run-in with her mother. Not for the first time, I might add.

Mellyn has issues, I'll say no more than that. I know you're her very good friend and if she wants to tell you more she will. Anyway …' Adelaide sighed and fell silent. 'Anyway, I asked her to come back to Sheffield, but she has just phoned to say that she'll stick it out a bit longer. She has a plan to help put things right, apparently.'

'Oh, I'm sorry to hear that. It sounds serious if you wanted her to go back home.' Rosie took a big swallow of wine. She didn't like the sound of that at all. She also didn't like the sound of Lu perhaps leaving either.

'I might be blowing things out of proportion, but I just fell that Mellyn's dangerous, somehow.' Adelaide paused and her words took good effect. 'That's why I'm ringing. I would be extremely grateful if you would keep a very close eye on the situation for me. Call me if you think I'm needed … day or night.'

Rosie sat on the arm of her sofa and took another drink. 'My goodness, you're worrying me now. If it's so serious should she be left on her own with Mellyn?'

'If it was up to me she wouldn't be. But what else can I do? Lu is a grown woman. I can't drag her out of the house kicking and screaming.'

'No. No of course not. Thanks for calling, Adelaide. I will be vigilant, I promise.'

'Thank you, dear. I know that you think the world of her, just like me.' Adelaide ended the call.

Was ten o'clock too late to give Lu a bell? There was no way she could sleep until she heard her voice. Rosie's finger hovered over the keypad and then she put the phone down. It stood to reason that Lu must be fine because she'd just called Adelaide. Perhaps Adelaide had been a little melodramatic and a phone call might put Lu's back up. She might suspect that Adelaide had said something too if she started asking about how things were with Mellyn.

Mellyn. She was definitely an odd one. Rosie pictured her face again and relived the interaction between them the morning she'd come to the B&B with Lu's watch … Jekyll and Hyde. But dangerous? Really?

The doorbell rang. Oh God. That might be Lu. Perhaps something had happened! Rosie ran down the hall and opened the door.

'Surprise!'

'Mum …'

As she was enveloped in a tight hug and expensive perfume, Rosie wondered how many more surprises she could stand in one evening.

Chapter Twenty-Five

Though Adelaide's voice has left my ears, I still cradle the phone to my cheek. When the news of me staying here with Mel had sunk in, she'd tried to be cheerful and said she'd understood, but the tone of her voice couldn't disguise the worry and concern behind the words. A calm feeling in my head means I have made the right decision, however. An unspoken bargain has been struck between head and heart. If Mel doesn't get help, it will be the end of our relationship. I can't afford to renege on it, for both our sakes.

I put the phone down, yawn and stretch my arms high above my head. This day has seemed to go on forever. A knock at my bedroom door makes me wish I'd turned the damned light out.

'Lu? I know you've just gone to bed, but I thought you might like to see this.'

Please, not now. Whatever it is can wait until morning. 'I'm a bit tired to be honest, Mum—'

'Yes, but this won't take a moment and I promise you'll love it.'

I'd bloody better. 'Okay, come in.'

Mel comes in wrapped in a black dressing gown, eyes afire, her hair still wild and windswept. Is she auditioning for a part in *Wuthering Heights*? Now, that I would love to see. She sits next to me on the bed and hands me two old envelopes. 'I've been rummaging through my wardrobe. There's one of me and your grandparents when I was about eleven or twelve'—she taps a finger on the first envelope—'and Joe's in the other.'

Photos? My hand shakes as I tip the first photo onto my lap … I want to save Joe until last. Against a backdrop of a seamless blue sky and ocean stand a couple in their thirties, their hands on the shoulders of a smiling freckle-faced girl in a yellow and black ra-ra dress. The man is tall and dark with the kind of face you could confide in. The woman is shorter, blonde, and looks a bit like me. Hard to believe that both had wanted me terminated.

I look at the smiling girl – Mel – and notice that her smile is restricted to her lips; the eyes don't have a trace of happiness in them. They look … angry. Her hand is on her dad's, but she seems to be leaning away from her mum's as if the touch of it on her shoulder is unwelcome.

'My goodness, you were so cute,' I say, and get a warm smile in return. 'And I do have a look of my gran, don't I? Not the hair, of course, but—'

'I was thinking you looked more like my dad. He had a kind face. Mum's was a bit angular,' she says with a sniff. Then she laughs. 'I can't believe how totally eighties I looked!'

Not a fan of her mum, then. Wonder why?

The second envelope is curled at the edges and sits like a precious butterfly on my palm. I shoot a quick glance at Mel – I'm almost too nervous to open the envelope – she sends a look of encouragement back and rests a hand briefly on my shoulder. I slip my fingers inside and feel an uneven edge. I draw it out and gasp in shock.

The image is of a beautiful young man with a smile to match, standing outside a chip shop in a fine drizzle. He has my nose and exactly the same hair colour as me. He's wearing a white T-shirt and drainpipe jeans and he'd had his arm around someone, but I can't see who. That's the second reason for my shock: the photo has been ripped in half.

I trace the jagged edge and look at Mel; there's no need to voice my question.

'It was me. I tore it in half at a low moment about six months after I'd … given you up.' She shrugs and bites her lip before continuing. 'I was so stupid, but I suppose I resented him for having a life without me. I never liked that photo of me either. Looked a fright – had Bananarama hair but on me it looked more like a pineapple!'

Typical Mellyn. I don't really care about her missing picture. At least I have a picture of him – my lovely birth father. 'He is very handsome.'

'Told you.' She nods. 'Looks like you too, eh?'

I trace my finger along his jawline. 'He does.' My voice struggles out from under a weight of emotion. 'I want to meet him one day.'

'Not sure that's wise,' Mel snaps. 'He hasn't broken his neck to find you, has he?' She deflects my glare and whispers, 'Sorry. Yes, course you do, love. We'll get my ... me sorted out and then see, eh?'

'Yes. And first thing in the morning you're making a doctor's appointment.' It isn't a question.

She nods and stands. 'You can hang on to the photos for now. Keep the one of your grandparents if you like, but I can't let you have the one of Joe. It's the only one I have.'

'Okay, thank you. Night.' I watch the door close and then look back at my ... dad. Thinking this in my head doesn't seem so much of a betrayal because the only dad I've ever known is alive and well and living in Sheffield. I might never meet my birth dad either, so it's all a bit academic really. It doesn't matter. I can say Dad out loud, but it doesn't feel real.

Then I look into his smiling eyes and I realise it does matter. I want to meet this man and one day I will, no matter what Mel says. And why does she only have one photo of him? Perhaps I can get a copy of this one somehow.

Before I go to sleep I prop the torn photo up against my water glass. Joe will be the last thing I see before I close my eyes and the first thing I see when I wake in the morning. It might be just a little scrap of a photo, a thread of the past, but it's more than I had an hour ago, and for that I'm grateful.

Early the next morning I finish my cornflakes and then write a note for Mel reminding her to ring the doctor. I know she can't wriggle out of it, or pretend she's phoned, because I'd said that I would go with her to the appointment. A gentle nudge won't hurt though ... or a phone call mid-morning either.

I set off down the street pulling my coat tighter against the breath of autumn; a fine mizzle beads my skin. It seems an age since I've seen Rosie and I can't wait to get into work. What a thought: Monday morning, damp and grey, yet I'm actually looking forward to my job. A little smile edges my lips. Must be 'summat wrong with my head' as my dad would say.

Rosie turns from the sink as I come into the kitchen and pushes her hair out of her eyes with a hand covered in soapsuds. The bubbles coat her fringe like ghostly frogspawn and she draws her brow into a deep frown. Her cheeks are pink, her jaw clenched. She's obviously flustered about something and I think it best to hide a smile.

'Am I glad to see you,' she says with a heartfelt sigh. 'Bloody dishwasher's packed up and the sodding chef has gone down with the flu! I've had to make a start on breakfast.'

'Oh. You should have phoned me and I'd have come in earlier.'

'I didn't know a thing about it until I set foot in here fifteen minutes ago. Sodding Pomp is still in bed! Vulture was still in his bloody pyjamas, hair stuck up like he'd had his finger in a socket, disgruntled that the chef's call had just woke him up. Just said, "So Rosie. You'll have to be chef today as well as waiting on people. Good job it's Lucinda's day too. I'll pop down in a bit to see how you're coping." I swear I'll swing for the pair of them one day.'

I'm having difficulty pushing a picture of a vulture in pyjamas out of my head, so look inside the dishwasher while I strangle my giggles. 'You sure this is kaput?' I say, just for something to say. I know there will be no calming Rosie while she's like this.

Rosie stops washing up, puts more frogspawn through her hair and glares at me. 'No. No, Lu. It works perfectly fine. I thought I'd pretend it's broken just to make my job even harder by having to washing everything myself!'

I hold my hands up and tuck my top lip under my bottom teeth. It's no use though. Laughter escapes through the sides of my mouth.

Rosie's tight pout relaxes, and her laughter joins mine. She gives me an apron and a soapy scutch upside my head. 'Okay, get that bloody apron on and help me.' She shakes her head and fires up the frying pan. 'What a morning. And you'll never guess who turned up on my doorstep last night at gone ten o'clock?'

'Um … the Queen?'

'Ha! Close. My mother!'

'Half past ten and it feels more like four!' Rosie leans back in her chair and puts her feet on the table. I'm not sure that's a good idea in a kitchen, but after the morning we've had, I couldn't really care less. 'Your turn to make the tea, Lu. There's some bacon left too if you feel like making breakfast.'

Her impish smile convinces me. 'A butty?'

'Yes please, and an egg if there's one hanging around.'

'Hanging around.' I look to the ceiling. 'Nope, not a one.'

'You okay?' she asks my back as I place bacon rashers under the grill.

'Yeah, why?' I'm not, but I'm surprised that Rosie has sensed it, given the whirlwind of activity we've just stepped out of.

'I think Adelaide was just worried about a big emotional goodbye. It wasn't that she didn't want to see you, Lu.'

I point a spatula at her. 'Sure, you're not a witch? You always seem to know exactly what I'm thinking.'

'Course I'm a witch. I have certificates and everything.'

I turn back to the cooker. 'Just seems a bit odd that she ordered a taxi so early. I really hope my decision to stay here hasn't broken our relationship.' Damn it. The words are out before my brain can stop them.

'No. She loves you to bits, trust me.'

Why does Rosie show no sign of surprise at my comments? 'What's Adelaide said to you?' I try to make my voice as normal as possible and crack an egg.

'Said? Nothing. It's obvious how much she cares.'

Rosie's 'said?' played an octave or two higher than the rest of her sentence. She's hiding something. There's been no curiosity about me mentioning a decision to stay here, but I haven't told her anything about what's happened over the last few days. I haven't even seen her.

'Adelaide often worries about nothing, Rosie. Don't pay too much attention to what she says.' I know I'm blushing and I'm glad she can't see it.

'Uh-hu,' she says and fills the kettle. 'I haven't had time to tell you about my mum turning up with all this going on, have I?' Rosie wears an egg goatee and a brown sauce moustache, but she's so involved in her tale to notice. She looks even cuter, if that's possible.

'I mean, it's not normal to just turn up out of the blue unannounced at bedtime,' she says. 'I hope her and Dad aren't splitting up. I couldn't bear it.' She takes a swallow of tea and then frowns at the rim of her cup. 'Have I got sauce on my lip?'

I hand her a bit of kitchen roll. 'Wipe your chin too.'

She wipes it and looks at the result. 'Why didn't you tell me I was covered in—'

'Just get on with your story. Why did she say she was here?'

'She thought we could do with a bit of mother–daughter time and that she missed me.'

'Sounds reasonable to me,' I say. Though it doesn't. It seems odd.

'But just like that? Without asking me first?'

'You mum might have thought you'd say you were too busy, or something …' My voice disappears into a mouthful of breakfast. Perhaps her mum was splitting up with her dad after all.

An arched eyebrow. 'Or something?'

'Look. You'll just have to take her at her word and see what happens.' That sounds wise and practical. I wipe my mouth in case errant egg stops me from being taken seriously.

'Guess so. Just not looking forward to going home. God knows what I'll find out.'

I watch Rosie chew her breakfast along with her thoughts. The tree through the window holds her gaze, yet I suspect that she might as well be looking at a brick wall.

'How about we all go out for a drink tonight?' My words draw her eyes back to my face and put a furrow on her brow. I push my plate away. 'You know – the four of us – our mums and us. It will take a bit of pressure off you if you're worried about her – might be fun.' I realise that my suggestion will take pressure off me too. Selfish, really, but another evening sifting through the ashes of Mellyn's problems is not an exciting prospect.

'No, I don't think Mum would go for that. She'll probably want to just chill out, me and her, you know?' Rosie looks at her cup.

'Don't tell her we're going then. I won't mention it to mine either 'cause she can be awkward.' My doggedness surprises me. 'Just turn up at the pub and we'll be there. They might hit it off and its ages since we had a chat – I missed you.' This last bit was true, but I do wonder if I'd over-egged it. I have eggs on the brain this morning. Better than on the chin, I guess.

'Aw, I missed you too,' Rosie says, an intense look drawing me into deep blue eyes. She blinks and it's replaced by a smile. 'Okay. Let's do it.'

Chapter Twenty-Six

I look at the notepad in my hand and then up at Mel's face. The ghost of a needy child hovers behind the defiance. 'See. It's there in black and white, Lu. Told you I'd make an appointment.'

'You did. Thursday at three. Well done, Mum,' I say. The ghost gathers up my praise and makes a smile out of it.

'How about we go to the pub after dinner to celebrate?'

The smile turns down at one side. 'Really? Thought you didn't like me drinking.'

'Not to excess. But one or two won't hurt.'

'Lovely! I'll wear my new boots, I'll show you them.' She runs upstairs, excited as a child, and I try to pretend that I'm not being manipulative and underhand. It isn't working – I have become the child catcher.

The Lifeboat Inn spells out its name in gold lettering; the roots of its old stone foundations are deep in history, and picture windows stare across the harbour from under lintel brows. Often these places lose something inside, but this old inn has retained its old charm. Huge blocks of stone hold up the ceiling, slabs of Cornish slate armour the floor, on whitewashed walls lifebelts remember past triumphs, and inside the frames of black-and-white prints the eyes of long-dead sailors gaze longingly at the bar.

'What a good idea of yours to come here.' Mel sits down, shrugs off her coat and crosses her long legs to show off the new black shiny boots. Her green woollen dress rides up her thigh and I notice a man at the bar notice. 'It's one of my favourite pubs.'

'It's perfect,' I say in a voice that's pretending not to be nervous but can't carry it off. While Mel's deciding what she wants to drink, my eyes flick a steady pendulum between the door and the clock on the wall. Any moment now Rosie will walk in with her mum. And … right on time. I look down at Mel while Rosie and her mum tip-tap across the Cornish slate. 'Sorry, didn't catch what you said, Mum.'

'No wonder. You aren't paying the slightest attention.' Mel sighs. 'I said I fancy a pint of Doombar.'

'Lu!' Rosie waves across at us and tugs her mum's sleeve. 'Mum, this is my friend Lu, the one who works with me.'

I wave back. 'Hello, nice to see you here. Want to join us?' I avoid looking at my mother, but if the glare in Rosie's mum's eyes is anything to go by, I fear for the jovial evening we'd orchestrated.

Her mum stops and says something to her daughter that I can't catch. Rosie acquires a namesake blush to her cheeks but gives a quick shake of her head and hurries them both over. I look at Mel, well, the top of her head, because she's staring at the sole of her boot as if the secrets of the universe have been revealed across it.

'Mum said that we shouldn't intrude, but I'm sure you don't mind, Mellyn?' Rosie says, and pulls out two chairs opposite us.

'No, of course not.' Mum looks up with a smile that she's borrowed from someone with a much wider face. 'Hello, Rosie's mum. You're very much alike.'

Rosie's mum's smile is all teeth and lipstick. 'That's so kind – I've a few more wrinkles though. My name's Val.'

'Mellyn,' Mel says unnecessarily as Rosie had just addressed her. 'Great to meet you.'

Rosie clears her throat. 'What can I get you all?'

'No, I was just on my way to the bar. Come with me and help carry the glasses?'

Mel's and Val's smiles have settled to straight lines as though all the stretching had exhausted their lips. 'Your usual, Mum?' Rosie asks and receives a brief nod in return.

Rosie nudges me as we walk away and whispers, 'Hope they get along, or we'll get back to a dead body.'

Knowing what I do about Mel, I think it best not to comment.

***

'Why the *hell* did you say we could join you?' Val hissed through a grimace, her eye line on her daughter at the bar.

'What else was I supposed to have said? There didn't seem a lot of bloody choice,' Mellyn said in a low voice, though the malice in it was deafening.

'We'll have one drink and then I'm having a migraine.'

'Yes, you always were a headache. And what the hell are you doing here anyway?'

'Come to visit my daughter to make sure she's okay. When she told me, she was big pals with your long-lost daughter I knew I had to get over here.'

'Really?' Mellyn turned down the corners of her mouth. 'Well, I think you should fuck off back to Spain. You're not welcome here.'

'Do you think I *want* to be in your company? The main reason I'm here is to warn you off. I didn't tell my Rosie what a monster you were while I was still abroad because she's headstrong, would have confronted you.' Val paused to try and calm her breathing, but it wouldn't be calmed; the look in Mellyn's eyes chilled her blood. 'And we know what happens to people that confront you, don't we?'

Lu looked over her shoulder at them and Mellyn gave her a warm smile. Then she twisted in her seat, leaned an elbow on the table, fluffed her hair to shield her expression and glared at Val. 'How *dare* you. You're good at being holier than though, calling me a monster, but there are some tales I could tell about *your* life. Not sure your precious little girl would like to hear them either.'

From the bar, Rosie flapped a packet of peanuts and raised her eyebrows. Val nodded and mouthed 'Thanks' while all the time her heart hammered under her ribs. 'You need help. I told you then and I'm telling you now,' she hissed at Mellyn.

'Fuck off back to Spain or I'll open your cupboards and let the skeletons out. That's why you left in the first place and nothing's changed. You *still* have that lump of a husband, don't you?'

'You wouldn't dare. You have more to lose than me.' Val's voice made a fist of showing strength but her insides turned to liquid under the gaze of those steely eyes.

'Really?' Mellyn raised a brow. 'Do you want to call my bluff? Our daughters are coming back now. It's your call.'

Val bit her lip and looked into the eyes of a sepia fisherman. Framed by the past, he stood on the harbour side holding a shark almost as big as himself, a hook through its gills. Val was caught on Mellyn's hook. She looked at the shark's serrated teeth and felt the bite of her threat sink in. There was nothing she could do. There was nothing she could do five years ago, and there was nothing she could do now.

'No. Just stay away from my daughter or you'll be sorry,' she whispered, and then swallowed hard as the futility of her words was exposed by Mellyn's laughter.

'What's tickling you?' Lu asked, placing a tray of drinks on the table.

'Just something Val said. We have a lot in common, it seems.' Mellyn winked at Val and started up a conversation about beer.

Rosie settled Val on the sofa, went to the bathroom medicine cabinet, and returned with tablets and water. The almost silent walk home had given Val precious thinking time and though what she was about to say was far from a perfect solution, it was all she could come up with right now. She looked at the pills in the palm of her hand and placed them on the coffee table. 'I won't be needing these, love. I ... I made the whole migraine thing up.'

Perched on the edge of an armchair and in the middle of taking off her shoes, Rosie screwed up her face. 'Eh? What for?'

'I wanted to get out of that damned pub and away from that crazy bitch Mellyn.'

Rosie stuck her chin out. 'Why? What did she say to you? I thought you looked a bit upset when we were at the bar.' She kicked off her remaining shoe and sat on the chair properly, leaning forward, elbows on knees.

'I knew her before. You were right when you thought we had been friends in the past. We met in her shop. I went in there to get something for your Aunty Sue's birthday and we got on really well. She didn't know many people because she'd not long moved here from St Austell. So we went out for a drink a few times and then one night we went back to her house.' Val paused and her stomach lurched at the bewildered expression on her daughter's face. 'We, err … we had more to drink and then we played a stupid game of truth or dare.'

'Mum, you're scaring me. I've never seen you look so … serious.'

'I am serious. And she's the one that's scary. She told me things about her past that put the wind up me. She's unstable, and that's putting it mildly.'

Rosie sighed. 'Oh hell. Lu said she's had a few problems with her, and Adelaide – Lu's old neighbour – she and her sister visited the other day. Adelaide wants me to keep an eye on Lu because she thinks Mellyn's scary too.'

Shit. This was just as she'd feared. 'Look, love, I know you're best friends with Lu, but it's not your place to keep an eye on her. I want you to stay as far away from her mother as possible. She's poison and she'll hurt you if she can. I can feel it.'

'Oh, for God's sake.' Rosie flung herself back in the chair and crossed her arms. 'Okay, perhaps Mellyn's a bit unpredictable, but aren't you being a little melodramatic? What exactly did she tell you in this truth or dare game?'

'Well, that's the problem. Mellyn didn't really spell out what she'd done in the past. But she hinted at things. Things that involved her parents' deaths – they died because of a dodgy gas fire. Her husband, a plumber, was implicated …' Val paused and shoved her hands through her hair. 'Things that implied that her husband's death hadn't been an accident … and that Mellyn might have been involved.'

Rosie's hand hovered over her mouth. 'Oh my God! This is mad! And how might she have been involved? What did she say to make you think that?'

Val threw her hands up. 'That's the trouble! I can't remember exactly what she said. We were drunk and it was a long time ago, but it was all very sinister.'

'Think, Mum. You must have some idea!'

Val looked into her daughter's eyes and realised that the anger and fear behind them came from her concern for Lu. 'Okay, as far as I remember she said something like, "He hurt my beloved parents but I was too scared to do anything …"' Val scrubbed at her eyes and sent her mind reaching into the past. 'Then she said words to the effect of, "But then I saw my opportunity and got my revenge."'

'Jesus, Mum. Why didn't you go to the police?'

'With what? A drunken conversation in which she never really admitted anything?' Val met Rosie's stare and blinked. She was never any good at hiding a lie.

Rosie thumped her fist on the arm of her chair and then realisation dawned behind her eyes. 'You didn't go because you'd told her something in the game that you regretted, didn't you? Something that she had over you.'

'Of course not!' Val hoped her plane wouldn't be struck by lightning on the way home.

'You must have told her something, or did you take the dare instead?'

'I told her stuff about sex. Nothing I want to share with my daughter, thank you. But nothing she could blackmail me with.'

Rosie seemed satisfied with that, stood up, began to pace. 'I'll have to tell Lu. She'll have to move out, move in here with me.'

'No! Haven't you been listening? The woman's dangerous and if you come between her and her daughter she'll hurt you. Give Lu a wide birth.'

Rosie stopped pacing, threw up her hands. 'How can I? She's my best friend!'

Val sighed, shook her head and said, 'Oh, Rosie … friends, is that all you are?' Then she saw the flash of anger in her daughter's eyes and cursed silently.

'What the hell is that supposed to mean?' Rosie's voice held a tremor.

This was a now or never moment. Val watched her daughter's face soak up heat from her neck like litmus and realised that it had to be now if she was ever going to support Rosie. 'I hate to see you hiding like this. There's really no need, love.'

Rosie folded her arms. 'Hiding from what?' The question was quick, defiant.

Val shrugged her shoulders. May as well get to the point. 'Your sexuality. I saw how you looked at Lu.'

'My … my what? How I looked at her? Have you gone bloody mad?' Rosie glared at her mother and then laughed humourlessly. 'You don't remember the boyfriends I brought home, I suppose?'

'Boyfriend singular, I think you'll find. Mike was a lovely lad, but in the year, you were together, you wouldn't let him get close to you.'

'For God's sake, we were eighteen. I didn't want to settle down.'

'No. But it was more than that. I overheard a conversation between him and our Jake. You dumped him because he wanted more than hand holding and a kiss or two. A year is a long time to wait …'

'Ha!' Rosie turned away from her mother and looked at the curtains. 'I see. Because I wouldn't shag him you've come to the conclusion that I'm a lesbian!'

'No. I did think it was odd, but it was only when Naomi started coming around that I came to that conclusion.'

'Naomi was a friend.' Rosie turned back to face Val, her voice icy, her eyes afire.

Val wanted to throw her arms around her little girl, tell her it didn't matter, and tell her she loved her. But this had to be said. 'Yes, but you lit up when she came around, moped when you were apart, jumped every time the phone rang … in fact, exactly as you should have been, but never were with Mike.'

'We were friends, nothing more,' Rose hissed through a tight mouth.

'Only because she wouldn't allow it. She was straight and you must have misread the signs. Her mum told me why she stopped coming around.'

The expected outburst never came. Val would have preferred that to the awful silence and watching her daughter's face trying not to crumble. She stood and went to embrace her, but Rosie held her hands up. 'I'd rather you didn't,' she said quietly and sat back down in her chair. 'I'd also rather you left here in the morning.'

Val's stomach rolled and she wished she'd been more tactful. 'Oh, love. Don't be like that. I only said it to show you that I've known about you for years and that it doesn't matter. I—'

'You say you know, but you never asked me, did you? No. You prefer to listen in on conversations and to friends' mothers.' Rosie said this to the floor but then she tossed her head back and looked directly into Val's eyes. 'Well, like mother, like daughter. I listened in on a conversation a few years ago between you and Aunty Sue. And though my sexuality is none of your damned business, I think it does matter to you, very much.' Rosie blinked and then stood. 'I'm going to bed. As I said, I want you gone tomorrow.'

Through a film of tears, Val stared at her daughter's closed bedroom door and slumped onto the sofa, her frame no longer able to support the weight of her heart.

Chapter Twenty-Seven

The squeeze of her heart and the tug on her conscience as she had slipped through the door in the early hours hadn't been strong enough to make Rosie stay and make things right with her mum. Making sure Lu was safe was the priority and another confrontation with Mum wasn't going to help that. The bloody cheek of her! Swanning over from Spain, full of melodrama and bullshit. Okay, she had come to warn her about Mellyn, but the rest was well out of order.

Breaking the news to Lu about her mother played much easier in her imagination as she'd walked to work through the crisp no-nonsense air that morning than it did in the tough reality of a busy breakfast kitchen. Even if she'd tried to say anything there had been no time for a quiet moment. Rosie returned Lu's smile across the dining room and placed two full English breakfasts in front of a young couple. For September, they were unusually busy, and Lu had been roped in for the morning.

'How's your mum?' Lu asked as she hurried a rack of toast to a portly man at the corner table.

'Mum's fine, why?' Rosie heard the snap in her voice. No wonder Lu looked surprised.

'Well, she had a migraine … just wondered—'

'Oh yes! Sorry, I've been rushing about like a loon this morning, I forgot.' Rosie realised she was babbling and cleared her throat. 'Yes, she's absolutely fine. Can we grab a coffee later…?'

'Yes. I said I'd pop in to lend a hand in the shop this afternoon, but I'm not tied to a time.' Lu frowned. 'Everything okay?'

'Yeah. Just that we didn't get time for a chat really last night. Not with Mum getting a headache.' Rosie acknowledged the portly man's beckoning hand and hurried over to him before Lu could say anything else.

***

There's something up, I'm sure of it. This morning Rosie had smiled, nodded, but mostly whisked herself away from me and my attempts at conversation since our brief chat at breakfast service. Perhaps her mum has decided to leave her dad as she'd suspected. Mum said that Val hadn't made much small talk while Rosie and I were at the bar, and she hadn't really said much when we returned. Then after half an hour or so she'd said she felt a migraine coming on. It didn't look great. And I'm not looking forward to coffee – I'm never the best at knowing what to say when people are upset.

I lick the froth off the cappuccino from my spoon and remember the last time I was in the Singing Kettle. Adelaide and Evelyn had been talking about black pudding and second breakfasts and I had tried to avoid looking at their twin eyebrows. Adelaide always knew exactly the right thing to say when people were upset. Perhaps she'd been to night school for it.

I look through the window at the cobbled street and the people walking along. Would Adelaide and Evelyn be walking the cobbled streets of Mevagissey now? I can't remember how long they were supposed to be there … perhaps they were back in Sheffield. Living in my home town seems a lifetime ago and so far, away. It might as well be the moon.

'How about a sticky bun?' Rosie's voice whispers in my ear, bringing me back to earth.

'I think a sticky bun is a wonderful idea,' I say and look up into her face. Her face that is pretending to be jolly, but the slightly puffy eyes are more honest. Before I can say anything, she hurries to the counter. Bugger. Her parents must have split up and I don't have the first clue about how to make it better.

'I got a chocolate éclair and a cinnamon whirl. Your choice.' Rosie puts the tray down and draws her chair back.

I pick the cinnamon whirl even though I want the éclair. I think she needs it more than me. We eat and make the obligatory appreciative noises while I surreptitiously scan her face for clues. Yes, she's definitely been crying, and not too long ago judging from her re-applied too-thick mascara. The lashes look like deformed spider legs that have waded through a pot of molasses. 'So how long is your mum staying?' I say, figuring getting to the root of the problem is the best option.

'Not sure,' Rosie says, and dabs at the corners of her mouth with a napkin. 'The thing is, Lu … I'm here to talk about your mum, not mine.'

The look in her eyes pokes a sliver of ice into my belly. Dear God. What on earth is it?

She keeps on looking directly into my eyes. Then she looks out of the window and sends her words out in a rush. 'My mum told me some very worrying things about yours last night. I was right, they had been friends a while back. Well, friends? They had been out for a drink a few times. They didn't know each other that well …' Her voice gets lost in her coffee cup.

The taste of coffee and cinnamon in my throat suddenly makes me want to retch. This is bad. Very bad. I need to know what Val had said but at the same time can't bear to hear it. I pick up a napkin and twist it. 'What did she say?'

Rosie folds her arms and dredges up a sigh from deep in her lungs. She won't look at me now. The table holds her focus. 'It was about a stupid drunken truth or dare game they played one night. Your mum hinted that her ex-husband had something to do with your grandparents' death – she said he hurt them and that his death wasn't an accident. Your mum got her revenge on him.' Rosie raises her shoulders and spreads her hands wide. 'Mum said she came back to warn me about her and that I should steer clear of her … and you.'

This can't be happening. Can. Not. I look at the napkin in my hands and watch my fingers twisting. I discard it and tuck my hands under my armpits, the heat of my palms seeps through into my cold skin. The café is warm, but I have goosebumps. My grandparents were killed? Killed by Neil? How? And why didn't Mel tell me?

I say, 'He killed them? My grandparents died in a car crash. I … don't understand.'

Rosie's eyes grow round. 'Well, that's not what Mum says. She says Mellyn told her it was because of a dodgy gas fire. He was a plumber apparently, this Neil. Not sure exactly what happened …' Rosie reaches her hands across the table, but I keep mine where they are.

'This is ridiculous!' I say, and a couple across the café glance in our direction. I lower my voice. 'Our mums were drunk and playing a game. My mum is prone to bloody melodrama and would have just said all this to shock yours. You know she struggles sometimes.' My brain hears every word I just said and screams at me to stop. Why was I defending her? I know she killed Neil, so why am I weaving some kind of plausible excuse to wrap her up in?

'That's what I thought at first, your mum is a bit … unstable, I suppose you'd call it. She was off with me the first time we met when she brought your watch to work. She was very cold to the point of rudeness and then switched into all smiles moments later. I didn't think too much of it, or say anything to you at the time, but added to everything else, well, I tend to believe my mum,' Rosie says, blue eyes sending sympathy from a face of worry.

I want to get up and leave, run away and hide from the whole bloody awful mess, but I have to stay, try and sort it. My heart continues to ignore my brain and I say, 'What do you mean, added to everything else? How do we know Val hasn't made the whole thing up? What did she admit to in the game?' I glance around to make sure nobody is listening and hiss, 'And if Val believed what my mum had told her, why didn't she go to the fucking police?'

Rosie's face colours and she looks at her hands on the table, picks at a thumbnail. 'That's exactly what I asked her. She said that she hadn't anything concrete to take to them. There had just been hints and generalisations, nothing really specific about how it had all happened.'

'Exactly, so let's just get a grip, eh?'

Sympathy is squashed by indignation. 'Yes, but what about the way she was at the dinner party? Saying she'd had a wonderful marriage when you'd told me that her husband beat the crap out of her?'

'I explained that to you already. She was ashamed that she'd allowed it to carry on for so long. She had concocted a nice picture of her life with Neil for the dinner party. I guess she didn't want you to feel sorry for her.'

'But it was all a lie, Lu. A whopper.' Rosie fiddles with her hair. 'And I may as well tell you that Adelaide phoned me the other night and said she wanted me to look out for you. She said Mellyn was dangerous, and—'

'I knew it! I could tell you'd talked to her because you weren't surprised the other day when I told you I'd decided to stay here and not go back home. Did she tell you why she thought Mum was dangerous?'

'No. She said it wasn't her place to tell—'

'It was over a silly argument about jewellery, that's all.' I try to smile but my lips tremble. My heartbeat is off the scale now and I dig my fingers into my armpits. 'Adelaide is a worrier, feels responsible for me, knows I'm still vulnerable after Mum's death. She got me through it ... she's over-protective.'

'God, Lu, I hate this. If you think everyone is making mountains out of molehills, and Mellyn made the truth or dare thing up, then so be it. I can't bear to see you upset, but I had to tell you what my mum said. How could I not?' Rosie's eyes well and she blinks.

I nod and swallow a few times. My brain gets the upper hand and forces a ban on speech while I gather my thoughts. How I wish I believed the rubbish I'd been spouting. I could turn my back on Val's revelations, ignore my darkest fears and carry on as before. But I might just as well ask the world to stand still. I hear the thump of my heart in my ears and the weight of the future threatening to crush any hope I've nurtured.

Images crowd into my head led by a memory of Mel's confession to murdering Neil … then her first meltdown at the gallery, the night at Joe's Crab Shack, followed by the vicious clown face when I wouldn't accept free jewellery, and the way she'd made me feel when I did, her wild attack on Evelyn over the 'stolen' necklace, the pain in my shoulder when she'd jabbed her finger into it, and so many other scraps of misery queued up behind, waiting to be seen. Too many. My memory slams the door on them.

Now there's this new story about my grandparents. I have to know the whole truth, and my suspicions argue that Val had been told some of it. Hints and generalisations needed clarity and I must have it. 'I could go and see your mum, ask her some more about what she remembers?' I say, hoping the hysteria in my head hasn't leaked into my voice.

Rosie shifts in her seat and bites her lip. 'You can't. We had an argument and I told her to leave.'

'What? Why?' I say, bewildered. Am I just wading through a bad dream? Nothing seems real today.

'She sticks her nose into my business. Thinks I'm still a child,' Rosie says through a sigh.

I can tell I'm not getting the whole truth, but what's new there? 'Has she gone back to Spain?'

'No. She texted me to say she's gone to Penzance to see Jake. Said she wanted to make it up with me before she goes back in a few days – she'll be staying at the Golden Sands.'

I sigh and rake my fingers through my hair. The walls are too close, the space too hot. I need to get out of here, away from Rosie and her big sad eyes, away from the easy chatter and laughter of the others in the café, away from the smell of coffee, away from my heart telling me to forget all about it, because if all this is real and this huge horrible nightmare is true it will mean the end of my new life, the end of Mel and me, the end of everything.

'I need to think, Rosie, make sense of all of it,' I say, standing and slipping my coat on.

'Yes, I expect you do. Shall I come with you, you know, for support?'

'No. I need to be alone.' I look at her tearful face. 'And thanks for telling me about it all. It can't have been easy.'

'I'm just so sorry. So sorry.'

'Me too,' I say and walk towards the door.

Chapter Twenty-Eight

Under the duvet I can pretend. The world is locked out; I'm safe in a pillowy cocoon of warmth and fabric softener. Bad thoughts can't get me here, make me do anything, send searching and painful questions stab, stab, stabbing at my conscience.

Mel is locked out too. I've had a, ahem, 'tummy bug' since yesterday afternoon. Must be something I ate. And no, I couldn't possibly accompany her to the doctor this afternoon, even though I felt a teensy bit more like myself. I can't face the prospect of sitting in the surgery and listening to more lies tumble from her mouth like circus acrobats. Sometimes living with her is like being inside a Big Top. Thrills, but mostly spills, with me walking a tightrope between happiness on one side and an open cesspit full of shit and daggers on the other. Overseeing and directing this spectacle is the ringmaster – Mellyn Rowe.

Mel might not even go to the doctor now that I'm not there to make sure she does. Her expression when I told her I wasn't coming was as though I had given her a get out of jail card. I groan and push my head into the pillow. Get out of jail … not the best metaphor. A seagull squawks with laughter outside my bedroom window and I tuck the cocoon tighter around myself. If a chink of light is permitted, the stabbing will start again. Now I can't breathe. I untuck, make a little gap at the edge of the bed and take a few deep breaths. Tea. I need tea. But that means leaving this sanctuary and I'm not ready to do that.

So, what if she doesn't go to the doctors? It's the least of my problems. Until we've established the truth there's little point. *Stab.* Yes, of course I know that learning the truth might mean there

197

would *be* no visit. *Stab.* Yes, of course I realise that she might need those get out of jail cards for real. *Stab.* Yes, I *do* know that I need to make a decision and stick to it!

I break out of the cocoon, but the mirror in the corner tells me I look less like a beautiful butterfly and more like an escaped zombie from a freshly dug grave. My nose tells me I probably smell like one too. It's been too long since my skin has seen water.

I close my eyes and screw up my face under the powerful jet of water. Then I reposition the shower head and look down at the chipped nail varnish on my big toes, the water, as hot as I can stand it, bouncing off my shoulders. When I was little, my mum had said that hot water invigorated the skin and soothed a troubled mind. I have to admit I do think a lot in the shower, and after a short while I can see what she meant. If I concentrate really hard, I might be able to squeeze a decision or two out into the swirl of steam enveloping my body – my replacement duvet.

I tug a comb through damp hair and I look out of the bedroom window at the seagulls perched on the roof opposite. I have arrived at two decisions. One is that I will repaint my toenails, and the other is that I will organise the best birthday meal in the world for Mel tomorrow evening.

We'll have the celebrations on the *Sprite* and we'll be normal, jolly, and try on the lives of a loving mum and daughter in the hope they'll be a good fit. One last lovely evening, and then the next day I'll sew a few questions into a conversation about the weather or something, but within the thread there will be snags upon which Mel's answers will be caught. With any luck I'll be able to examine them, smooth them out before my needle sets to work again. And if luck deserts me? One seagull flies to the roof of a shed in the next garden and cocks a glassy yellow eye up at my window, as if waiting for an answer. I huff at it and draw the curtains.

'Oh, lovely. You're up and about.' Mel comes indoors with the scent of wood smoke in her hair and brushes cold lips against my fire-warmed cheek.

'I am indeed and feeling much better now. How are you?'

'Wonderful!' She hangs her coat up and runs water into the kettle. 'You were so right to make me go to the doctor's. Doctor Roebuck is such a lovely woman. I'd expected a big hoo-ha – did I have suicidal thoughts, did I have a troubled childhood, yadda yadda. She did ask those kinds of questions, but only in passing. Mostly she just let me talk, share my feelings, you know?'

'That's great,' I say, and point at a glass of water on the coffee table when she shakes a tea bag at me.

She raises her voice above the roar of the kettle. 'So anyway. I'm going back in a few weeks when she's managed to book me in to see a counsellor. It's a twelve-week thing where we'll go over my main concerns and work through my anger issues.'

I watch her back as she makes the tea and hope that she's actually been to the surgery. She seems much more up and cheerful than she's been for weeks, so if this is another lie it's a bloody convincing one. 'That's great, Mum. No medication?' I say as she sits down opposite my 'sick bed' sofa.

'Nope. Not even a smell of any.' She raises her cup to her lips but doesn't drink. 'And for that I am very grateful.' She takes a sip of tea. 'Oh, I needed that. I've been run off my feet all day, and all the time worried sick about the appointment.' She cocks her head a little like the seagull earlier and narrows her eyes at me. 'So, have I been a good girl, then?'

'You have. Very good. And because you have, I'm organising a birthday treat for you tomorrow evening. A meal and a celebration on the boat.' I smile and it feels genuine.

Mel's face can't seem to decide if it's happy or confused. 'Oh, Lu. That's lovely … but don't you remember I said no fuss? People aren't coming, are they?'

'What people? You've never introduced me to your friends.'

Relief curls her lips. 'Oh, I'm glad it will be just us. I thought you might have invited Rosie and Val. I don't mind Rosie, but Val is a bit odd.'

Funny, that's what she says about you, and worse. Much worse. 'No. Just us, as you say, unless you want me to invite your friends?'

'I told you I don't really have many.' She winds a strand of hair around her finger and winks. 'A woman on her own and all, they think I'm going to gobble up their husbands.'

Or maybe it's because you're psychotic and you scare the pants off them. 'Yes, okay. Just as you like – it's your party.'

'And I'll cry if I want to?' Mel laughs and then a frown silences it. 'I hope you haven't gone to a lot of expense. There's no need. It's not as if it's the big five-oh or anything ... not yet, anyway!'

'Never you mind. You'll just have to wait until tomorrow night.'

Chapter Twenty-Nine

Rosie is possibly the only person I want to talk to now, apart from Adelaide, of course, but I can't talk to either of them. I picture Rosie's lovely face, her big sad eyes and wobbly chin the last time I saw her. If I saw her today I'd crumble, and a big soggy mess in Pomp and Vulture's dining room would take an age to clean up. If I phone Adelaide, she'd be down on the next coach and I couldn't cope with that either.

Rosie has texted me a few times over the last few days to ask how things are between Mum and me, was my illness genuine, and could she do anything? I told her Mel and I were working through things, of course it was genuine and no she couldn't. I text her now to say I'm still under the weather and won't be in to work. I hate letting her down, but the lying is worse. No use worrying about that though. I must have a clear head and put Mel first. Tonight, is the party, but tomorrow the serious stuff starts.

In the garden I pull the zip of my fleece all the way to my ears. The September early morning air has just been a bit nippy recently, but today, nip has turned to pinch. Searching for a rose for Mel's breakfast tray isn't an option, they had long since gone over, as Adelaide would say, but a few sprigs of lavender and honeysuckle yet hold on to life. They would be more appropriate; I admire their determination.

I clear away the breakfast dishes and watch Mel smell the little bouquet. She was thrilled that I had stayed home to make her a birthday breakfast, and her 'Oh dear' when I told her I'd lied in order to do so sounded less like reproach and more like a triumph.

'Oh, my goodness!' Mel picks a turquoise cashmere sweater out of its box and holds it to her face, her eyes wide in surprise. 'This is the one I saw last week! Oh, Lu …' She looks at me and shakes her head. 'This cost a fortune – I don't want you spending all that money on—'

'Well, I did, you're my mum. Just think of all those birthdays I missed.' I hadn't planned to say that, so I quickly hand her another gift to cover my words. Mel had said something similar to me that day in the shop when she was trying to get me to accept all that jewellery, and I could tell by the wry smile that she remembered. I hope she didn't remember her behaviour too.

'Something else? Oh, this is really all too much.' She takes the silver gift bag and pulls out a bottle of her favourite perfume. Her eyes fill and she fans her hand across her cheeks.

'Hey, don't start blubbing. This is your birthday. Oh, and here's your card.' I pass a little yellow envelope to her. Buying everything else was so easy compared to that little slip of verse and paper. The only card I'd ever bought with 'Mum' on the front was for the woman who had loved me and nurtured me all my life. A woman who had so carelessly played chicken with her own. Betrayal whispers in my ears, even though I try not to listen.

In the shop a few weeks ago, I had thumbed through generic birthday cards with nature scenes and seascapes on the front, but then my conscience prodded me over to the Family Birthday section. Even though I call her Mellyn in my mind, I call her Mum out loud, so why is it so hard to send a bit of card that will be in the recycler in a week? I know the answer. The verses in the cards were flowery and love-soaked and I haven't felt comfortable enough to say words like those out loud yet. I've tossed a careless 'you too' at her 'I love yous', but that's not the same as buying a card with it written in black and white. Mel would adore a verse like that, however; she's been hungry for a public show of affection and there it was in my hand. So, I bought it.

I watch her face as she opens it and traces the words inside. 'What a lovely, lovely, card.' Her eyes swim and she fans her face again. 'Such beautiful words.'

'Glad you like it,' I say, and scrunch up the tissue paper from the sweater box to mask her sniffs. 'And now I have things to do, places to go, before I see you this evening. Off to work with you, you'll be late.'

'Is that wise?' Mel frowns and places the card on the kitchen table. 'It's a small town and if you're seen out and about when you're supposed to be poorly ...'

'Yes. I'd thought of that but it can't be helped.'

'You need to think of a big fat fib in case you're spotted,' she says, pats me on the cheek and takes her presents upstairs.

I stand at the foot of the stairs and listen to her hum a merry tune, open and close drawers, run water in the bathroom and lean my head on the whitewashed stone lintel. *And you're the master of big fat fibs, aren't you?* Thoughts like that won't help, won't help at all.

Unhelpful thoughts thankfully haven't been my companions today and, as far as I can tell, I haven't been spotted going about important birthday business. All my tasks are now accomplished and, in an hour, or so Mel will be the beneficiary. Jack looked as if his face had been squashed into a troll mask when I walked into the Crab Shack this morning. His mono-brow had bristled like an overweight caterpillar and he'd folded his arms protectively over his dubiously stained apron.

Once he learned that I wanted two of his lobster specials delivered harbour side this evening, and that I was paying top dollar, he unfolded his arms and face and grinned like a clam. Or was it happy as a clam? Either way, he was very courteous and accommodating and wished Mellyn a very happy birthday. I chose a delicate pâté from the deli and fresh rye bread that I'd toast for the starter. The cake shop was next, and my order was everything I'd dreamed it would be, and a bottle of fine champagne cooled itself down in the fridge. Now I look at the clock. Right, I must get changed, grab ice for the bucket, toast the bread, throw everything else in the cooler and off to the boat. Mustn't forget the cake. I'll need two trips – glasses, plates and cutlery in the same bag would tempt fate. Everything has to be perfect tonight and perfect it will be.

The *Sprite* looks like a dream. White fairy lights twinkle on her deck and clusters of balloons shake in a zephyr. I can't believe how mild the evening air is compared to the pinch of morning. It isn't warm, but it's much better than I could have hoped for an alfresco dinner. I've just finished putting the finishing touches to the starter and rearranging chairs that were perfectly fine, when I hear, 'Lu! Wow how wonderful!'

I watch Mel hurry alongside. She looks wonderful with her hair floating around her shoulders, jeans tucked into boots, and a smart wool coat over her birthday jumper. Holding on to the handrail she steps aboard, her smiling face illuminated by the fairy lights, but mostly it shines from within. She puts her arms around me – her new perfume's overpowering. 'I can't begin to thank you for all this,' she says into my hair. 'Nobody has ever done anything so lovely for my birthday before. Not even special landmark birthdays!'

I hold her at arm's length. 'That's awful. Didn't your parents do anything for your eighteenth ... twenty-first?' The pain etched into the lines around her eyes and the downturned lips signal *back off*. Damn it. Why do I always uncover the weeds in her past? Why are there never roses?

'Never mind,' I say. 'Look, we have a starter.' I wave my arm with a flourish at the candlelit table.

Mel claps her hands in delight. 'That looks delicious.' She reaches into her canvas bag. 'I brought both red and white. I didn't know what we'd be eating.'

I take the bottles and just in time remember that admonishment won't be a good idea. Not tonight. 'Well, we have champagne for the main course. Let's have white with the pâté.'

The starter over, Mel pushes her hair from her forehead and says, 'That was so good.' Then she leans across the table and cocks her head. 'Tell me. How did you manage to make the main course without me knowing? When I got home tonight there was no smell of cooking.'

'You'll see.' I laugh, looking over her shoulder at a young man hurrying along the slipway and down the steep cut steps balancing two white boxes. 'And that jumper really does bring out your eyes.'

Mel snorts into her wine at the in-joke. 'How macabre.'

I stand and take the boxes from the young man and slip him a tip. Mel swivels in her seat, opened mouthed. I place one box on the table and lift the lid. 'Lobster special, madam?' I watch her mouth open wider and laugh. 'And before you ask, I paid for them!'

A full moon peeps at us from behind a silver cloud, and stars show up our fairy lights. The champagne is on standby for a birthday cake presentation and I have to congratulate myself on orchestrating such a good evening. I realise I have never taken so much trouble over anyone's birthday before, so in an odd way it's been a first for both of us. Mel has never had anyone make a fuss, and I have never made one. A little glow of a good omen hangs around in my belly and, even though tomorrow is tell-the-truth time, I have a feeling it won't be half as bad as I imagine.

I sing happy birthday and the zephyr helps Mel blow the candles out. She cries when she sees the heart-edged *Happy Birthday Mum XXX* decoration and says over and over that she's had the best birthday ever.

Then the zephyr brings reinforcements and I button up my cardigan. 'Shall we go back home in a bit for a coffee by the fire?'

'Home already, when we're having so much fun? I was thinking about taking us out for a sail in this gorgeous moonlight!' Mel waves her arms at the sky.

'It's getting a bit blowy now. Is that a good idea?'

'I've been sailing for thirty years, trust me. And I only aim to go just past the harbour mouth to get away from the light pollution of the town. We'll have the last of the booze and a toast. The moon is stunning out at sea. It will end the evening perfectly.'

I shrug and agree. Though I do wonder if having the last of the booze is a great idea. She's had two glasses to my one all evening. Still, she definitely isn't drunk and she certainly wouldn't do anything to jeopardise our safety, would she? I'd be a killjoy if I insisted on going home. Besides, I want to see the moon and stars illuminate the black velvet sky just as much as she does.

The *Sprite*'s engine thrums, the moon lights a silver path across the waves, and we set out along it towards the open sea.

Chapter Thirty

With the engine stopped and the anchor dropped, Mel switches off the fairy lights and then we wrap blankets around our knees and make ourselves comfy on the back seat. The lights of the harbour are in plain view, but we're beyond the reach of their wiggly fingers. I close my eyes and listen. Gentle waves slap the *Sprite*'s bow and shush the noisy shingle a little way off, and one or two clanks of rigging join in now and again as a breeze invites them to dance.

'Look up, Lu,' Mel says.

The reverence in her voice opens my eyes. I tilt my face to the heavens and open my mouth. Oh, the moon … The enormous bright, round, moon rolls centre stage, frightens away clouds and asserts its rightful place amongst a supporting cast of stars. In depth and multitude, stars hold darkness in contempt and draw navy paths from the centre of the sky for the moon to sail upon.

'Oh, my goodness,' I say. Pretty lame in the face of such beauty, but the rest of my words have decided they are inadequate.

'Told you it'd be worth it,' Mel says quietly, the moon reflected in her eyes.

'I have never seen anything like it.'

'Well you have now, my love.' She leans across, switches the fairy lights back on and flaps a hand at my puzzled face. 'We need a bit of light so we can pour the champagne!'

I look at our two glasses raised to the moon, the bubbles caught in starlight, and Mel says, 'To my wonderful, clever and beautiful daughter. I thank you for this wonderful birthday surprise, but I thank you most of all for coming back into my life.'

'You're very welcome,' I say as we clink glasses, 'and I'm very glad to be back in it.' *At least I hope I will be when we've got to the truth.*

'Tonight, is so perfect, and what you've done for me is so perfect that in a while I'll tell you some things I've been keeping from you. Secrets between mother and daughter can only lead to mistrust in the end. Trust is so important don't you think? I've never felt this close to anyone before, barring Joe. My lovely, lovely daughter.'

More secrets? Dear God, I hope they're nice ones. I pat her hand and nod because I'm not really sure what to say apart from, 'I feel close to you too, Mum.'

'Bottoms up,' she says, and to my dismay downs the champagne in one and then lifts the third-full bottle of white. 'Another?' Her eyes dance with mischief.

'No thanks. I'm fine with this.' I make my tone polite, but allow a bit of disapproval to filter in.

'Well I'll have it then. We've a bottle of red unopened too.'

I looked at her and frown. 'Mum, you have to sail this boat back to—'

'It was a joke, Lu. You never can tell when I'm pulling your leg!' She laughs, but I notice that her eyes don't find it funny.

We sit quietly for a few moments and then I say, 'Rosie must have been cursing me today. Poor girl will have been so busy she'd be meeting herself coming back.'

'Cursing? Hmm. Like mother like daughter then.'

'What do you mean?' My heart rate quickens.

'Look. I might as well tell you. Her mother and me knew each other a few years ago. I said I didn't know her because I didn't like her. She said the same to Rosie for the same reason.'

Now what? Damn it. I don't want to have this conversation tonight – it will ruin everything. But my gut says that to feign surprise isn't an option. I sigh. 'Well, actually, I did know. Val mentioned something to Rosie.'

Mel downs half her glass in one and my stomach lurches. 'Interesting. What did she say, let's be knowing? I don't like people having secrets behind my back.'

'Not secrets, just that you were friends but that … well, you fell out.' I look at the moon for help.

'Look at me, Lu.' Mel's tone won't be ignored. I look at her and swallow. The moon has abandoned me to the steel in her eyes. 'You are a terrible liar. What do the three of you know that I don't?'

'Please, Mum. Let's not do this now. We've had the perfect evening and all this talk of—'

'What has that bitch said?' Mel's vicious clown face waits under her skin. 'Tell me, Lu, and I'll know if you're lying.' She drains her glass and pulls out the bottle of red from her bag.

'Mum. Please don't open that, it really—'

'It really isn't a good idea. Yes, I know. Now tell me what she said or I'm downing the whole fucking bottle, and don't think I don't mean it.' She pours half a glass and then screws the top back on. 'That's all I'm having … for now.'

My stomach rolls as if copying the waves further out at sea and I fold my arms across my noisy heart. If I tell her the truth she'll have a meltdown and drink the whole bottle anyway, but if I don't, she'll know I'm lying, and the result will be the same. What the fuck am I going to do?

'I'm waiting,' she says quietly, but the clown face has almost broken through and she takes two quick gulps of wine.

'Okay. She said she came to warn Rosie away from you because you were dangerous.' I hesitate and then catch the glint in her eye. 'She said you both got drunk in a truth or dare game … and you hinted about Neil having something to do with your parents' death and that you got your revenge on him. That's ridiculous, because they died in a car crash … didn't they?'

She ignores the last question. 'Hinted? Is that it? Nothing else?'

Isn't that enough? I look at her. The clown has borrowed a calm expression and that scares me more. 'More or less. She said they'd died because of a faulty gas fire. Neil was a plumber and had done something to it. You knew he had hurt your beloved parents and—'

'Beloved – that's a joke,' Mel says, linking her fingers and stretching her arms to the sky. She yawns and puts her feet up on a chair as if she's totally unconcerned. It has the opposite effect on me. 'But yes, the fire was faulty.'

'I don't understand.'

'No, I don't suppose you do.' She examines her nails and yawns again.

'I thought they died in a car accident.'

'That's because I told you they did. I also told you I loved them and miss them every day, blamed myself and all that crap. I haven't told you everything.' Mel flicks her eyes to mine and then back to her nails. 'I told Val half-truths too. As you rightly say, I was drunk again. Cursed myself the next day, but there we go. Anyway, I sorted it pretty quickly. First, I told her it was all made up, but she wasn't buying that. So, then I told her that if she ever repeated anything I'd said, I would tell everyone about her own nasty little secret, her sordid affair. I'm good at blackmail, as you know.' She sends a brittle laugh into the sky.

The laughter fades and I wonder if I have somehow fallen down a rabbit hole.

Nothing is real. There's just us on a boat in a huge black snow globe, but when it's shaken, instead of snow, the stars will fall.

I look at Mel and she smiles at me as if everything is normal, as though the things she has just said were ordinary. I have become a reluctant spectator, detached and bewildered.

I listen to the waves slap the bow and, oddly in such a situation, wonder when her voluptuous laugh has gone. I haven't heard it lately. Perhaps that wasn't real, either. Perhaps it had been pretend, rehearsed, borrowed from someone else. Lies upon lies upon lies, twisting, deceiving, hoodwinking. She raises her glass and a scream builds in my chest. What do I actually know about this woman I'm calling mother? Who exactly is Mellyn Rowe?

Mel sighs and gives a chuckle. 'I shut that bitch up so fast it was hilarious. She'd trusted me in that game, told me her boring little secret about an affair. I said I'd tell her husband, children and the whole town about her and the next-door neighbour. Said I'd make stuff up, too – ruin her reputation. She was already considering buying a bar in Spain and I made her mind up for her. Clever, eh?'

'Oh, Mum,' I say with a sigh.

'Oh, Mum, what? I couldn't afford the risk. If you'd had my life you'd learn to trust nobody, look out for nobody but yourself.'

'I think we should head back in now.'

'Do you? Well, tough, I don't. And I think it's time you learned the whole truth about everything. If we are to be mum and daughter properly, you need to know. You also need to love me unconditionally – just like I love you.' Her fingers on my hand makes my skin crawl.

'Okay, but let's do this tomorrow.'

'No. It has to be tonight.' She spreads her arms wide and tilts her head back. 'Tonight, under the stars, this perfect end to a perfect day with a perfect daughter. I need to share it, don't you see?' She stares intently into my eyes. 'It's all part of the healing process, as Doctor Roebuck said. If we wait until tomorrow it won't sound right, you'll not understand.' Mellyn throws her arms around me and it takes all my resolve not to push her away. I don't want to hear any more. My heart can't take it.

'I'm just worried that it might be upsetting and you'll regret tell—'

She releases me and pours more wine. 'I'm telling you now, and that's it.'

'That's the last glass, Mum.' I grab the bottle and thrust it into the bag. I put the bag behind my legs and wonder if I can drive the boat back. I'd watched her loads of times and she'd let me have a go once or twice. Guiding a boat back to its mooring was a different matter though, and if Mel kicked up a fuss, it would be practically impossible.

She looks at me over the rim of her glass, her bone-chilling smile obscene under the fairy lights. 'Okay. Are you listening?' I push my hands through my hair, say nothing. 'Right. I hated my parents ... so I killed them.'

Chapter Thirty-One

The scream that has been building in my chest reaches my vocal cords and I have to put my hand over my mouth to prevent its escape. No. *No*. NO! This can't be true. She's delusional, her psychosis has taken over, surely ... surely it couldn't be true. Please, God, don't let it be true. I bite my lip and look at a blur of stars.

'Well, when I say parents, I mean Dad. She wasn't my mother. He married again after my mother died when I was only a few months old.' She leans forward and does the manic staring thing again. 'Isn't it awful I don't remember my mum at all, not even a little bit? I have a photo of her holding me but it could be anyone.' She sniffs, sits back and tucks the blanket over her chest. 'Anyhow, Dad and my stepmother were always so wrapped up in each other that they never had time for me. I felt like an inconvenience, an appendage. Dad never talked about my mum either, it was as if she'd never existed.'

I can't speak. Literally. My mouth's so dry that my teeth stick to the inside of my lips and adrenalin wants me to run. I look at the dapples of silver on the waves and close my eyes. Mellyn doesn't seem to notice. Her words are relentless.

'I never felt loved. Oh yes, they fed, clothed, sheltered, all the usual stuff, but never loved. Then when I got pregnant it was the living end. It drove us further apart. I hated them for trying to get me to kill you, so in the end they got what they deserved.'

She strokes my arm but I don't react, just sit there like a statue, immobilised by her story.

'Sorry, love. I know it's not easy listening but it has to be done.' Another sip of wine. 'So, on that night, I told Val I was convinced that Neil was somehow involved with my parents' death. Not true. Neil had serviced their gas fire and said it needed a new part. It was an old fire. He'd been on at them for ages to get it done, but Dad thought he was fussing for nothing. Neil said that on no account should it be used, he'd broken a filter or something when he was fiddling.' Mellyn twisted her mouth to the side and sighed. 'I can't remember now what he said, to be honest, but I do remember him telling me that I should tell them not to use it. Neil was busy on a job and said he'd fix it the next day. But I didn't tell them, Lu. I let them die. I came back from Christmas shopping and found them both sitting in their chairs by the fire watching a rerun of *Morse*. Well, they weren't watching it, of course, because they were dead. Just sat there, grey faced. Dead.' Mel shakes her head and tries to look remorseful.

A noise in my throat that sounds like a sob escapes me and I wipe my wet cheeks. She doesn't notice or chooses not to. I want her to stop – need her to stop. My heart races so fast that my head feels like one of the party balloons. She doesn't stop though. Won't.

'Neil was distraught when he found out what had happened. I said telling them not to use it had just gone out of my head. It hadn't, of course, how could it? Not something as important as that. He was suspicious, but in the end, he blamed himself. He said he should have gone around there, told them himself not to use the damned thing. I made him keep quiet though when the police started asking questions. I told the police that I'd seen my dad taking it apart the day before when I'd popped round, said he always liked to sort things out himself, was a bit of a DIY enthusiast. I explained that I told Dad not to do it himself, but that he wouldn't listen.'

My heart misses a beat and I put both hands over my mouth. This can't be happening. Cannot.

'Neil struggled with his guilt over the next few months and in the end, he couldn't cope. We were at my parents' house doing it up, like I told you, and he just comes out with it, says he's going to the police to tell them what had happened. I pretended to break down and agreed that honesty was the best policy, but that we should think about what exactly we were going to say and go together the next day. Later on, I pushed him off the ladder.'

My voice broke free. 'NO! No. No. No,' I sob. 'So many lies ... you said he beat you ...'

Her expression is neutral, her tone matter of fact. 'No. He never beat me at all. The things I told you about him being cruel to me when he was pissed ... it was the other way around. He adored me, but he was just dull. He didn't even drink. I never loved him, not like I loved Joe.'

Sobs threaten to engulf me and I want to surrender to them, roll up into a ball and cover myself with the blanket, block out her face, her story, her terrible, terrible secrets. Then instinct tells me that I have to fight it, can't let it happen. Yes, I'm on a boat with my mother, but she's a dangerous woman. My heart says, *But she's my mum ... my mum, and she loves me.* But she's capable of anything, my mind reminds me. It fights with the child in my heart and fleshes out a plan. I wipe my eyes and gather my wits, force my breathing into a regular rhythm.

'Show me how to get the boat to shore. You've had too much to drink and we need to get you home,' I say, relieved to hear calm in my voice, though I'm anything but.

'I'm not drunk, Lu. I'm also not ready to go in yet. What do you make of the truth, eh? You haven't said anything. Just sat there crying.' Mellyn stands and draws the blanket round her like a cloak. 'I have bared my soul to you, for fuck's sake, and you say nothing!'

'This is not the time or the place.' I stand too and set my legs as a wave buffets the stern. 'We'll go home, get some sleep, and then tomorrow we'll get you the help you need.' Too late I realise that might not be the best thing to say. The resurgence of the clown mouth confirms it.

'Jesus. You sound just like Neil,' she spits, and takes a step towards me.

Panic squeezes my heart when I think about what happened to him. Then I remember that sometimes when I've challenged her, she's backed off. I would try that. Besides, I don't have a lot of options. 'What do you expect me to say? You told me you killed my grandfather, his wife and your husband in cold blood. Of course, you need bloody help!'

'Don't you have any compassion for me at all?' she asks quietly, a tremor in her voice. 'I'm you mother ... doesn't that mean *anything*?'

'Of course, it does. And I do care about you, very much. That's why I want to help you.'

'Tell me you love me then.' The tremor is gone. 'You said it in the birthday card but I'd like to hear you say it out loud. Don't you see, I've given you all of the truth because I love you? We are bonded forever now, and those bonds can never be broken.'

I can't think of anything I'd like to do less right now. I walk to the control and turn the key in the ignition. Nothing happens. I try it again and then my hand flies to my face as the sting of a slap spreads across my cheek.

'You don't have a clue what you're doing, you idiot, and I told you, we're going nowhere!' she shrieks.

I turn and glare at her. 'How dare you!'

'You want to run to the police, just like Neil. I told you everything and you turn your back.' Her lips make themselves into a snarl and her eyes send jets of venom into mine.

'Look, calm down. I never mentioned the police. Come on, start the engine and we'll—'

'You want to turn me in. I can see it in your face. I can't trust you, Lu.' She reaches out and shoves me in the chest and I'm forced back so hard that the steering wheel digs into my kidneys.

'Stop that!'

'Stop that!' she mimics.

'Just get this boat started, now!'

'Just get the boat started, now!' She cackles and shoves me again.

I shove her back and she stumbles to portside. 'That's enough!' I yell.

With a look of pure hatred on her face, she picks up her wine glass and swings it down hard against the edge of the handrail. The moonlight catches the shard of glass in her hand and nausea rolls in my throat.

'Sit back down, Lu.' She looks at the shard in her hand and then back at me. 'We have lots more to discuss.' She makes her mouth a thin line.

'I don't think so,' I say.

'Well I do.'

I run my hands through my hair and look at the harbour lights. So close and yet so far. She steps forward and motions with the broken glass for me to return to my seat. What was left of logical thought in my panic-stricken head whispers, *How is this possible? She's my mother... she loves me ...* Again, adrenalin tells me to run, and this time I have to listen. I kick off my deck shoes.

'What are you doing?' Mellyn says, stepping forward again.

She sounds like my mum again, but I can't afford to believe it. I undo my chunky cardigan and let it fall to the floor.

'Lu. You can't be serious ...'

I leap up the step, onto the cabin roof, and strip off a second layer. 'I can't see I have a choice, can you?'

She studies the glass shard in her hand and sends me a smile almost as wicked and lethal. 'Stop right there or you'll be sorry,' she growls.

'I'm already sorry, Mellyn,' I say, a catch in my voice.

'Mellyn again ... not Mum any more. That's how you really feel about me, isn't it? It's all been fake on your part. You won't ever tell me you love me, will you?' A growl in her throat, she says, 'Okay, you asked for it.' Her manic smile turns my guts to liquid. 'Your precious so-called mum's death was no accident either. You know why? Because I killed her, too.'

Chapter Thirty-Two

I find my legs have given way and someone is screaming. A horrible animalistic scream of despair, pain and fury. I look at Mellyn's calm expression and realise the scream is coming from me. On all fours on the cabin roof, I draw in great gulps of air and try to think, form words. My brain, my intellect is shutting down, leaving only instinct and emotion. Mellyn watches me from the deck, expectantly. I feel like some caged animal, an exhibit, entertainment for her audience of one.

'I did it for you, of course. Well, for us,' she says, her eyes never leaving mine. 'I knew as long as she was around you'd never come and find me. You'd proved that already, getting Maureen to make contact and then changing your mind.' Mellyn's voice is calm, yet she gouges the shard of her wine glass into the wood of the deck rail. She blinks a few times and the calmness leaves her voice. 'Can you imagine how that made me feel? *Can you?*'

My breath comes in short huffs and I can't control my body. A shake starts in my fingers splayed on the roof of the cabin and spreads through the rest of me. I hear myself say, in a voice I barely recognise, 'That's impossible – you couldn't have killed her. It was just an accident, a terrible, terrible accident. She'd been to the hairdresser ... ran across the road to get out of—'

'The rain, yes. It was my suggestion that we made a dash for it. We linked arms and everything, wasn't that sweet?'

I shake my head a few times. This was another one of Mellyn's lies – a product of her illness. 'No, you're lying. You didn't know where we lived ... or, or anything.'

'I'm not lying, I'm afraid. And I did know where you lived. Once Maureen had kindly told me your basic details – your name, the name of your adopted parents and your city – it wasn't hard to track you down at all.' Mellyn sighs and makes herself comfy back on the seat as if it's the most normal thing in the world. She still holds what's left of the glass.

I go from all fours to a kneeling position and shove my shaking hands under my armpits. Emotion still rules me, but instead of fear and disbelief, pure anger wears the crown. 'You're telling me that you tracked us down just so you could murder my mum?' My voice cracks with a mixture of disbelief and fury.

'I am. But as I said, I did it for us, so we'd be together, just as we always should have been.' She leans forward, picks up the bottle of wine and takes a long slug. Then she fixes me with a pleading stare. 'Don't imagine it gives me any pleasure to tell you this, but you have to know. I was sorry as soon as I'd done it, told Hannah I was too, even though I knew it was for the best. In fact, I knelt by her for a few minutes while a man shouted he was calling an ambulance. It was the least I could do. I had tears streaming down my face and you know what? She just looked at me as if she understood.'

'NO! She wouldn't have understood. How could she?' Mellyn raised an eyebrow and shrugged. 'And how, how did you do it? How did you end up with her at the side of the road?' I realise I'm sobbing and stop my mouth with my discarded cardigan.

Mellyn actually smiles. Smiles with pride in her face. 'Oh, that wasn't hard. I came up to stay in a nearby hotel for just over a month. Paid someone to run the shop. I followed you all, got to know your daily habits. I followed Hannah most often though, that's why I was there, after all. Though it was hard not to tell you who I was one day when I sat behind you in a café. My lovely, lovely baby. So near, but yet so far.' Her bottom lip wobbles and I want to scream. 'Anyway, she was a creature of habit. Had her hair done once a week at the same time. On the day of her *accident* I arranged to have my hair done too, and we got chatting.'

'I can't … I can't believe how cold, calculating and—'

'Well, to be honest I wasn't exactly sure what I was going to do that day, so it wasn't really planned. I had initially just thought I'd get her chatting and then hopefully befriend her. How to remove her would come a later date, really.' She takes another swig and looks out across to the lights in the harbour.

'But we left the hairdresser's together, laughing and joking, and as we watched the lights at the crossing, the slippery tarmac and her silly sandals gave me the idea that this would be as good a time as any. I linked arms with her, we ran for it, and I elbowed her into the path of a car. She … well, you don't need to know the finer details. Once the crowd began to form and a man that knew first aid came over, called for the ambulance, I slipped away. I did pay my respects at the funeral, though. You looked at me, remember? I was under that tree. But I had to leave … couldn't have you recognising me later when we met up.'

My God … she was the woman in the hat and glasses. I look into her eyes and know that this is the truth. Not one of her fantasies, but the honest, cold, vile, gut-wrenching truth. Then a series of images flashes in front of me. Mum and Dad laughing about Adelaide's eyebrows, family holidays and Christmases, Mum tucking me into bed, all lost … replaced by the pain, heartache, and the grey man Dad has become, all because of what this evil woman has done.

Instinct takes over and fury drives me down from the cabin and on top of her before she's had time to draw breath. Because I've taken her by surprise, her 'weapon' is useless, easily falling out of her grasp and into the ocean as I smash her wrist against the deck rail. I feel my fingers wrapping themselves around her throat and watch her eyes bulge as a deafening roar of anguish leaves my lungs.

A pain in both my forearms clears a way through the suffocating red fury inside my brain and I see that Mellyn has dug her nails into my skin and drawn blood. I release her and step back, my chest heaving, shocked at what I'd been attempting to do. She might deserve to die, but it won't be at my hands. Then I would be just as bad as her. I can't … I won't allow that.

She doubles over, retching and coughing, and I run back up to the cabin roof.

'Lu ... Lu, my baby girl.' Mellyn pulls herself upright, reaches out her hand and rasps, 'I'm sorry. I don't blame you for what you just did ... but please ... let's just talk about it. You're my daughter and I'm your mum.'

I snort and spit on the deck. 'You might be the woman who gave birth to me, but you will *never* be my mum!'

As she moves towards me, I take three steps and dive into the ocean.

Chapter Thirty-Three

*C*old ... *cold* ... *move* ... *strike out* ... *kick, KICK!* Adrenalin comes to my rescue and I exhale into the icy water and power my body towards the harbour lights. After a few more strokes, the chill clutching my skin relaxes its grip, and a few strokes later, I glance behind. Thank God. There's a comforting distance between myself and the *Sprite*, easily identified by its fairy lights. Then an engine kicks into life and the chill comes back. I must keep focused; there can be no room for anything else but reaching land. I draw a breath from the bottom of my lungs, and swim.

The hammering of my heart in my ears can't drown out the engine's thrum and I realise that swimming the narrow path of moonlit water is a dangerous course. The first shadowy shapes of moored fishing boats bob along a darker channel about a hundred yards to my left, so I strike out for these as hard as I can. A few moments later, a mooring buoy looms out of the shadows and I narrowly avoid a painful collision. My hands grab for it but slip on the submerged rope, so I grab it again, feeling the seaweed squelch through my fingers. I shudder as the anchored chain of the buoy skims my leg, my heightened imagination offering images I'd rather it kept to itself.

Behind the head of the buoy I watch the *Sprite* come closer and as it draws alongside I hear, 'Lu! I'm sorry. Lucinda! Come out, you'll catch your death.' *I nearly caused yours tonight ...* and then the enormity of what she's done punches me in the gut. *No time for tears.* I submerge until the engine grows quieter and then swim to the end of the first craft. The *Sprite* is a little way along the channel in front and then she stops, her engine idling. Mellyn looks over the side and sweeps a powerful torch beam along the water to port and starboard. *Shit. I can't make my way to the beach safety now, she's blocking my way!*

'LU! FOR GOODNESS SAKE, ANSWER ME! THIS HAS GONE BEYOND A JOKE!' She cocks her head and listens for a while, sweeps the torch again and then moves the *Sprite* on.

My teeth are chattering and bone-chilling cold is numbing my legs. The longer I'm inactive the worse it will be for me. Immediately I swim out into the moonlight again and strike for shore. The *Sprite's* further ahead now, but the wash she leaves slows my progress and every time I take a breath I gag on diesel fumes. Treading water with leaden limbs, I see the boat take a right turn away from the beach. Perhaps she's going to moor up and try to head me off as I come out of the water. Rational thought soothes my worries. Even if she was, she wouldn't be able to moor the *Sprite* in time and catch me. I'm too close to shore …

I set off again and then stop at the sound of an engine growing closer. Bloody hell, she's not mooring at all, just sweeping round in an arc! I'm not too hard to spot either: a black head bobbing along a mercury strip. Turning around I see the *Sprite's* bright fore-light bearing down on me, and though my own mother is the pilot, it only takes a second for me to realise her intentions. She can't risk my escape. Not now I know the extent of her madness. I summon every remaining scrap of energy and once more swim to the left, moments before the boat powers past. I grab the mooring rope of another trawler and peep around it at the stern of the speeding boat. A lesser swimmer would now be under it, limbs shredded by the propeller. Vomit surges to my throat and into the water.

Think. Think! Did Mellyn know I'd survived? Odds said yes. The impact of my body would have damaged the engine or at least slowed it. Perhaps she thinks I've been struck by the bow and knocked clear somehow. Whatever the case, I guess she will arc round and be back to check before very long. The little harbour beach is tantalisingly close now, but I can't afford to take the direct route.

I move in the inky black shadows from fishing boat to rowing boat, to rowing boat to fishing boat – swimming, ducking under ropes, wriggling past chains – until there's only one boat between me and the beach. An image of me stealing a rowing boat flashes but is dismissed. There isn't time. One last sprint and then I'll be home and dry. I hang my arm over a rope to support my weight, hold my breath and listen. My stomach lurches at the sound of an approaching engine and the *Sprite* comes level, idling her engines. I hold on tight as her wash slaps against the sides of the boat I'm hiding behind and the torch sweeps the water again. Mellyn's voice drifts towards me, sweet, cajoling, she must know I'm close.

'Lu? I know you're here somewhere – I saw you swim away. You got the wrong idea. I wasn't trying to harm you, I was trying to rescue you, my love. I SAID I WAS TRYING TO RESCUE YOU.' She pauses and I'm glad I can't see her face. 'Lu! Answer me, damn you. *Answer me!*'

I hear her curse and then she moves on, no doubt to complete another circuit. This is it. I need to go. Right. Now.

I break cover and force my limbs to begin a front crawl, and this time my speed matches the title. *Come on, COME ON!* I reach within and find … nothing. My reserves are empty… and then my foot strikes sand. I put both feet down in waist-high water and sob with relief. Wading as fast as my unsteady legs will allow, I struggle from the breakers and collapse on all fours, gasping for air.

My hair lashes my face as I whip my head to face the sea and the sound of a boat coming along the moonlit channel. There's no way Mellyn could land the *Sprite* here on the beach … could she? *She's mad enough to do anything … go!* A crazy half-hop scramble takes me up the beach and on to the cobbled street that runs along the harbour. A man walking his dog says something to me but I don't answer, just put my head down and keep going until I reach the main street.

I lean against a wall and my whole body starts to tremble. Though I'm wet through to the bone and only wearing leggings and a T-shirt, I don't feel cold. I'm shaking because of the shock … the shock of having your own mother … Stop. No time for this. Where to go? Can't go home she'll find you there. No key to get in anyway. Rosie's? Yes, Rosie's. My feet take a few steps. *Fuck*! I can't. I don't know exactly where she lives!

A racking sob escapes and I slap both hands over my mouth. Can't get hysterical. Will *not* get hysterical. *Think*. Police? Yes, the obvious choice. I wrap my arms around myself and the shaking increases. No. Can't face them, all their questions … no, not yet.

Fear jumps under my ribs and I look behind along the dark street expecting to see Mellyn bearing down on me, broken glass in hand, but I'm alone. Oh God. Where can I go? A breeze whispers down an alley and with it an answer: *Val. Go to Val!*

Chapter Thirty-Four

'I'm sorry, Miss Lacey. You can't just come in here at ten o'clock at night demanding to see guests! You're obviously distressed—'

'Of course, I'm distressed. Someone just tried to kill me! I want to see Mrs Green right now!' I wave my arms to emphasise my point and droplets of water land on the reception desk.

The Pompesque woman behind it takes a step back and points at the phone. 'If that's the case then I suggest the police might be the best—'

I run through the inner doors and to the foot the stairs. 'Val! VAL! It's me, Lu!' I yell. I hear a door open and Val appears in a dressing gown.

The receptionist catches up to me and says, 'I'm calling 999 this minute!'

'No, it's okay,' Val comes halfway down the stairs. 'I know this girl. Hell, Lu, you're soaked!' She tucks her blonde bob behind her ears and hurries down the remaining steps. 'What's wrong, love? Is it Rosie?'

I shake my head and look at the worry and sympathy in the lines of her face. I try to speak. My words are stuck somewhere under shock and bewilderment, but tears squeeze past and roll down my face. 'I … I …' My tears become a river and I cover my face.

'Come on, sweetheart. Come with me,' Val says, slipping her arm around me and helping me to my feet.

'Just so long as you know that room is single occupancy,' the receptionist says.

'Oh, for goodness' sake. Can't you see the state she's in? And for the record if she needs to stay here I'll pay for another room, okay?' Val snaps.

'Just want to be clear, that's all,' the receptionist mutters and leaves us.

Once inside Val's room she closes the door and puts both hands on my shoulders. 'Now, are you sure nothing's happened to Rosie?' She searches my face.

I wipe my eyes. 'No. It has nothing to do with her.'

'Right. Then before you tell me what it's all about, I want you to go into the bathroom and get out of those wet things. Have a shower and I'll make you a cup of tea.' She slips off her dressing gown to reveal red candy-striped pyjamas. 'Put this on after, it's lovely and warm.'

Hot water, at first painful, works the chills from my body and I realise that shock hasn't been the only cause for my shakes. I had been freezing. Thank God I'd come to Val. There's no way I'd be shampooing my hair and washing seaweed from my skin if I'd gone to the police. Val is my saviour. Yes, I'm still trapped in a nightmare, but I can at least hope for daylight now.

'Sit on the bed, love. You look a lot better for that shower. I didn't like that blue tinge to your mouth. Now, you might not like it, but I'm putting lots of sugar in your tea for shock.' Val places her hand gently on my cheek. I have to look away to stop the tears coming again.

The sweet tea makes me gag but instinct urges me to drink. The sugar rush is instant and its heat warms my insides. My brain wakes up and I take a few deep breaths to steady my giddiness. 'Thanks, Val. I'm beginning to feel more like myself now.'

'Tea is wonderful for shock. I'll make you another when you've had that.' She reaches out and pats my hand. 'Take your time. You don't have to tell me what's wrong until you feel like it.'

'I'm ready now. I have to tell someone else to make sure it's real … that it all happened.' My throat grows thick with emotion as a series of flashbacks from the evening whirl in my head. I draw a breath and tell her everything.

During the time it takes to tell her, Val looks like my shock has jumped across the room and into her. I need two more cups of tea and half a box of tissues to explain, and at the end of it all, Val pulls a bottle of red wine from a bag in the wardrobe and takes a few pulls straight from the bottle.

Pale faced, she grabs a handful of tissues, sits opposite in an armchair and wipes silent tears from her face. 'I'm so, so sorry, Lu. If I had been braver a few years ago … gone to the police, you would never have had to go through this terrible nightmare.'

'But as you said to Rosie, you didn't really have anything, did you? Just hints and half-truths from a drunken game. Mellyn would have denied it for sure.'

'Yes, but I could have at least tried. The thing is, I had an affair with the man next door. Just a one-night stand, didn't mean anything, and luckily, he and his wife moved house afterwards … but it would have killed my husband. We've been together since school, and …' Val flaps a tissue at me and shakes her head.

'Mellyn did mention it—'

'She did? Oh, I am so ashamed. I regretted it as soon as it had happened. I love my husband so much. I was such a bloody fool. I only told her because she told me about Jack at the Crab Shack.' She sniffs and raises an eyebrow. 'Not sure you knew about that.' I say I did. 'So, my sordid little secret seemed the logical *truth* to tell Mellyn.'

'Mellyn told me she silenced you with threats and lies. I don't blame you for keeping quiet. You had so much to lose, and you didn't have any evidence about what she'd done.'

Relief lights the contours of Val's face and she puts a shaking hand to her mouth. 'Thanks for understanding, Lu. I don't deserve it, but do you think you could keep this from Rosie? For her sake more than mine.'

'Of course. There's no reason for her to know. What would be the point?'

'Thank you. So, what will you do now?' Val takes a deep breath and exhales.

'I would be grateful if I could stay here tonight – in another guest room like you said. I'll pay you back, of course, when—'

'No, love, I don't mean tonight, I meant about Mellyn. Will you go to the police in the morning? I'll gladly come with you.'

I want to answer, but the little kernel of guilt that has lived in the pit of my stomach for the last few months swells to gigantic proportions and stops me opening my mouth. I look into Val's kind blue eyes and know it has to come out. I tell her that I knew about Mellyn killing her husband, but the version she had told me. 'So, I'm to blame too, aren't I?' I say.

'No. No you aren't!' Val shakes her head and sticks out her chin. 'You didn't know that she killed him in the way she did until tonight. You thought you were protecting your mum's secret and felt sorry that she'd endured years of bullying from a brute of a husband.'

She sniffs into a tissue, comes to sit next to me on the bed and puts her arm around me. 'You poor, poor, girl. You had no choice. You'd just lost your lovely mum and then at last found your birth mum after all these years. Betraying her would mean the end of everything. And now to find that Mellyn killed your mum ... well, it doesn't bear thinking about. You must be in such turmoil, not to say shock.'

I wonder if Val is in fact a guardian angel. She understands completely. 'Thank you, Val. That's exactly why I kept quiet. And I don't know how I feel just now. It all feels like some vile nightmare to be honest.'

'Yes, it would do. And I will keep quiet. If Mellyn tries to drag you down with her, just deny you knew anything at all until tonight.' She strokes my hair and says, 'You do know you have to go to the police now, don't you? Even if she is your mum. She's dangerous, love, and if you let her off the hook, there's no telling what she might do.'

I sigh. 'Yes, I know. I kept quiet in the past, but that was before I knew what she'd ... what she'd done to my ...' My throat closes over and I blow my nose.

Val pats my shoulder and rings reception to organise another room for me. I walk over to the window and peep through the curtain, half expecting to see Mellyn staring back. The dark street is empty, and I know how it feels. My mother is a cold-blooded killer, a criminal. She also needs professional help, so telling the police won't be like a betrayal, it will be a kindness. And let's not bloody forget she tried to kill me tonight … so why do I feel so bad? I turn from the window.

'Mellyn will probably deny it all anyway. It'll be my word against hers.'

'Not quite,' Val says. 'Didn't you say you'd recently made her go to the doctor and she'd talked about her past?'

'Yes, but you know her. She's a very good liar. She told me so many lies in the end I never knew what was true and what was false. She changed and swapped the past around to suit her. She was even going to change her name to Tamsyn at one time.'

'She … she … wanted to change it to Tamsyn?' Val frowns.

'Yes, she wanted to change it to that because she said kids teased her at school or something …' I stop as the colour drains from Val's face and her mouth drops open. I feel my heart jump. 'What's wrong?

'I … I'm okay. It's just all this trauma I suppose. And if I'm traumatised God knows what you must be.'

I don't think she's telling the truth; her voice went high at the end and she is definitely flustered. But she's right that I'm traumatised. I watch Val's mouth moving, hear the sounds of words coming out of it, yet my brain refuses to make sense of them. I'm halfway down the rabbit hole and Val is the only thing from this world, *this* reality, keeping me from falling. Part of me wants to fall, to escape from the last six months, to find myself back behind my desk looking at the clouds and remembering Megan in the playground. No. Not to that moment … I had to escape to a few hours before it, so I could stop Mum from linking arms with Mellyn and stepping into the road. Everything would be normal again.

I would have to go back to the old, boring, timid me, existing day to day, never looking up, going through the motions, but right at this moment, I have never wanted anything more. I watch Val's mouth come to a stop and she shakes my shoulder gently.

'Lu? Have you been listening?'

'No. I haven't really been taking it in ...'

'Not surprised. Perhaps you should go to bed now. I was just telling you that the receptionist's left the key in the door and it's just two doors down—'

'No. I'll never be able to sleep.' But even as I say this I'm yawning. I nod and stand up. 'Yes, I think I'll go to bed now, Val. Thanks so much for everything, you'll never know how much—'

'Hey, no need to thank me. Come on, you're exhausted.' Val puts her arm around my shoulders and guides me out into the corridor.

I thank her again and turn off the light, but as soon as my head hits the pillow I pass into oblivion.

***

In the half light, Val rubbed her eyes and reached an arm out of bed, her fingers patting the bedside table. Where was her damned mobile? At last she found the switch of the bedside lamp and followed the sound of the insistent ringing to the chair a few feet away.

'Hello?' she said, unable to see the caller ID without her reading glasses.

'Mum, it's me. Sorry to bother you so early, but I need to speak to you.'

Val got back into bed and peered at the clock. Six forty-five. There was something the matter with Rosie's voice. It was hiding tears. 'What's wrong, love?'

'Oh, Mum. I've had an awful night! It's Mellyn, she's gone crazy!' Rosie's voice cracked and her racking sobs down the line twisted Val's stomach.

'What's she done? Has she hurt you? Because if she has, I swear I'll—'

'No. No, don't worry, I haven't seen her. But she called me at midnight last night.' Rosie took a few deep breaths and her voice became calmer. 'She was obviously blind drunk, cursing, swearing, and demanding to see Lu. She was convinced I had her with me, or knew where she was.' Rosie paused and blew her nose. 'I've never heard language like it. She wouldn't believe me when I said I hadn't seen Lu. She yelled at me that I was sheltering "the devious bitch" and that when she caught up with her she'd kill her. And then she called me some more vile names and then put the phone down.'

'Oh, my goodness!' Val wanted to reach down the phone and hold her daughter tight. 'You poor thing, I wish you'd have phoned me last night. I could have told you about—'

'I didn't want to disturb you, especially as we didn't part on good terms.' Rosie rushed on before Val had a chance to explain. 'Anyway, I phoned the police and told them what happened, that I was frantic for Lu's safety and I was going around there. They warned me to stay away but I had to do something.'

'Rosie, it's okay, listen—'

'The police got to Mellyn's just before I did, but she wasn't there. The officers wouldn't let me in, but said they'd found half a bottle of brandy on a table and a glass had been smashed against the wall. I told them they should search the *Sprite*, but the boat was gone.' Rosie ended on a sob. 'Mum, I think Mellyn's taken Lu on the boat and … God knows what she's done! I must have phoned Lu's mobile about a hundred times and it goes straight to voice—'

'Listen to me! Lu's safe. She's here at my B&B.'

An intake of breath. 'What? I … oh, thank God! But why, what happened?'

'Look. The best thing is for you to come around and I can tell you all about it then. I'll meet you in reception in fifteen minutes?'

'I'll be there in ten.'

Chapter Thirty-Five

To Val, her daughter looked more like a little child than a grown woman today. After Val had told her everything, Rosie sat in the armchair hugging her knees, huge blue eyes focused on nothing, her face a snowdrop under honey curls.

'Are you sure you don't want breakfast? I could have it sent up here and—'

'No thanks, Mum. I won't be able to eat anything until I've seen Lu.'

'Sleep is the best thing for her right now. I'm worried about you. You've had a right night of it and then had to come to terms with everything I've just told you too. Please let me order breakfast. If not a full English, then just some toast …'

A knock at the door drew Rosie from the chair. Val opened the door and Lu walked in, her raven hair a bird's nest; dark shadows under her eyes sucked khaki from the moss-green. 'Rosie,' she whispered, looking as if her whole face was hiding behind a stiff upper lip.

Rosie didn't bother to hide and burst into tears, wrapping her friend in a tight hug as she did so. 'Thank God you're alright,' she sniffed. 'You wouldn't believe what happened to me last night.'

Lu frowned over Rosie's shoulder at Val. 'I'll go and sort us all out some breakfast,' Val said in answer. 'Leave you two to catch up on all the'—she stopped and shrugged—'madness, I suppose you'd call it.'

***

Once Val leaves, Rosie pulls me close again. 'I have been so worried about you,' she says into my hair. Then she draws back, and her eyes hold mine with such intensity that I feel heat rise in my cheeks. 'I don't know what I'd have done if ...'

I clear my throat and pat her back. God, all I need is an 'awumah' and I'd be Adelaide. Adelaide. Hell, she'll be beside herself when she finds out about all this. A picture of two Adelaides side by side smacks me in the funny bone and I hear myself laugh, but the laugh sounds awkward and uncomfortable. Rosie frowns and walks towards the window. Does she think I'm laughing at her?

'I'm not laughing at you, Rosie. I'm not laughing at anything, really. I don't feel right in the head at the moment, to be honest ...'

She turns and gives me the sweetest smile. 'I'm not surprised, with everything you've just been through.' When I hold her gaze, she looks at her hands and her face grows very pink. This puzzles me. Before, she'd looked into my eyes so intently I had become embarrassed, and now the situation is reversed. It's as if ... as if we ... no, that's a ridiculous thought. It isn't even a real thought, just the tail end of madness, a blink of emotion in the eye of the storm.

She stops looking at her hands and I see her skin has gone back to its normal colour again. 'Sit down and I'll tell you about last night,' she says, 'and I'm sorry, it's more bad news.'

I sit by the window while Val and her daughter fuss about finding clothes for me to put on, and think about what Rosie has just told me. It's no shock that Mellyn had said she'd kill me when she found me. She tried to kill me last night. She'd killed her parents, her husband ... why not her daughter? I watch the first few early morning people spill from buildings into streets and go about their business.

Two bearded young men in bohemian clothes and blond dreadlocks shove hands in their pockets and talk together on a street corner. I make up a whole story about who they are and what their lives are like. An elderly woman aided by a walking frame turns the corner and eyes the young men with contempt. They're blocking her path but, deep in conversation, they haven't noticed. She thrusts a whiskered chin and shuffles closer. One of the men gives her the biggest smile and alerts his friend to her presence. They stand aside and I watch the smiley one's lips say sorry. The old woman makes her mouth small, tight and mean and quickens her shuffle as if she's afraid of being infected by their proximity.

Even though the old woman looks nothing like my m … Mellyn, there's a trace of her in the tight mean mouth, the quick shuffle. I can tell the old woman's manner is born of fear and prejudice, and what little I know of Mellyn's real truth makes them similar. Perhaps the origin of her psychosis was in fear. Fear of being unloved. There might also be abandonment issues and certainly jealousy.

The men embrace, and then the street corner is empty. A conversation about breakfast goes on behind me and I decide there's little point in trying to understand Mellyn's actions until I know the whole truth.

Will I ever know the whole truth?

'Lu, we thought that these might be okay?' Rosie tries not to laugh as she holds up red skinny jeans and a lacy white T-shirt.

'Your underwear is dry, Lu,' Val says, taking a second breakfast tray from a girl at the door and setting it on the bed. 'I know my clothes aren't ideal, but Rosie's wouldn't fit you. What with her being the size of an elf and all.'

Good, a normal conversation. That's what I need. My brain needs respite. I say the clothes are fine and that the proffered flip-flops would be great until I manage to get my clothes from Seal Cottage.

'We've been thinking,' Rosie says, and passes me a tray full of breakfast. 'We need a plan. The first thing to decide is where you will stay. You can't stay at the cottage in case Mellyn comes back.'

'No. That's just occurred to me,' I say, and apply myself to sausage, scrambled eggs and bacon as if there was a time limit on their consumption. I presume stress, heartache and a night swim brings out the survival instinct's desire for fuel.

Val butters toast. 'You can stay with Rosie. I was going to – we've made up'—she winks at her daughter—'but your need is greater. I'll stay put here in the B&B. I'm going to stay for a few more days until I can be sure you're both alright.'

I point to a mouth stuffed with breakfast and make a big show of nodding while I give myself time to come up with an excuse. The intense look Rosie gave me earlier is still hanging around, doing odd things to my feelings. Looking at her pouty lips now, I flush as an image of me lying in her bed planting kisses along her neck shows up. Madness. I don't think staying at her house would be a good idea. Not while my brain resembles a bowl of cold spaghetti.

'Thanks so much for the offer, but I could do with some time alone to think. It's all been a huge shock.' Rosie wraps herself around a slice of toast, but Val nods her understanding. 'I'll stay at Pebble House for the time being.'

After breakfast, Rosie and Val decide to take my matters into their hands. I'm incapable of logical thought for more than a few moments. Not surprising. The shock is wearing off a little, but emotional turmoil kicks around my insides. The matters in hand amount to a visit to the police station to see if they have discovered more about Mellyn's whereabouts.

The officer in charge says they have nothing so far, but they would like me to make a quick statement. The quick statement takes over two hours and leaves me battered and bruised. Even though I told it all to Val last night, this time Mellyn's vile secrets are out and in the hands of the authorities, and for the first time it all feels completely and horribly real.

Val's flip-flops slap down the corridor, leading me back to the waiting room and their owner. I have to get in the cottage and get my clothes. This T-shirt made me feel like a virgin prostitute. The desk sergeant looks up as I push the double doors open and Val and Rosie hurry over.

'You okay, sweetheart?' Val slips her cardigan around my shoulders. I frown at her but then I realise I'm shaking.

'Yes. I just need to ask the sergeant here if someone can take me back to the cottage to get some things.' I send a smile to smooth the furrow from Rosie's brow.

The sergeant opens his mouth, but the phone rings and he holds a finger up and answers it.

An expectant silence fills the room as we wait for him to finish the call and into it Rosie says, 'If Mellyn's still on the boat they have a good chance of finding her, we think. The coastguards do a grand job and given that she was pissed out of her head, she won't have got far. Mind you, if she fell off somehow, then—'

Val rolls her eyes at her daughter. 'I'm not sure that's something we want to be talking about at the moment, Rosie. I mean …' Then her voice tails off at the sound of the sergeant clearing his throat, and when I turn from her to look at his sympathetic eyes and set mouth, I'm right back in my parents' living room on the day my mum was killed. I'm glad of Val's arm through mine.

He clears his throat again and says, 'That was the coastguard. I'm sorry to tell you that the *Sprite* was found a few minutes ago washed up on the beach at Godrevy.' His heavy sigh must have shaken the floor because my legs tremble. 'It's matchwood, I'm afraid. The rocks around there are lethal.'

'And Mellyn?' Val speaks for all of us.

'No sign as yet. The coastguard's organising a search right now.'

Chapter Thirty-Six

I expect Seal Cottage to feel cold, barren and resentful as I walk through the door an hour later. It doesn't. It feels just as calm and peaceful as always. The officer makes himself comfortable at the kitchen table with a cup of tea and a newspaper and I go upstairs to pack.

It's nice to be alone. My head's stuffed with puzzles and other people's conversations. I need to time to breathe ... to think for myself.

Rosie has gone back to work in case the Pomp explodes and finally sacks her, and Val has gone back to Rosie's to phone her husband. I stuff my things into cases and wander over to the window. It wasn't very long ago that I looked out of it on to my bright new future. Impossible to think that the woman I'd hoped to share it with, my long-lost mother, might have gone, disappeared ... Okay, to be realistic, according to the coastguard, given her condition last night, most likely dead. The rip tides around here take no prisoners and if the ocean made matchwood of the *Sprite*, what would it do to a human body?

How do I feel about that? Sad? Yes, of course. I would feel sad for anyone that died in that way, let alone my ... my mother. I can't just turn my feelings off completely, and even though she was a very dangerous woman, had done vile and despicable things, she'd needed help. Help that I·couldn't get her in time. It will take me a long time to come to terms with arguably her most despicable act, however: taking the life of my mum.

What to do now? My future looks cloudy and unsettled and I wish I had a crystal ball. I walk away from the window, pull another bag from under the bed and feel something heavy shift to one side. I smile. It's the travel iron I have never used.

I heave it out and it turns into a crystal ball right there in my hands. It says go back home. That's where your decisions are waiting. You can't think here, suffocated by the ghost of Mellyn. Go back home to your dad, Adelaide, and the comfort of their love, their genuine love. Go back home to the calm, order and certainty that you desperately need after so much madness.

Go back home to heal.

Just then the phone rings. I answer it and then run to my car. The entrance to the beach has been cordoned off with yellow tape and a lifeguard vehicle is making its way to an ambulance parked nearby. Rosie had called to say she'd seen on social media that a body had just washed up a mile down the coast. It had to be Mellyn. I need to see with my own eyes, though, macabre as that sounds. I recognise a few of the policemen from earlier milling around and speed over to them. 'It's her isn't it?' I ask one of them, panting.

'How did you know about this?' He frowns, obviously annoyed. I tell him. He sighs and says more gently, 'Damned social media has a lot to answer for. We haven't contacted you yet because the body hasn't been formally identified.'

'It's her.' I know it is, how could it not be?

'Okay, you'd have to do this sooner or later anyway. She's over here in the ambulance.'

Unexpected late-afternoon sunshine strips jumpers and coats from beach walkers and an accomplice breeze strokes fingers through tousled hair and kisses roses into cheeks.

'Are you sure you won't change your mind, Lu?' Rosie says as she rolls her jeans up over her knees. She joins me at the water's edge and turns her freckled face to the sun.

I walk a little further into the waves and then stop as an errant breaker soaks my cotton trousers up to the thigh. 'Bugger!' I say, and harrumph when Rosie laughs. I back up to her more sensible approach in the shallows and have a sudden and unwelcome thought of Mellyn struggling for her life far out at sea in the black depths.

'So, are you?' Rosie nudges me.

'What?'

'Sure, you won't stay for a while. I get that you need calm and quiet, but you might need someone to talk to as well, you know? Someone to discuss things with?'

I glance at her hopeful face and part of me wants to say yes. But that part isn't nearly big enough or influential enough to have much of an impact on the rest of me. 'I can call you if I do,' I say. 'And yes, I've made my mind up, I really am going home. I *need* to go home. I called Dad this morning and he was so happy. I didn't tell him what had happened, of course. I'm not sure I could have found the words. It all seems so …' I sigh and look out at the blue horizon.

'Surreal?' she asks, and I nod. 'I still have trouble believing it's all happened to be honest.' She bends and pulls a pebble from the foam. It's black and wrapped in grey stripes. 'I was busy at work this afternoon, folding towels, not really thinking about anything and wham! There it all was in my head playing out like some scary movie. You know?' She hurls the pebble into the waves.

I do. 'That's one of the reasons I need time away. The memories are all so relentless here. Mellyn in the streets, the pubs, shops, the harbour … cold and dead, snow-white face with seaweed in her hair on the trolley in the ambulance.' I swallow. 'I had to walk past her shop earlier and it really freaked me out, I can tell you. And something I love, just standing here looking out at the ocean, is spoiled.'

'You sound like you're not coming back,' Rosie says to her toes in the wet sand.

'Hey, of course I'm coming back. Just not for a while.' I slip my arm through hers and feel her stiffen. 'I will miss you, you know.' I speak to a dog walker in the distance.

'You'd bloody better.' She squeezes my arm against her side and I can feel her heart pounding. 'When are you going?'

'Tomorrow.'

She turns to face me and puts her hand to her eyes as a shelter against the sun slanting over my shoulder. 'That soon? What about giving notice at work?'

'I phoned the Vulture earlier. He was more than happy to let me go straight away. He said bookings were pretty slack for the next few weeks.'

Rosie sighs and walks up the beach and into the shade of rocks. I follow her until she stops and folds her arms. 'I have something on my mind and now seems as good a time as any to say it,' she says, and turns serious eyes to mine.

Oh dear. I don't like the sound of that. I can't hear anything serious … be expected to juggle my battered emotions into some sort of coherent response. 'Okay, what is it?'

'I know you might think it's a weird thing to come out with, but as you're leaving I want to give you something to think about while you're gone.' Rosie finds a smile from somewhere. 'Might take your mind off all the misery too.'

My heart throws itself against my ribcage and my head tends towards giddy. I nod and bite the inside of my cheek.

'How do you feel about you and me … you know, in the future … you and me starting up that business we mentioned? I know we said it only in fun, but we work well together and I'm sure we could do a better job than Pomp and Vulture!'

I hadn't really known what to expect, but this wasn't it. I laugh and shrug my shoulders. 'Well, it's certainly an idea. I promise I'll give it some thought.'

Two hours from home, I think about Rosie and Val. We'd had a goodbye meal of takeaway fish and chips at Rosie's and a very tearful parting on her doorstep at the end of the evening. Val gave me a bear hug and made me promise to keep in touch, and then left me and Rosie to say our goodbyes. We shared a goodbye hug and a kiss on the cheek and then Rosie looked deep into my eyes and the atmosphere turned into something else. Something else that I couldn't define and something I have to run away from right now. I will have to face it sooner or later though, this much I know.

I step out of the car and the front door opens even before I get halfway up the path. Dad comes out, and when I see his wobbly smile and swimming eyes, a sob I didn't know was there escapes before I can stop it. I run into his arms so fast that he nearly falls over, and then we're laughing, crying and trying to talk all at the same time, but of course neither of us is making any sense.

Dad puts his arm around me and guides me through the front door, the familiar smells and sounds of home wrapping me in a welcome hug. Another welcome hug is waiting in the kitchen. 'Adelaide!' I say, and step into her awumah.

'It's so good to have you back, Lu!' she says. 'So glad you changed your mind. I hated leaving you there.' She glances sidelong at Dad. 'Um … what with things not being as great as you'd hoped with your birth mother.'

'Not as great as you'd hoped? Were you having problems then, love?' Dad asks.

'Oh yes. You could say that,' I say, and then hysteria bubbles in my chest and I have to sit down.

Adelaide's eyebrows shoot up. 'Things got worse after I left?'

'You have no idea, Adelaide … no idea.'

Chapter Thirty-Seven
Three weeks later

From the top of a hill, I can see that October in St Ives has shrugged off the muted smokiness of September and presents a crisp tableau courtesy of a coin of a sun in a blue sky. I can't go straight into town though. I need time to collect my thoughts.

In the National Trust car park at Godrevy, I get out of my car and walk to the cliff edge that overlooks Godrevy beach and the lighthouse. A wide sweep of beach leads to St Ives on the left, and to my right, the lighthouse, so much closer than I have ever seen it. Oddly, close up, it looks smaller than before, though it's still formidable. I watch it fearlessly command the waves at its feet and encourage seabirds to sail their reflections past its windows.

A week after I had returned to Sheffield, Rosie called to ask how I was and told me that she missed me. I told her I missed her too, very much. I was shocked by just how much. I listen to the ocean shush the sand and look at the St Ives tableau again. Somewhere behind the dark outline of the first buildings and up a ridiculously steep hill is Seal Cottage, just waiting for me to walk through its door. I think about all that might mean. I think about turning the car round and driving straight back home. I think about all the questions swimming around my brain and what would happen to it if they were never answered. I say goodbye to the lighthouse, go back to the car, and set out along the coast to St Ives.

On the scrap of a drive outside Seal Cottage, I turn off the ignition and déjà vu slips onto the passenger seat beside me. I'm here to see someone very special … again. I place my hands on my jeans and am glad of the warmth of my thighs under my cold fingers. All of my upper body's cold, and I realise that my heart is the source. I had put it in cold storage just before I left home this morning. It made sense. It's fragile and battered and has to be protected from unexpected and sudden emotion.

The touch of the stone seal head feels rough and cold this time under my fingers, and I can hear no one singing inside. Even if there was, the pounding of my heart in my ears would have made it hard to detect.

Why am I doing this?

Nobody forced me to.

I turn and take a few steps back to the car and I hear the door open and a woman's voice say, 'Lucinda?'

The sound of it wraps around my heart and pulls me back round.

There stands my mother. My real mother.

Nobody could argue otherwise, because apart from her dark blonde hair, it's as if someone has held up a mirror – reflecting me, sixteen years ahead. She puts a hand to her mouth and I watch tears well in her moss-green eyes.

I walk back towards her on legs that feel as if I've borrowed them from a newborn foal. My mouth opens, but words slide back down my throat.

'My baby, my darling,' she says so quietly that I wonder if I've misheard. She grips the side of the door for support and says again as if in disbelief, 'My beautiful, beautiful baby … my darling girl.'

My heart comes out of cold storage. Her words have melted it, because they aren't false, contrived – just full of love.

I start to sob. Big, embarrassing, unexpected, racking sobs and then her arms are around me and I hold on tight. For her, my love doesn't have to grow; it's there immediately, as is the name 'Mum' impatient with waiting on my tongue.

'Come inside, let's sit down before we fall down,' she says, and leads me to the sofa. 'I've just made coffee. Would you like some?' I nod and accept the bunch of tissues she hands me. She wipes her own eyes and we both laugh a little self-consciously.

'My God. It's been a while since I cried like that,' I say, and picture the police officers in our living room with my broken dad.

'Mine are tears of happiness, but yours must be mixed and coming from a place of turmoil with everything Tamsyn put you through.'

That was it, exactly. I smile and nod. 'It will take a while to get through, I think. You must be in shock too ... Mum,' I say, relieved to have ended the waiting.

I watch her face crumble and having caught my bout of sobbing, she sinks to the edge of the sofa. 'Thank you for calling me that, it's so wonderful, and so much more than I deserve.'

'Believe me, I don't use that name lightly,' I say, and hand her more tissues. 'My heart told me it was the right thing to do.'

We sit and talk about how wonderful Val is and, if it hadn't been for her, we might have had to wait much longer to find each other; we might never have found each other in fact.

I had been right that Val wasn't telling me the truth that night I'd run to her. When I'd mentioned that Mellyn had wanted to change her name to Tamsyn, Val's face had drained of colour, but she'd denied anything was wrong when I'd pressed her. She'd kept what she suspected from me until she could be sure she was right. But she had told the police.

Two weeks ago, I received the phone call from them that had brought me here today, about a matter that had sent waves of shock crashing against my stomach walls just as forcefully as the ones I'd watched smashing on Godrevy rocks. They said they had reason to believe that the woman who called herself Mellyn wasn't my birth mother at all, in fact her name was Tamsyn. She was the half-sister of my birth mother, Mellyn Rowe, and they were tying up a few loose ends but would be back in touch very shortly. They also said that they had acted on information from Val about something Mellyn had told her a few years ago. Val had almost forgotten it because of everything else that had happened, until I'd mentioned the name Tamsyn to her. When I finished the call to the police I immediately called Val and she told me all about it.

'Well, I asked Mellyn once if she had any children, but she deflected my question by talking about her family instead,' Val said. 'When my Rosie told me about you, I imagined that Mellyn had never mentioned you to me because she'd been ashamed of having you adopted, perhaps. But I did think it was really odd, though, because of two of them in one family doing the same thing. Then all the other stuff that happened buried it all in my mind, until now …' Val trailed off.

'Two of them in one family doing what? What do you mean?' I asked.

Val sighed. 'Sorry, I'm not making much sense, am I? The thing is, Mellyn said that she had this half-sister called Tamsyn who she hated. Said she was the golden girl and Mellyn had always felt second best … but Tamsyn had fallen from grace when she got pregnant as a young girl. Their parents had been ashamed and forced her to adopt. She got to be the golden girl again, though, because she's a doctor now, apparently, working with the Red Cross abroad. Then I remember Mellyn just changed the subject, and that was all she ever said about her.'

I could hardly process what I was hearing. 'The half-sister got pregnant early too, was forced to adopt … a bit of a coincidence to say the least. So, the truth is that the woman who pretended to be my birth mother was called Tamsyn and she stole Mellyn's whole story? Just swapped the names round?' I asked, bewildered.

'Seems like it.'

'But why the fucking hell had Mellyn, I mean Tamsyn, pretended to be my mother in the first place? What would be the point? Jealousy? Longing? And how did she get the letter from Maureen telling her I was looking for my birth mother?'

'I don't have the answers to all that, love.' Val said. 'Perhaps Mellyn will if you get to speak to her.'

The police called back a day later. It appeared that Seal Cottage didn't belong to the woman that pretended to be my birth mother at all, but instead to her half-sister, Mellyn. The officer told me that they had found her pretty quickly and she'd explained that Tamsyn was looking after the cottage while she and her husband were working abroad. They had been in Africa for six years but were planning on a return to Cornwall next year. Of course, once she'd heard about the whole tragic mess, Mellyn had arranged to come back straight away.

That information had answered my question of how Mellyn had got Maureen's initial letter. She'd just picked it up from the floor when it landed on her mat at Seal Cottage. Another little bit of pity I'd originally felt for her when I'd found out she was dead was stamped out by my anger. *What kind of a person would take the identity of another in order to steal her daughter?*

The officer said that Mellyn was in shock, of course, but had given him her details and would he please pass them on to me. For the last week I had looked at the scrap of paper with her phone number and email address on it, and more than once had screwed it up and put it in the bin. The last time I retrieved it, I had to wipe chopped tomato from the last three digits of the phone number, but they remained stained and red and illegible.

Before I could change my mind, two days ago I wrote Mellyn a very short email just to say I would come down today if she wanted to meet and discuss what had happened. It was businesslike and to the point, as was the one I received in return. I printed it off and I've read it a hundred times already. I wondered if I could go through all that again? The green shoots of love I had begun to grow for the woman I believed to be my birth mother had been pulled out by the roots, and my battered heart was now supposed to launch itself at yet another 'mother'?

Dear Lucinda,
*   Thank you for getting in touch at this extremely difficult time. I will be at the cottage all day. Come when you like.*
*   Best wishes,*
*   Mellyn*

How different it was from the much folded and unfolded email I'd had from Tamsyn. No bubbly gushy words, kisses, or declarations of love this time. For that I was glad. My heart would have hated it. Those few lines were honest and open. I decided that no matter how tough, if I passed up a chance to meet her I'd never forgive myself.

I'm so happy I did now as I sit opposite my mum. For the next few hours we talk about Tamsyn and fill in each other's gaps. The police had explained to Mum the terrible truth about what Tamsyn had done to her parents, her husband, and my adoptive mum, and of course how she'd pretended to be my mother. I tell her all the awful things she'd done to me and how it all ended on the boat.

She tells me that she and Tamsyn had had the normal love–hate sibling relationship growing up, but she'd never realised how much Tamsyn had really hated her until she'd come down to St Ives after her husband 'died'.

'Tamsyn was in bits. Now I know the truth it's not surprising,' Mum says, and shakes her head. 'Anyway, we had a big heart to heart just before I went abroad to work. We'd …' Mum bites her lip as if she's let something slip but carries on. 'We'd only bought this place a month before, we'd not even had time to move in here, before a post came up to work abroad, for a year initially, so … I said she could stay here in the cottage. It might do her good to get away for a while. The while ended up being six years.'

'So, what did Tamsyn say in the heart to heart you had?'

'Ah yes. That was an eye-opener. Really cut me up. She said she'd always felt second best to me, that our parents pushed her out, that I was the golden girl and she'd hated the sight of me in the end. She hoped that when I'd got pregnant, things would change, I'd be shamed, but no. Once Joe and I had agreed to have you adopted, it was all back to normal.'

I pull a sigh from the base of my lungs and say, 'So it sounds like as well as your identity, she stole your entire life story and made it hers?' I tell her everything Tamsyn had told me about Joe and the way she'd felt about him, the parents conspiring against them, forcing them to put me up for adoption, and the sing-song voice she used to tell it.

Mum nods, the sadness in her eyes reflecting mine. 'Yes, she always used a weird voice when she lied. And yes, what you've told me, that was my story. I confided in Tamsyn, you see. During the pregnancy I felt shut out by my parents and needed someone to talk to. Someone who I thought was on my side. On the day she told me all this, she said she hated me for taking *her* boyfriend.'

'She went out with Joe?' I ask.

'Hardly. They were in the same tutor group and a gang of them went for a burger on the way home from school once. That was all. Then she asked him round on the pretext of homework or something. I was at home at the time and when he walked in … he and I just fell for each other right there. Love at first sight.'

I frown. 'He'd not seen you before? But didn't you all go to the same school?'

'No, I went to another, "better" school, my mum wanted to stretch me. She was pushy, and in that respect, I can see how Tamsyn's jealousy was justified.'

I try to find some sympathy for Tamsyn, but it's all been used up. Something occurs to me then and I say, 'I wonder why she switched some of the story, though.' Mum frowns. 'Well, she said she expected that Joe went on to be a doctor. But it turns out it was you that did instead.'

'We both did. Like Tamsyn, he was a year older than me and so had a head start.' I go to interrupt but she hurries on. 'Anyway, though I was worried about Tamsyn after she'd told me all this, she said she felt so much better for getting it all off her chest. I apologised about Joe, because in her own warped way I could tell she had loved him. I said she could live in the house rent free, anything at all I could do to make amends. She said it wasn't my fault as I hadn't done any of it deliberately, and that our parents had been at fault really in the way they had treated us differently growing up.'

I place my hand over hers as she looks close to tears again. Mum squeezes it and sighs. 'She said she was so glad we'd had this out and that we could now move on. Said she'd forgiven me, which was odd if she didn't think it was my fault, but obviously she did, and she hadn't at all. She stole you from me – her ultimate revenge.' A tremor ends her words and she looks through the window. 'And we let it happen. I never looked for you because I felt I didn't deserve you. You know why we had to give you up, because Tamsyn told you, but even so. Anyway, we didn't want to upset your life. Of course, we so wished that you would come looking … one day.'

That's the third time she's said 'we' and she hasn't told me anything about her husband. I know she has one because the police told me. 'Your husband knows about me then, obviously?'

'My husband, he's, um … I mean he …' She puts a hand to her mouth as if to stop her words. Her eyes can't hold mine. But her hand reaches out.

A prickling sensation begins in my spine. I look at goosebumps along my forearms. I watch Mum's face and something in it tells me a secret. No. It can't be, can it?

'Mum, what happened to Joe?'

The window still holds her gaze and she tightens the grip on my hand.

'Oh, Lu.' The window releases her and she looks right into my eyes. They tell me a story of guilt, and love. 'I so much want to tell you, but I think you've had enough shocks just recently—'

'Yes, but because I have, I can cope with it. Tell me.' *If he's dead I can't.*

'We stayed together. We'd both wanted to be doctors since we were kids. This shared dream was just another reason why we were made for each other. We went to the same college and uni – he was the year above, of course. Then we did our training, became doctors and got married.'

I rake my fingers through my hair. This was more than I could ever have hoped for. I take a moment to calm my breathing and say, 'So that end part of Tamsyn's story – well, your story actually – when she said you and Joe drifted apart and he probably made another life as a doctor without you ... was a lie?'

'Yes, seems she added a bit for reasons best known to her.'

'Well, where is he now?'

'He was working with me in Africa, and now he's right here in St Ives. We thought it best that I see you alone ... as I said, it's a hell of a shock for you.'

'My God,' I say, picturing the lad in the ripped-in-half photo again. I realise now that the other half of the photo wouldn't have been of Tamsyn, but of Mum. A few thousand questions queue up in my mouth so I swallow most of them back down and ask just two. 'Do I have any siblings? Does he want to meet me?'

Mum shakes her head. 'No siblings, we felt it wouldn't be fair. We never got over having to give you away.' She cups my face in her hands. 'And yes, my darling, of course he wants to meet you. He loves you just as much as I do.'

'Oh, Mum,' I say, and hug her tight. My heart is so full that I can't squeeze any more words past it, but it doesn't matter. Right at this moment, nothing does.

Epilogue

Six months later

Rosie looks at me and says, 'So this is the one, yes?'

I look at the old cottage standing window deep in grass and wildflowers and then back at her hopeful eyes. 'Bloody hell, Rosie … it's going to take a hell of a lot of work.' I turn my back on the cottage and look out over the sea; I listen to her sigh and shuffle her feet on the gravel path.

'Yes, we know that, but both our dads said they'd help put it right,' she says, and then laughs. 'Well, not your doctor dad, not sure Joe would know one end of a hammer from the other.'

'Hm,' I say, and listen to her waffle on behind me about savings from my birth parents and offers of help from Adelaide and Val regarding decorating, making curtains and God knows what else. I smile and am glad she can't see it. I'd already decided that this cottage was ideal for our new café the first time I laid eyes on it last week, but enjoy pretending I'm still considering it. Rosie's so easy to tease.

And to fall in love with.

Of all the shocks I had last year, that one's pretty high up on the list. Rosie had eventually plucked up courage and told me how she felt about me and I hadn't known what to do or say. I couldn't deny that I felt strongly about her, but I was straight, wasn't I? I'd had a couple of boyfriends in sixth form and that disastrous fling with a married man that I told Tamsyn about one night in a weak moment. Stupidly I hadn't known he was married, but the shame of it when I found out put me off relationships for good. And if I'm honest, the sex was a little boring to say the least – felt like I was going through the motions most of the time. I told Rosie I needed to think, and in the end had opened up the whole confusing bag of emotions with Adelaide, of all people.

I didn't mean to, of course, but as usual Adelaide yanked words out of my heart like a champion fly fisherwoman. I didn't expect her to understand at all, but she did. She unravelled my tangled feelings and made sense of my puzzle in just a few sentences.

'It seems to me that you've fallen in love with a person and your heart couldn't care less if this person is male or female,' she said, and raised her wonderful eyebrows. 'And why should it? Love is love, if you ask me. It's a precious gift and you could do a lot worse than to share it with Rosie.'

Rosie slips her arm through mine and rests her head on my shoulder. 'You look serious, what are you thinking?'

'Just about Adelaide and what a wise woman she is,' I say.

'Yes, she is. And she thinks this place is perfect. I was chatting to her about it again only yesterday—'

'Something we all agree on then.'

'What? So, you want it then?'

'You could say that. The vendor's accepted the offer I made this morning.'

Rosie steps in front of me and thumps my shoulder. 'You bugger! Why didn't you tell me?' Her brow furrows, but a huge smile waits at the corners of her mouth.

'What would be the fun in that?' I say with a laugh.

She laughs too and we both look out to the blue horizon. 'I can't wait to start this new venture ... my life, with you,' she says, her voice suddenly serious. 'We'll have fun whatever happens. I promise.'

'I'll hold you to that,' I say. Then I kiss her, take her hand and we make our way back down the road to St Ives.

Acknowledgements

A big thanks to Mandy Blake who advised me on adoption issues and shared some of her personal experience of adoption with me. This gave me a valuable insight into the adoption process in the UK over the years. I'd also like to thank Imogen Howson for believing in this story from day one and championing its entry into the world. It has had a few title changes since then, but the story is the same. A huge thanks to the wonderful Betsy Freeman Reavley and everyone at my publisher Bloodhound Books. I am very lucky to have found such a dynamic and hardworking team of people.

26006471R00153

Printed in Poland
by Amazon Fulfillment
Poland Sp. z o.o., Wrocław